Promise

ROGUE RIVER BOOK ONE

L.B. DUNBAR

L.B. Dunbar Writes, Ltd.
https://www.lbdunbar.com/

Cover Design: Lori Jackson Designs

Cover Photographer: Regina Wamba

Editor: Emerald Edits/Nicole McCurdy

Editor: Gemma Brocato

OTHER BOOKS BY L.B. DUNBAR

Rogue River

Promise

Patience

Prudence

Sterling Falls

Sterling Heat

Sterling Brick

Sterling Streak

Sterling Clay

Sterling Fight

Sterling Touch

Sterling Stone

Lovewell Landing

The Holiday Post

Fall Love

Holiday Hotties (Christmas novellas)

Scrooge-ish

Naughty-ish

Grouch-ish

Elf-ish

Chicago Anchors

Elevator Pitch

Catch the Kiss

Parentmoon

Road Trips & Romance

Hauling Ashe

Merging Wright

Rhode Trip

Lakeside Cottage

Living at 40

Loving at 40

Learning at 40

Letting Go at 40

Silver Foxes of Blue Ridge

Silver Brewer

Silver Player

Silver Mayor

Silver Biker

Sexy Silver Fox Collection

After Care

Midlife Crisis

Restored Dreams

Second Chance

Wine&Dine

Collision novellas

Collide

Caught

The Sex Education of M.E.

The Heart Collection

Speak from the Heart

Read with your Heart

Look with your Heart

Fight from the Heart

View with your Heart

The Heart Remembers - a sequel

BOOKS IN OTHER AUTHOR WORLDS

Smartypants Romance (an imprint of Penny Reid)

Love in Due Time

Love in Deed

Love in a Pickle

The World of True North (an imprint of Sarina Bowen)

Cowboy

Studfinder

THE EARLY YEARS

Legendary Rock Stars Series

Paradise Stories

The Island Duet

Modern Descendants – writing as elda lore

For those who adopt.
Thank you.
From an adopted child

WARNING

For your own mental health,
please check my website for trigger warnings.
www.lbdunbar.com

PROLOGUE

[Trinity]

Twenty-four years old

"Dart Rivers, you are ridiculous." I laugh at the man handcuffed to my bed.

A man who apparently handcuffed himself to the metal headboard.

"Told you I'd chain myself to this bed until you agreed to marry me."

As I'd said, the man is ridiculous.

And ridiculously good-looking with whiskey eyes and a seductive smirk. Bristly scruff on a jaw as structured as the ridges of the mountains around this small West Virginia town. His laugh compares to the river that flows through it, roguish, rugged, and rushing at high speed. Like the flutter of my pulse when he looks at me like he is.

Like he wants to devour me. Like he's truly happy. With me.

His best friend's younger sister.

He claims he's pined for me for years.

But we both know this is only sex. Incredible, mind-blowing, toe-curling sex.

An internal sigh floats through my sated body. My limbs are stretched from the positions this man has put me in. My heart is soaring. This feeling cannot be trusted.

We were only lust, right? Temporary and unfettered. Fleeting and fun.

Yet we've been hooking up for weeks.

"I don't recall you asking me a question to be answered," I tease, sauntering toward the bed. I'd been in the ensuite bathroom, cleaning up after round number I've-lost-count because this man is insatiable.

Of course, I felt the same way.

I mean, look at him. Upper body leaning slack against my pink, ruffle-edged pillow. Head tipped back against the white wrought iron headboard. His bare chest on display, showing off the sleek lines of his abs and long length of his torso. One arm outstretched, wrist clamped in a fur-lined handcuff. The other cuff secured around the top of the frame. His free hand is flat on his belly, low, teasing, just above where the fold of the sheet drapes over his angled hips, exposing that tempting trail leading south and pointing at something distinctly hard. A giant arrow suggesting all roads lead here.

To Dart Rivers and his ridiculousness.

"What question do you need asked, baby?"

He purrs like a king cat, a lion giving a gentle rumble, while I climb up over his body, my gaze focused on the flat disks of his taut nipples. The dusky skin surrounded by summer-sun-kissed flesh.

Fuck, he is so beautiful. Almost as blinding as a sun himself. My insides warm just looking at him. My lower belly flutters, pulse racing, and another part of me clenches, reminding me of all he'd already done to me.

I settle on his lap, wearing the T-shirt he'd tossed to my floor last night when we tumbled into my room. My inner thighs hug the outside of his, resting just below that tempting stiffness beneath the sheet. The hand on his belly comes to my hip, electricity ripples over my skin, crackling like lightning in a summer electrical storm. Something vibrant and neon and invigorating.

I'd pinch myself to wake from the dream of having sex with this man, if my body wasn't already sore in delicious ways, telling me I am not imagining things.

Dart Rivers and I have been having sex for weeks. Repeatedly.

"Trinity?" His lazy, mountain twang draws my attention. "What worries you, baby?"

His own vulnerability seeps into the question. A reminder of how many times he's said he isn't good enough for me. His past weighs heavily on him. He says he doesn't have anything to offer me, other than a promise.

He'll love me forever.

Actually, his exact words were, *I'm going to love you so hard, Forever.*

Forever with a capital letter, like a proper name, a nickname he'd given me.

He whispered it during the quiet of us coupling and playfully teased it in public in front of others, ones questioning how he ended up with me. Something I still wonder as well. Knowing it's going to hurt like hell when this ends.

Dart has a reputation for being a flirt. He's easy on the eyes and easily swayed others into bed. It's difficult to believe there is anything remarkable enough about me that he'd choose me for eternity.

"Marry me, Forever," he says as I smooth my hands over the ripples on his abdomen.

"You're just saying that, so I'll find the key and unlock that handcuff." I keep my tone light, coy even, while my pulse skitters.

He sets his hand over one of mine on his belly and nods toward the key on my white nightstand, implying I don't need to search anywhere for the mechanism.

"You're the key to me."

Something in his voice has me tilting my head. Dart is always joking around, tossing out cheesy lines like swiping playing cards off a stacked deck.

My gaze pinches the slightest, questioning the vulnerability in his eyes.

"Come on, Trin. Put me out of my misery."

He gently bucks his hips, and I lean deeper into his stomach with the motion.

"You want to have endless sex, with only me, for the rest of your life?" I tease because marriage is sacred to me. It means monogamy, faithfulness, and unending trust, like my parents have.

"I do." His response is sharp and serious, like he's making that vow at an altar before a priest.

I laugh, but Dart tightens his fingers around my hand. The chain attached to the cuff at his wrist clangs against the beam of the headboard, reminding him, in case he forgot, he's handcuffed. He doesn't look toward the clinking reminder but keeps his gaze focused on me.

"Dart?" I whisper, no longer certain if he's toying with me or being heartfelt.

"I mean, I do want to have sex with you forever." His mouth twists, the corner pops up. A teasing fishhook catching me unaware.

"See." I smack his bare chest, the thwack snappy and loud, cracking through the momentary quiet that lingered after I'd exhaled his name. "I knew you couldn't be serious."

Still, my heart blooms. Petals unfurling from the mix of reality and fantasy.

"But I am." His voice drops again, those eyes killing me with their sincerity. Their fear.

What could this man possibly be afraid of?

He races cars for fun. He was a philandering flirt, having countless women before me. He stood on rooftops and built houses.

"Say yes, Forever." The emotion in his voice emphasizes the nickname. The infinity in it.

"Dart." My throat thickens as I spread my fingers and coast them up his chest. His heart races beneath my palm.

"Trinity Haven, please be my wife. My life. My forever."

With my knees on either side of his hips, my body stiffens from his genuine plea. As if something deep inside me hears the quiet truth.

I might still feel puzzled that he'd want me above anyone else. Maybe, a little afraid of his restless, almost reckless, spirit. But the love inside me is nearly suffocating. Instantly, I imagine a life with this man, who I believe is good at his core and faithful to a fault, at least with friends. With the few people he truly allows close to him, like me.

He really wants to marry me. No more fucking around. No more endless flirting.

Just me. Permanently.

"I won't break you, Trinity." He slides his large palm to my knee, skimming up my thigh, along my side, to pause over my heart.

A promise.

One said more like a reminder to himself to never be like his parents.

He'll love me. He'll never leave me.

Forever.

"Yes," I whisper.

Shock registers in those amber eyes with rays of gold, and my heart wilts, thinking this might be another one of his jokes. A cruel one.

But suddenly, he's jostling me, twisting at his hips as he stretches his other arm across his body, seeking the handcuff key just out of his reach.

"Unlock me, Trin," he strains. "Get me out of this cuff so I can hold you properly."

Laughing at the sudden movement and urgency in his voice, I slap my hand over the key and insert it in the lock. I continue to jiggle with laughter at how frantic he is to be released.

The second he's free, he jackknifes upward, wraps an arm around my lower back, and flips our positions.

I laugh even harder, giddy and high, at the suddenness of him wedged between my legs, his arms banded around my back, uncomfortable as I lie on them.

"God, you're quick." I'm breathless as I clutch his firm biceps.

"Say it again, Trin."

"God, you're quick?" A schoolgirl giggle escapes, like I'm fifteen instead of twenty-five years old.

"The other word."

"Yes." The word clogs my throat, rough with emotion. Like more of that summer storm effect, one moving from crackling lightning to a refreshing downpour.

His brows slowly crease, eyes searching mine. Whatever he sees slowly smooths his forehead and deliciously curls his lips. A sunrise after a stormy night.

"Yes, I'll be Mrs. Dart Rivers," I repeat to reassure him. The name has a nice ring to it.

"No, baby. You'll be my forever."

And when he kisses me, like we have all the time in the world to spend locked together in this fuzzy shift from lust to love, I believe him.

Forever.

1

[Trinity]
Forty-one years old

There is something provocative about Georgia O'Keeffe's painting *Grey Lines with Black, Blue, and Yellow*. The obvious slit up the middle of the image. The sliver of a petal pink center. The outward folds of blue and purple, distinct from the contrasting outer rim with a slash of yellow and green before the swollen plume of white and gray.

Dart said the image looked like a giant pussy.

But I no longer care what Dart Rivers thinks about art, especially the framed poster that hangs on my entryway wall.

A dozen years of marriage, swept away like petals falling from a wilted flower, followed by three years since our divorce.

His opinion on anything no longer matters to me. And I remind myself of this as I drop my keys in the glass dish on the slim table below the picture in my front hallway.

In the house I now own alone, without him.

The problem with fighting thoughts of my ex-husband is that looking at this picture reminds me of my own body part, long forgotten by him. A part of me he once loved. Said he couldn't get enough of. The scent. The taste. The feel of me opening around him.

Ha.

He was a real piece of poetic work. And his best poem was titled: he left me.

"I love you, baby," he said, his voice breaking. The unusual sight of tears in his eyes. "But I can't give you what you desire most . . . not a family, not the life you deserve. I hate the thought that I'm holding you back. We're both chasing dreams, feeling unfulfilled. And I can't give you the one thing you really want."

Trouble was, I'd only wanted him.

My older brother's best friend had paid me no mind for years. Then one day his eyes seemed to open, and all he saw was me, until he was no longer looking.

Unfulfilled.

I ignore the dull ache that never leaves my chest, even after all these years.

He'd made a choice. It didn't include me.

Shoving aside the loneliness that hovers over my shoulder like a shadow, I head toward the stairs leading up to my bedroom.

Book club is tonight. A weekly meeting of women from the Milton County area.

We call ourselves the Sterlets, starlets of romance reads and sexual treats, named for Sterling Falls, where we meet. Self-fulfilling pleasure toys are sold by one of the older women in our community. Although you wouldn't be caught with a dildo in your hand, because she would not sell you one if you called Meredith Mulligan old.

"I'm just getting started," she'd say about the sexual revival she had back in her fifties.

Meredith is my idol.

Loud, proud, and owning her sensuality.

I owned mine as well, because I'd been on enough failed dates in the past few years to prove no one satisfied me better than . . . me.

Still, I feel unsettled lately. Restless.

I get this way every spring, with racing season in full swing. When flowers, like my Georgia O'Keeffe painting, start to bloom. And the second quarter of the year means rebirth.

Babies recently fill the NICU—neonatal intensive care unit —where I work as a nurse.

The ache grows sharper when I recall another area where I felt like a failure. Even though I knew all the science behind why I hadn't carried pregnancies to full term.

And I wouldn't even be thinking of Dart and my situation except it had been a particularly harrowing day in the unit. A baby nearly lost his life. So small. So innocent. So helpless.

But he'd been a scrapper and made it through a difficult day.

Dismissing the near-loss from my thoughts, I focus instead on getting out of my head, and scrubs, and into a dress. One that is flirty and loose, flowing over my wide hips and hitting above my knees, flattering my short stature.

One that says spitfire, not forever.

As I run my fingers through my short, blonde waves and freshen up my lipstick, I hear the soft, elongated yelp of a cat. The stray tabby has been coming to my back door for a week, reminding me I fed him once, and he demands more.

Tonight, his cries seem especially loud and incessant, but I smile at his call.

"At least somebody loves me," I mutter aloud as I make my way down the stairs and head for my kitchen. The room is at the back of my shotgun-style house. The place is narrow and long and was ramshackle when we bought it. But there had always been something I loved about this two-story clapboard-sided home, just over the border of Sterling Falls, in Rogue River.

The whispery, willowy, elongated yowl sounds even louder when I enter my kitchen, flicking on the lights, before heading for the fridge.

"I'm coming, Oliver." After several visits, I'd named the scoundrel still crying for me.

I pick up a low bowl set in the dish strainer after I washed it last night and fill it with milk.

Balancing the bowl in one hand, I twist the knob for the back door with my other one.

Then I fumble the bowl, hands suddenly trembling at the sight on my low stoop.

Milk spills over the rim, coating my numb fingers.

Because Oliver the cat isn't on my back steps.

The high-pitched cry is coming from a bundle wrapped in a pink blanket.

A newborn baby in a laundry basket.

2

[Dart]
Forty-four years old

Parked in the lot designated for drivers and their car trailers, I stare down at my phone, thumbing through photos I have no business looking at. I should have deleted them years ago, but I could never do it. Could never let them go, like I would be erasing a part of me. My past. My heart.

I stare down at one of my favorite images. A blonde-haired beauty, head surrounded by a halo of sunlight, making her look almost angelic. Her long lashes are lowered, her nose pressed to the yellow-orange center of a daisy. The white petals nearly kiss her lips.

I'm jealous.

Because it's been three long years since I've kissed those lips.

With a brush of my thick thumb, I swipe the image aside, forcing another photo forward. A black-and-white one of the same woman. Her head is tipped back, laughter in her smile, while my nose is buried in her neck. I don't have to see my face to know I'm smiling against her throat. Breathing in her unique scent that reminds me of summertime and fresh sheets on a bed with her next to me.

I swallow thickly, knowing my head should be on the race. I have a lot riding on today's outcome. Every event, I'm seconds closer to a new personal record at the finish line. Then again, I've had a few mishaps this season. And a time clock score doesn't feel as rewarding as I once thought it would. The financial payout rises as the end result lowers, signifying I'm racing better, faster, but I'm still not getting where I thought I'd go.

Fulfillment.

The racing circuit is a rush. A dream I never knew I was dreaming, but there's a hole in that dream.

A chip in the windshield.

A tiny crack that has spread and grown over the years.

Like driving without a taillight. Not impossible, but no way to signal when it's time to change your path. Go left or right. Go home or stay the course.

A life in one direction: alone.

Lately, I've been questioning all of it. Decisions made. Comments said. What I thought was for the best for both of us.

I think I've made a mistake.

No. I knew I had as soon as I left.

They call restlessness in a marriage the seven-year itch. A time when the honeymoon phase ends, and reality begins. Satisfaction drifts. Boredom might even set in.

We had a dozen years together. It wasn't always perfect, but it was ours. And I never experienced dissatisfaction or boredom. Not directly. Not with her.

Trinity Haven. My wife.

Because of her, I had a better life and nicer things in it. A woman devoted to me through good times and bad. A beautiful home we worked hard to renovate and make our own. An honest life, forging our own path, until I couldn't give her the one thing she wanted most. The one thing we both desired. A family.

We were good as a couple, until we weren't anymore. When two wanted to become three or four.

Empty bedrooms stood finished and waiting. And waiting and waiting.

I swipe to one final image. The one that hurts the most. Our foreheads pressed together. A smile on both our lips. Her eyes are closed, but mine remained open, afraid if I shut them, I'd discover I was dreaming. In that moment, I marveled at our position. That she'd said yes to me. She married me. She became my wife.

Twelve years around curves and along straightaways, over speed bumps and through potholes, until there was a crevice too wide to drive around, along, over, or through.

Failure.

The one thing I promised never to do. I would not fail her. I tried my damnedest and had done my best, and yet I still hadn't given her everything. *I* hadn't been enough.

You'll never amount to anything. My grandfather said it best, and his insults still haunt me in moments like this.

I blink at the image and run my thumb over her half of the photo. One of the happiest days of my life. Our wedding anniversary is approaching. Another marker of time.

What does one call a three-year itch after divorce?

The point where dissatisfaction still exists, and boredom might be setting in. When loneliness outweighs financial gain, racing goals, and getting ahead.

And the hurt still lingers. The healing didn't come as I expected.

I sigh, toss my phone to the table, and scrub at my face, letting out a deep groan.

The simple motion rocks the camper on the back of my

pickup truck. I didn't own an RV like most of the other guys. I don't stay in expensive hotels between races as some do. Every penny of my first few successes went one place, and I lived a frugal lifestyle thereafter.

The space isn't large or lavish. The foam bed needs replacement, but there is no mending for the ache of lying on it alone each night, missing my home, missing Trin.

Pressing on the pop-up tabletop, I stand and reach for the mini fridge mere inches away. I retrieve a water bottle, crack the lid, and drain the cold liquid in one long gulp.

I need to hydrate. I need to focus.

I toss the empty bottle into the camper sink and pick up my ball cap. The one embroidered with my team's name. Velocity.

Clicking the handle on the door, I step into the lot overflowing with expensive RVs and extensive trailers for hauling cars. The crew already has mine in the pit, waiting for my arrival.

The day feels exceptionally warm for late spring. Not officially summer yet.

My fire-retardant suit made out of Proban dangles open, the arms flowing like wings from my waist. Safety standards vary in the racing industry, but my team is strict about protection. The fire-resistant material they require for socks and shoes, suit and helmet, doesn't eliminate burns but cuts down on their potential damage.

For some reason, the suit feels itchy today, despite not being fully on yet. The white tank I wear underneath the one-piece outfit is already damp. A combination of nerves and memories.

Before every race, I wish Trinity were here, selfishly wanting her to see how far I've come.

I doubt she cares about the race, though. Or me anymore.

Closing my eyes, I try to center myself, taking a deep breath of the atmosphere around me.

NASCAR feels less like attending a sporting event and more like entering a living, roaring machine.

You hear it before you see it.

Even from the parking lot, the low thunder of engines in pre-race checks is like distant storm clouds. The air smells of gasoline, hot rubber, sunscreen, and grilled burgers.

In the fan lot, coolers undoubtedly thump against tailgates. Race day visitors wearing car logoed tees and faded caps will cheer loudly and razz other fans, all in the spirit of the sport.

Concession stands and food trucks gear up for rowdy race enthusiasts eager for beer, brats, and speeding cars.

Ah, race day. Nothing like it.

Forever. The word whispers through my head, reminding me of something infinitely better than any race.

Shrugging into my suit, I zip up the front and tug on the ball cap. The closer I get to the arena, the heavier the sound grows, deepening until it vibrates through my ribs. The grandstands rise ahead, massive and metallic, shimmering in the early sunlight. Somewhere in the distance, a speaker crackles with pre-race commentary.

I weave my way through the crowd, finding my team, my pit. On autopilot, I go through routine checkpoints and pep talks before slipping into the Chevrolet Camaro ZL1. The red exterior with a yellow stripe is a beauty, but that strip of sunshine color reminds me of a certain blonde today.

I shake the thought and settle behind the wheel, engine purring around me, vibrating up my shins and over my knees, filling my belly and matching the thunder in my chest. My fingers flex and fist, gripping the steering wheel a second and third time before I exit the pit and pull into position.

After a slew of rough races in the early months of this season, there's a lot on the line for me today.

My pulse accelerates. My heart rate spikes.

In the crowd, hats come off, and fans rise. The national anthem plays.

A command follows. "Drivers, start your engine."

Thirty-plus cars ignite at once, a wave of mechanical thunder that sweeps across the speedway. The roar is primal.

A pace car sets us rolling forward until that sacred green flag waves and we're off.

Go time.

Then, in a matter of mere seconds, everything happens in slow motion.

I crash.

3

[Trinity]

"Congratulations." The brunette-haired child services agent offers me a shaky smile before her gaze dips to the baby in my arms. The poor thing has tired herself out from crying so much.

I glance at my mother. With short, white hair in a wavy bob, she looks like a model in an older woman's magazine. In her early seventies, Mary Haven is one of my best friends, and the first person I called after discovering a baby on my back stoop.

I am still in shock.

Seconds after discovering the baby, a robust, ebony-skinned woman, wearing a sharp-looking, black pantsuit, came around the back corner of my house.

"Oh good, you are home." She appeared out of breath, ample chest heaving, but her smile was kind, her eyes sympathetic.

Had she buzzed the front door, and I hadn't heard it?

"I hate to drop and dash like this, but if I can get back on the road, I can make it home by midnight." She shrugged a diaper bag off

her shoulder and held it out to me, then pulled a large manila envelope from the outer pocket of the bag.

"Everything is explained in here."

I'm not certain I blinked, staring at the outstretched rectangular envelope in one of her hands and the strap of a pink bag in the other.

"She's all yours."

Without thinking, I took the bag and the offered envelope, watching blindly as the woman bent at the waist, set her hands on her knees, and cooed at the baby.

"Be a good girl." Her voice softened. "Make your momma proud."

With that said, she stood to her full height again, reminding me of a bear. A great brown one you want to cuddle despite knowing she's dangerous.

Seconds later, she was gone, and I was holding a screaming baby in an attempt to soothe her.

I still didn't understand what was happening.

My first call should have been to the sheriff. I glance at Stone Sylver seated across from me in one of the two chairs opposite the couch next. The tall, broad, mustached-in-the-modern-way man is an old family friend. Heck, he was practically family. His younger sister is going to marry my older brother one day. Plus, Stone grew up side-by-side with Cortland. The two were inseparable for most of my childhood years.

Stone offers me a kind but cautious twist of his lips. From the law's standpoint, he doesn't like this situation. A baby dropped off on a doorstep in the early light of a spring evening. The ring camera on my front porch didn't detect the make or model of a vehicle outside my house. As the baby was dropped off on the back stoop, and I don't have a camera facing the backyard, she must have parked down the block and slipped onto my property from the side. The outer limits of my camera's projection only caught a bulky shadow along the edge of my driveway before she was out of range.

In the envelope provided was a birth certificate, naming the baby: Baby Girl Olsen. Along with the certificate was a letter explaining how I'd apparently helped care for the baby in the NICU.

The mother had no immediate family.

The baby was one month old.

I vaguely remember a young woman recently having a child. No family present. No partner at her side. She didn't visit the baby in the NICU, at least that I'd noticed during my shifts, and we were on the verge of calling child protective services when someone came to claim the newborn. I was not on duty that day.

Apparently, the mother saw how deeply I cared for the infant from the start. She felt confident I was the right person to take her child.

She also recognized my last name and produced an ancestry report showing we were somehow fifth cousins. I haven't been able to process the chart.

I still couldn't quite process what was happening.

Was I being cruelly punked? Or had I been dropped into a scene from *Baby Boom*?

I was no Diane Keaton. And I definitely did not have a Sam Shepard in my life.

The letter included with the birth certificate further explained how Marissa Olsen was a college student, twenty-one years old, and on the cusp of a bright future. Her parents were dead, and she didn't want to raise a baby. She wanted the sweet thing to go to a family member, albeit a distant one. The baby had been delivered to me by a former nanny trusted by the co-ed.

"Is any of this legal?" I direct my question to the case worker.

She shrugs, though the motion is not dismissive. "At this point, the situation is considered abandonment. With consent to offer her up for adoption." She nods toward the envelope on the low table in front of my couch.

"With your background, and our area's lack of baby placements, I'd appreciate if you could keep her here with you for a few days while I sort everything out. If you'd like to proceed with adoption, the process can take up to twelve months in West Virginia."

"Adoption?" I roll the word over my tongue.

The option was one Dart wanted to consider when the doctors told me the older I got, the harder it would be to conceive, even with medical assistance.

Geriatric pregnancy. What a term for a woman over thirty-five having a baby. Insulting, and surprising, when over thirty percent of current pregnancies involve women over thirty, some well into their forties.

It's still possible, I'd argued with Dart. *I could still get pregnant.* Having faith in science and biology and anything else that gave me hope. But after three miscarriages, the last one nearly killing me, Dart had had enough of trying.

I almost lost you, Trin.

I didn't see how it mattered. He'd left me anyway.

I look down at the sweet, cherub-faced baby swaddled tight in a pink blanket. The wrap tucked around her gives her a sense of security as she dozes on my lap.

I'll keep you safe, too. It shouldn't be a thought.

Yet, something deep within the well of my gut says this little one belongs with me. We've both been abandoned. We both have so much love to give. We both need love in return, and I'm open to sharing my heart with her.

All the stored-up heartbreak shatters just by looking at her round cheeks and button nose. Her little lids are closed and flutter. She shudders a wispy breath like she can hear my thoughts, and agrees.

We need each other.

Hope rushes up my sternum, settling behind my ribs,

constricting my airway, and yet wrapping around me, like the security blanket around this child.

Hope is literally in my arms. All my dreams, right in my hands.

Still, I say, "Let me think about it."

The current situation is dangerous. The risk of attachment is great. Hope is a risky pill.

Yet, I stare down at the sleeping babe.

What a gift.

A baby.

Delivered by a giant stork, who looked like a bear, dressed in a black pant suit like a modern-day Mary Poppins.

My heart fills with love, like the slow slosh of the first pour of liquid into an empty cup.

Stone clears his throat. "Gives me time to find the girl. Talk to her."

The case worker gives Stone a skeptical glance.

"I'm happy to keep her a few days," I acknowledge, drawing the child service worker's gaze back toward me. She gives me a grateful smile. She's just as overworked as I am. And I briefly wonder if she overworks herself to drown loneliness, like I do. Helping others compensates for being alone.

She already knows about my extensive background. The formal education and hours of experience in my line of work are on file with the state. I'm clearly qualified to take care of a baby.

Emotionally, however, this is a lot to process.

An hour ago, I was preparing for book club, ready to buy myself a new self-soothing plaything after a rough day at the hospital, and now . . .

I gaze down at the sleeping baby once more. Her little lips pursed, occasionally quivering. A natural instinct to suckle. Her eyelids flutter again, a sign she is dreaming. She doesn't have eyelashes yet, but her cheeks are pink cherries.

She's perfect. And apparently, mine. For now.

Again, I glance at my mother. Her dark eyes are damp with both love and concern. She'll support any decision I make.

Within twenty minutes of my stunned call to her, she was here, baby formula and diapers in hand, plus infant hand-me-downs from my niece, Ruby James.

Which reminds me, this baby needs a name. Something precious like her. Something unique.

"I think I'll call her … Mirabelle."

Wonderous miracle.

4

[Trinity]

It's been four days, maybe five, since Mirabelle came to me. The days and nights are running together because I have not been sleeping.

While Stone sorted out the background of Marissa Olsen and the mysterious nanny, Mirabelle remained with me. Then, child protective services returned, wanting to know how I'd like to proceed with Mirabelle.

The answer was instant. *Adoption, please.*

Baby Girl was going to become Mirabelle Mary Rivers.

I hadn't kept my maiden name when I married Dart. I'd been proud to be his wife, excited about the idea. The new name felt like a fresh start, which was silly, really, because I wasn't any different than I'd been before I married him.

But I was certainly different after the divorce.

And while I introduced myself to everyone as Trinity Haven, legally, my name remained Trinity Rivers.

In the NICU, babies are often put on intense schedules for feeding and sleeping, the two necessities for growing stronger when a baby is premature, as Mirabelle had been. She'd been born a month earlier than her due date, but she hadn't needed the intensive care unit for long. Her development showed no signs of distress or delay.

Just a normal five-week-old at this point.

Because of her schedule, Mirabelle needed to eat every three hours around the clock, and I woke up from her small cry just after ten.

After lifting her sleepy form out of the bassinet that belonged to my brother Clint when his daughter was an infant, I carry Mirabelle down the dark staircase and along the hallway leading toward the kitchen.

Then . . . I stop right before my toes cross into the room at the back of the house.

A cold chill runs down my spine.

Certain I am imagining things, I take a hesitant step backward, not even turning around to retrace the distance. As if I can reverse time. My second step is a slightly longer stride, setting my foot quietly behind me, so as not to disturb what I really hope I imagined. Or rather, who.

Fear doesn't race through me as much as confusion.

Like, why would well-worn cowboy boots on manly feet be dangling over the armrest of the couch in my living room?

But with a shaky final step backward, keeping my back to the front door, I pause outside the archway into the living room and stare at the distinct shape of masculine boot-covered feet.

Boots I recognize because of a definitive mark on the bottom of the right sole. Like Andy was written on Woody in *Toy Story*, claiming the raggedy cowboy toy belonged to the young boy who owned him, my name is etched into the bottom of a boot.

Trinity.

I squint as bright moonlight beams through the front window, highlighting those size thirteens over the arm of my couch, noticing how much brighter my name looks on the bottom of that boot. Like a permanent marker recently traced over the original engraving, etched with the sharp tip of a roofing nail one drunken night near a fire pit in the backyard of this house.

We'd just bought the place and worked long days to make it semi-livable. Dart built a fire in the yard for us to cook our dinner. Hot dogs and beans heated in a can.

To many more nights in our yard, he'd toasted to us, tapping his warmed tin against mine.

Later, he used the nail from our construction site to mark those old boots, telling me he belonged to me.

Heart and soul, house and footwear.

Always ridiculous.

And apparently, sleeping on my couch.

"What the fuck?" I shout, causing Mirabelle to flinch in my arms. Her tiny body curls against me like a little snail tucked into its shell home. The space against my shoulder and my chest is her comfort spot.

Dart jolts upright, forcing his feet to fall off the armrest and thud against the rug. He turns his head left to right like he searches for danger, then struggles to register his surroundings. With a hand on the back of the couch, he slowly turns toward me.

The gold in his eyes stands out, giving him a hawk-sharp gaze that narrows in on me.

"Jesus, Trin. You scared the piss out of me."

I ignore his easy tone mingling with the casual way he's sitting on that couch.

"What the hell are you doing here?"

With a shuddering mewl from Mirabelle, who shivers and shifts against me, Dart ignores my question to ask one of his own.

"Whose baby is that?"

"Mine," I snap, running a protective hand up her back while straightening my spine. I hold my head high, claiming this child like he has my name written on his boots.

"When the fuck did you have a baby?" His gaze drops to my belly. His voice is a mix of shock, disbelief, and . . . hurt? Impossible.

He'd only be surprised to learn that I might have moved on, slept with someone else, and had a baby.

It could have happened, I'd argue. But it hadn't. Not like he must think, as expressed in the lines across his forehead and the tightness around his mouth.

"You still haven't answered *my* question," I counter, not giving in to his. He doesn't need the truth. Not yet.

Slowly, he rises to his full height, taking one cautious step toward me before stopping. He slips his hands into his jeans' pockets. The denim is worn and faded. He also wears a dark T-shirt with the emblem of a car manufacturer on it.

Dart is tall and lean but solid. His dark brown hair is a little longer and messier than he'd previously worn it. His biceps are muscular. His chest is wider than I remember. The tight shirt accentuates both areas on him.

Dammit. Why does he still look so good?

A thin layer of scruff on his jaw is unfamiliar. He used to keep his face clean. Racing standard, he'd told me in a message I hadn't responded to but couldn't help but listen to.

The first six months of separation were filled with disbelief.

One day we were arguing; the next, he was gone.

Despite his attempts at keeping up communication, I didn't know what to say to him.

Eventually, I had to stop. Stop listening to messages. Stop reading texts. Just stop.

Near the one-year mark of his absence, I'd filed for divorce, signed the paperwork, and sent it to him to sign and mail in.

When the deed to the house arrived, along with a statement

that the mortgage was paid in full, I wept for days. Not out of relief after more than a decade of struggling to make ends meet, but at the finality of it all.

We were over.

And he shouldn't be here.

"Honey." He chews his lower lip. "I'm home." His voice drops, sheepish while playful, and his arms spread wide before falling to his sides. Those whiskey eyes, burnt orange with flecks of gold, give me a look that once dismantled all my ire when we argued over things, like who should take out the trash.

And dammit, I will not permit those eyes to have an effect on me now.

Thankfully, his gaze drops from my face to the floor, like he's a child about to be scolded. Which he would deserve.

Instead, I keep it simple. "Get out."

The words leap from my lips, bold and loud, like I've been waiting three long years just to kick him out, as if he hadn't left me first.

His head sharply lifts, his shoulders falling. "Trin . . ."

"Don't you *Trin* me. And don't you dare sneak into my house and settle on my couch like you still live here."

He sighs, turning his head to the side briefly before looking back at me again. Those eyes are fierce, frightening in a way that says he knows something I don't.

"I do live here. This is my house."

"This." I stomp once and tighten my hold on Mirabelle. "Is *my* home."

Dart pulls his hands from his pockets and takes a large step toward me, mouth falling open like he's about to speak.

With the suddenness of his approach, I take a step back, and Mirabelle shudders again.

He glances at the baby and clamps his lips tightly, like he's holding back words he knows he'll regret.

Oblivious to the fight around her, but possibly sensing the tension within me, Mirabelle squirms. I hold onto her even tighter, like I want to be that snail, coiling into a protective shell, and taking her along with me.

Dart tilts his head to the side, letting his gaze rest on Mirabelle. His eyes roam over the back of her downy-haired head and along the short length of her curved back to her little bottom, settled on the ledge of my forearm.

His shoulders fall even further. His eyes soften. He turns his head one more time.

The distance between us is a valley of vast separation and undeniable pain. Of questions without answers.

Over time, I no longer knew who to blame. I only knew I couldn't continue to love him.

I *had* to stop loving him.

And he needs to leave.

As if he read my thoughts, he steps back toward the low table between the couch and two chairs, swipes a ball cap off it, and sets it on his head, tugging the bill low, shielding his eyes.

"I see I'm not welcome here this evening."

Welcome here? Is he serious right now?

"However, I'll be back tomorrow so we can talk."

He steps toward me again, and this time I hold my ground, not moving back at the suddenness of his approach, not shifting to the side to allow him to pass.

He pauses next to me, the heat of his arm warming my bare shoulder. A spark tickles my skin. One I dismiss as familiarity. I've known this man most of my life and have . . . *had* been in love with him for almost two decades. Been his wife. But not anymore.

Still, I'm dizzy from the erratic rhythm of my heart, like I've twirled in place too many times. My pulse is so strong, I'm certain Mirabelle can feel it where her head nestles near the side of my neck. Even Dart might be able to detect the ragged beat.

Watching as his own chest rises and falls with staggered breaths as he stands beside me, I imagine chaos running rampant inside his chest as well.

"We'll work this out," he mutters, side-eyeing Mirabelle.

Work what out? I want to shout, but he steps toward the front door faster than the words can peel off my tongue.

There's nothing left to work out.

It's been three years. Over one thousand days and nights of working to get him out of my system.

But if he's truly gone, why do I suddenly feel a scratch in my throat and an itch along my skin?

Dart walks out the front door, shuts it softly behind him, and sets the LOCK button on the automated keypad, explaining how he got in here, but not why he is here.

"I knew I should have changed the code," I grumble aloud, also knowing why I didn't.

But that's a thought for another day.

For now, I'm left wondering why my heart feels like it is tearing in two again, watching him walk out.

5

[Dart]

Parking along Dock Street in Rogue River, I sit and stare out the windshield at the darkened town. The lights outside The Ferryman's Rest. The white-covered dock, a town landmark, in the distance. The river flowing like black ink in the background.

Everything looks the same and yet completely different.

Flexing my fingers over the steering wheel, I watch them tremble. Aftershocks of the accident, along with the black and blue bruises on my ribs, and the concussion diagnosis. I shouldn't have driven such a long distance, but I'd waited as long as I could to get here.

The accident comes back to me again, like a slow-moving reel in my head.

The crash came out of nowhere.

A blink-and-you-miss-it-mistake at nearly 190 miles per hour.

Mid-pack, my car caught a faint tap to the left rear as I surged into turn three. The back-end snaps loosened, the tires wailed across the asphalt with a scream swallowed by the roar of engines. I fought the wheel, but the car was already out of my control, sliding sideways, then hooking hard as the tires bit again.

The impact was violent.

The front end slammed into the outside wall, folding the hood upward and sending a shock through the chassis like a hammer blow. The car ricocheted, spinning across the track in a cloud of smoke and debris. Another hit followed, this time on the right side, steel and SAFER barrier grinding together in a shower of sparks that lit the grandstands. For a breathless second, the car lifted, all four tires skimming above the surface before crashing back down and coming to rest against the wall.

Silence—then the hiss of steam and the crackle of the radio.

In the driver's seat, I sat stunned, heart pounding, ears ringing, nose filled with the smell of burnt rubber. The safety straps had done their job, holding me tight. My head throbbed from the force of the impact, and my hands trembled as I flexed my fingers, testing myself piece by piece. Pain flared in my shoulder and ribs, sharp but manageable.

I was hurt—but I was alive.

In an instant, a beautiful image flashed in my mind. Hair, long and blonde. Eyes deep wells of darkness, and yet still a beacon. Face round, smile wide, laughter always on her tongue.

Trinity.

Get out of the car, Dart.

My mind played tricks on me, her voice a whisper just above the ring in my ears and thump in my chest.

Still, I quickly unbuckled and scrambled out the window. I stood on the door frame for a split second, swaying slightly, then raising a hand to let everyone know I was okay.

Bruised and shaken, I still walked away under my own power.

I blink at the bright light of The Ferryman's Rest, a local bar near the river, and an old haunt of mine and my friends.

Home, it was the first word that whispered through my head after Doc diagnosed me and Max said I was done for the season.

Come home to me, Dart.

My mind had definitely been fucking with me, hearing her sweet voice like a whispered plea. Damn concussion caused that plea to return to the scene of a different crash. A damaged marriage.

The analogies were endless. The heart of a car is the engine, and her heart was certainly dead toward me. Her tone flat as tires. Her enthusiasm at my return was like a shattered windshield.

Every mile put between me and Florida was a range of emotions. Questions like speed bumps of doubt. Hairpin turns ripe with an urgency to get here. The home stretch was all anxiety.

The finish line was Rogue River, West Virginia, that house, and Trin.

And I am a jackass.

Sneaking into the house was stupid.

I didn't know what I expected. I shouldn't have expected anything.

And she had a baby.

Just what the fuck? Why didn't any of the guys tell me she was pregnant? That she'd met someone? That she'd moved on?

The trembling in my hands could no longer be attributed to the memory of the accident. My sides were black and blue for more reasons than the crash. My heart hammered against my ribs, banging at my chest.

You idiot. You lost her. You've actually lost her.

Yet, what did I really think? That she'd be sitting here, waiting for my return? Holding her breath while I raced around a circle, chasing my tail and my pride? That she'd keep her hands at ten and two on her heart, like I've kept mine?

I pump the brakes on my racing thoughts.

Her moving on is why I left, right? I wanted her to be happy again. Wanted her to heal. Make new dreams, maybe love someone who wasn't a failure.

I need a drink, and I shove open my truck door, breathing in the subtle smell of moving water and thick pines. Even the scent of the town is similar and yet not quite the same as I remember.

The Ferryman's Rest is my destination. A purposely dingy-washed exterior looks like the outside of a well-worn riverboat. The kind used for hauling cargo, not people. The interior walls are weathered wood with captain's wheels and knotted rope décor, along with low-lit lanterns hanging from the ceiling. But most of the decoration is overshadowed by the neon beer advertisements, fishing paraphernalia, and river-related quotes that litter the walls. This place feels a little like entering a bait and tackle shop that serves beer.

And the inside remains the same as it was three years ago, as if time stood still in my absence.

Trinity might have moved on, but The Ferryman's Rest has not.

I used to come here after a hard day working construction, or on long evenings when Trin had an overnight shift at the hospital.

Here was where I hung out with friends.

The same guys currently sitting at a table near the back.

Hutch Hudson.

Marshall Grant.

Jon Pettington, who went by Petty, and was the last person I'd expect to see sitting in this bar.

"Holy shit," Hutch hisses.

"Well, look what the cat dragged in," Marshall drawls, exaggerating a Southern twang.

"Last man I expected to see here," Petty states, stealing my thoughts.

"I could say the same about you," I counter as he slowly rises from his chair. His riot of blond curls features streaks of gray. Wrinkles near his eyes give away the years of living the life of a band member for Collision, an alternative rock group who'd hit their peak about fifteen years ago. He's tall and lean and smacks my back hard as we embrace.

Unlike my short absence, Petty has been gone since college, although we've all kept in touch. Maybe we didn't always reunite here in Rogue River, but we didn't let our friendship disappear, like I had from this town.

With a final slap, Petty spins toward the table, his hand lingering on my upper back.

"You remember Hutch." He points at the burly beast in our friend group who still looks like a linebacker but has a heart of gold.

"And Marshall." Petty nods toward the slick one in our gang. Black hair. Blue eyes. Back in high school, every girl wanted to be his.

"And I'm Petty." He pats his chest.

"Ha-ha-ha." I mock at the implication that I'd forgotten them. "I just saw you guys in February."

The second month of the year marks the start of the racing season. They'd come down to Florida for a time trial. We met up back in November to attend one of Petty's concerts. We met in Vegas last summer.

Of course, there was always one man missing from those visits.

Originally, our crew was like a five-point star, each of us a highlighted arm of the shape.

For half a second, I'm relieved the fifth member is not present.

Then, I hear a low hiss behind me, accompanied by a sharp, "What the fucking hell?"

I slowly spin to see a man with reddish-brown hair, a thin

layer of scruff on his jaw, and eyes that match his sister's—coffee brown and pissed.

"Tate," I choke around his name.

Tate Haven made up the final point in our friend group. Tate, whose younger sister should have been off limits, yet I flirted with her forever, because I'd known from the moment I met her, she'd be just that for me.

Forever.

Despite the three-year blip in time, Trinity is always going to be mine.

"You have some fucking nerve," Tate continues, setting down the four long-neck bottles between his fingers and standing to his full height to face me.

"Tate," I state his name a little stronger this round, shifting my eyes from him to the guys and back.

In a flash, the sympathy in Hutch's face is apparent, as is the concern in Marshall's. Petty's hand comes to my shoulder again, standing in solidarity with me as the other man who left our pack long ago.

"I'll pull up another chair," Petty says before he drops his hand from my shoulder and reaches for a seat at the table behind us. A group of women giggle as they allow Petty to steal the chair.

"I'm leaving," Tate states at the same time I say, "I should probably go."

"Sit your asses down," Marshall grunts, pointing the long neck of his beer bottle at the empty chairs around the table.

Petty waves at the one next to him. Tate takes the empty seat beside Hutch, across from me.

This is fucking awkward layered on uncomfortable and perilous, and yet, Tate's wrath is as warranted as his sister's. He'd been one of my best friends, and I assured him over and over again that I'd never hurt her. Never leave her. Never stop loving her. Promised him with everything I had, which wasn't much. Then I did the exact opposite of what I vowed.

I broke her heart. And mine.

"Whatcha doin' back here?" Hutch asks with genuine interest, before bringing a beer to his lips.

"Does Trin know you're back?" Tate interjects before I can provide an answer, glaring at me while lifting his bottle and taking a sip. He continues to evil-eye me over the end of the tipped-up bottle.

"Saw that accident, man," Marshall says next, shifting topics.

I glance at him first. "Yeah, I got lucky."

But had I? My wife had a baby without me. And any hopes of a racing career are now on hold.

"Luck is like licorice; it eventually runs out," Hutch states, arching his brow.

Not certain what licorice has to do with anything, but I understand his meaning. Luck is sweet but transient. It never lasts.

"This candy shop is empty then," I confess as a waitress approaches the table.

"Need anything, honey?" Her voice is sweet, the question innocent, but the tension at the table jacks up a level.

"I just got us a round of beers at the bar, Prudy. Where were you five minutes ago?"

The blonde narrows her eyes at Tate. "I don't work for you, Tate Haven. Not here."

"Uhm, you kind of do. You're a waitress." He snarks back at her, a flare in his eyes. A bull about to charge, only I'm sensing the rush is to get in this woman's pants.

Tate is a total *himbo*, and there probably isn't anyone left in this town he hasn't slept with.

Except, apparently, this woman.

She ignores him and turns toward me. "What would you like?"

"I'll just have a beer." I tip my chin toward the one Petty holds up. A local brew.

She nods, gives Tate another stink eye, and walks away.

"Woo-wee," Petty chuckles. "I don't know whether to drink this beer or bathe in it. That was one dirty look."

Petty has always been a jokester, and goading Tate is easy.

"Fuck you, pretty boy," Tate mutters, taking another sip of his beer, But I don't miss how his eyes shift back toward the blonde waitress. "She's a pain in the ass."

"You wish she was a pain in your ass," Marshall teases, leaning back in his seat.

"Or wants you up her—"

"Stop right there, rock star." Tate slams his beer bottle on the table and narrows his eyes at Petty, who breaks into a peal of laughter.

"Yeah, that's what I thought," Marshall adds, smirking, while Hutch just casually sits back listening to these guys.

For a hot minute, it feels like I never left Rogue River. Other than the tension coming off Tate toward me. And the fact that Trinity had a baby.

Fuck.

The waitress returns and sets my beer down, giving me a friendly smile before turning her back on the table, ignoring the darts in Tate's eyes focused on her ass.

"She new around here?" The question is nothing more than making conversation.

Those darts aim at me next. "She's fucking off limits."

"Superstar race man here doesn't need your girl," Petty teases, squeezing my shoulder and jostling me.

"She's not my girl," Tate grumbles, a bucket of disappointment beneath the gripe.

For his part, Petty likes to think we share camaraderie because we both live in a fast-paced world. Rock stars have groupies. Race car drivers have pit lizards.

But there's one fact these guys don't understand.

"I'm married," I snap, raising my hand up to show them the black silicone band around my left ring finger.

Tate slams his hand on the table. Petty stares at me. Marshall sits forward. Only Hutch gives me a knowing look. The corner of his mouth curls up just the slightest.

"I knew it," he whispers.

"Knew what?" Tate barks at the big man sitting beside him. Tate always had to be in the know. He's as gossip-hungry as the teenagers in the high school where he works as an athletic director. He slowly turns his head back in my direction. His voice is almost sinister when he says, "Since when?"

Does he think I'm *remarried*? What about his sister and marriage? Impossible.

"June third, fifteen years ago."

I watch as the wheels spin in Tate's eyes.

Petty lifts his hand, counting on his fingers, trying to do the math. "That would be . . ."

"Holy shit," Marshall chokes out. "What are you not telling us?"

With a glance at our blue-eyed buddy, my attention stays focused on him. He's the smartest in the bunch, and I watch as he calculates the truth.

His brows lift. His shoulders fall. "Why would you lie to us?" Hurt fills the question.

"Never lied to anyone."

Maybe I hadn't been as straightforward as I should have been, though. The guys knew Trin and I were having trouble. Well, three of the four knew there were issues. Sharing about our fertility struggles had been difficult, but telling them about my feelings of failure relating to the situation felt impossible.

Like I'd be admitting too much. I'd be giving proof about how I never felt good enough for Trinity in the first place.

And they think I'm divorced.

I might have walked away from Trinity, but I did it for her. She'd been so unhappy because of me. Because of us. I couldn't stand her mental suffering, and then I almost physically lost her. It was too much. I thought if I left, she'd find what she wanted, what she deserved, elsewhere.

But damn, it fucking hurt that she had.

Seeing her hold a dream, snuggling that baby, I should have been relieved. It's what I'd wanted for her.

But also looking at her, cuddling *our* dream in her arms, was a bruise on my already tender ribs. She finally had all she wanted, and all I hadn't been able to provide for her.

"Why didn't any of you guys tell me Trin had a baby?" I argue defensively.

The entire table falls silent. No one offers Trinity's relationship status or an explanation for the baby.

The bruises on my ribs ache worse, like someone is pressing on the massive black and blue marks, purposely making my eyes burn. I chew the inside of my cheek, fighting the anger conflicting with reason.

I wanted this for her. I wanted her to find happiness. To heal. To feel whole.

"Think you need to talk to Trinity about that," Hutch says quietly, lowering his eyes, then flicking them back up at me, offering me a sympathetic look.

He's right. Trin and I need to talk, but where do we start? The silence between us has grown as wide as the miles that separated us. The blame is all mine for walking away in the first place. I might have called her at first, tried to re-ignite communication, but eventually it just got too hard. Her silence. My unrequited pursuit. In a blink, three years were gone.

Luck running out like licorice. Time, too.

And crashing the house certainly wasn't a good start to a conversation.

"Gonna need to find a place to stay tonight." I'm simply stating a fact. I've got the camper still on the back of my truck, and I could have parked in the yard, but the house was too tempting, too inviting.

Home.

Tomorrow I'll approach Trin with a clearer head . . . maybe.

Because my heart is wrecked in a new way. One I can't fully process as thoughts come at me in fits and dribbles. *How? When? Who?*

"Go back to Florida," Tate mumbles, taking another sip of his beer but not disguising his irritation.

"You can crash on my couch," Hutch offers, giving me a sympathetic smile.

"Thanks, man. It's only for tonight."

Suddenly, it's like I'm a teenager again. The lost boy in the lot of them. The one without a family, who roamed from house to house, avoiding home.

You'll never amount to anything, just like your parents. I didn't want my grandfather to be right.

And I never wanted to be a burden to my friends or their families. But that's what made these guys special. None of them ever treated me like I was putting them out. They'd been by my side, offering their homes, giving me their brotherhood. Hell, the Havens gave me the longest stay, allowing me to share a room with Tate for our entire senior year of high school.

Russell and Mary Haven were afraid I'd drop out otherwise, and I might have, if not for their kindness.

I can't think about Trinity's parents yet. Her father was gone before I left, but I don't know how I'll face her mom.

But first, I need to face Trin again.

Tomorrow.

I'll be waving a yellow flag, a warning to proceed with caution.

A crash was on the track up ahead.

Me. I am the wreck.

6

[Trinity]

I hated how I hated that Dart had disappeared last night, but it was a good reminder that he was as unreliable as a cool breeze on a hot summer day.

The morning progressed like a well-oiled machine, as in no structure. I woke when Mirabelle cried out, fed her a bottle, then snuggled with her a bit before attempting to clean. Laundry was suddenly a daily necessity, and bottle washing was constant. I needed to get to the store and—

The distinct clatter of a metal ladder stalled my mental list of things to do. I glance at the ceiling as if I can see through it to where the noise is coming from. Everything in me says *don't panic*, but I rush up the staircase to my bedroom, double-checking all was well with Mirabelle in the bassinet.

Then I hear a thump on the roof, like Santa decided to visit early, followed by the distinct thud of someone walking above my head.

"What the . . ."

Leaving Mirabelle sleeping, I race down the stairs and yank

open the front door with enough force that it slams against the interior wall. I am only slightly gentler with the screen door that makes a distinct *crick*.

Rounding the house, when I probably should have been calling the police, the sharp rip of shingles being torn from my roof hits my ears.

"What the hell are you doing?" I shout at the intruder who thinks breaking into my house by going through the roof is a viable idea.

Within seconds, Dart is standing on the edge of the roof, two stories up, staring down at me. A god on a mountaintop gazing down at a minion.

"I'm replacing the roof," he shouts down, like the situation is obvious.

I don't need him to fix the roof, even if I had been trying to get my brothers over here for weeks. What was the point of them owning a home exterior company if they couldn't put family first? Then again, I would be getting the lifetime guarantee of free service along with a friends and family discount on roofing materials.

"You're going to wake Mirabelle."

"Who?" he hollers back at me.

"The baby," I growl.

He stiffens before turning around and climbing down the rickety extension ladder that had been gathering dust in the garage. Something on my list of things to do was to clear out the space that once belonged solely to Dart. His man cave, he'd tease, about the collection of automobile memorabilia and a Chevy Camaro he'd been working on in hopes of racing her one day.

He eventually did get to race her.

As he scrambles down the ladder, like the professional construction worker he once was, my gaze falls to the butt of his jeans. Ones where the worn denim clings to the firmness of his fine ass. His legs are long, yet the rest of those jeans still outline the strength in them. A small tear just below the back pocket shows a sliver of skin.

As he *clomps* to the ground, feet landing without touching the final rungs, the sound snaps my attention away from his backside.

Because I don't care how well those jeans fit him.

"About that . . ." he starts, spinning toward me and approaching.

"About what?" I blink, my hand coming to my chest, as if I can slow my pulse, which races through my veins because of the way he's staring at me. Like he wants to rush me, devour me.

But he couldn't possibly want those things.

His amber eyes scatter my thoughts for another beat before my brain catches back up to our conversation.

I scowl. "She's not a *that*. She's a she. A baby. A— You know what? I don't owe you an explanation. Stay away from my roof."

His mouth ticks, one corner lifting higher than the other, like I suggested something dirty. Like it had whenever I did suggest something dirty. His gaze roams down my body, taking his time to coast over my breasts and settle on my hips.

"It's my roof, too," he mutters. His gaze snaps back to my face and his expression sobers. "And I think a baby . . . Mirabelle . . . resting under it, is a pretty big deal between us."

"There's nothing between us," I argue.

Dart flinches. The edge of his jaw clenches like I've taken the hammer dangling off his tool belt and whacked him in the knees.

"Trin," he whispers, strained and winded. Hurt is handwritten in every letter of my shortened name.

Exhaling, I cover my belly with my hand, like I'm the one who took a punch to the gut, knowing that lashing out at him isn't going to get him out of here. And I need him gone.

I need him out of sight and swept back to the recesses of my mind where I keep him filed away between broken heart and failed marriage.

"Look." I take a deep breath. "I don't need your help. Clint or Cort will get to it." *Eventually*.

I'm so proud of my eldest and youngest brother, who own Haven Exteriors, an exterior painting and roofing company, that has really grown since they started.

Dart used to work for them. He'd not only been Tate's best friend as a kid, but he was practically one of the family by association with Clint and Cort. Then he officially became family when he married me.

"How are your brothers?" he asks, casual, calm, like it hadn't hurt either of them that he'd quit their business. Quit their brotherliness with him.

"Don't," I choke, weakly warning him my brothers are off limits.

Don't act like he cares about the rest of my family, especially Clint, who worked side-by-side with Dart before he and Cort started their own business and brought Dart into the fold like one of them. Don't even think about Tate, his best friend since childhood, who took the breakup of our marriage almost as hard as I did.

All of this was off limits. Dart taking interest in the roof. Him standing in my yard. Him standing so close to me.

He squints toward the front yard. "Still gonna fix the roof."

My roof, I want to argue. Instead, I say, "Mirabelle is sleeping. *I* need some sleep." I should be napping, but a load of laundry calls and baby bottles need washing.

I'd taken a leave of absence from the hospital, but I was only given six weeks off. So much for FMLA—Family Medical Leave of Absence. The hospital was short-staffed. Every nurse mattered. At one time, I'd taken on more responsibility in my department. Took every extra shift. Worked doubles to avoid coming home.

Most of that time away hadn't mattered. Dart wasn't here either. He'd been out at an old coal mine canyon, running circles in that Chevy Camaro he'd finally fixed up. Around and around and around he went, until he caught the attention of someone.

"You look tired." He reaches for my face, thumb ready to swipe under my eye, but I jerk back.

His intended concern mingles with another flicker of hurt in his eyes, causing my stomach to ache once more. Then again, he doesn't really care about me.

He left.

I do not want his concern. I do not want him looking at me like he is. Like he wants to take my burdens and carry the load a while.

"Let me fix the roof," he says finally, softly, like he truly wants to tackle the protective layer of this house.

"Go away," I mutter with no fight in the demand.

"Not happening." He straightens and hooks his thumbs into his tool belt. Construction worker porn is a real thing, and once upon a time, seeing Dart in a tight tee and faded jeans with that thick belt at his waist would set my heart fluttering. Home renovations were like an aphrodisiac. He'd fix something, and I'd want him to break me in the most pleasurable ways.

But not anymore.

When the silence between us becomes too much, he turns back for the ladder. His boot-covered foot hits the first rung with a clang. The distinct sound of metal rattles against the house. The hammer at his belt swings forward, adding another clank to the symphony of noise.

And a sharp cry comes through my phone.

A baby monitor app is almost always open on the device, and I pull it from the back pocket of my shorts.

Dart freezes as the quiet wail rings like a tornado siren. He twists toward me. "Sorry," he whispers from feet away, then hitches his thumb toward the ladder, continuing to keep his voice quiet. "I'll get back to this later."

Later.

A word that holds a thousand promises. Implies a future.

We had our time. It's now the past.

"I gotta hit the hardware store anyway." He steps closer to me again. "I'll be about an hour."

The nearest hardware store is almost to Huntington, the closest large city near us.

"Don't rush," I mutter, spinning toward the house as Mirabelle's cry grows more insistent.

Having the strange sense Dart is watching me, I step through the screen door without a glance back at him. But before I shut the front door, I pause, finding him at the edge of the yard, looking at me.

With his hands on his hips, nostrils flaring, he looks like an eager racehorse behind a starting gate. Like he can barely contain the energy waffling around him, the need to charge. The flicker in his eyes is recognizable.

I've seen that look before.

When I'd tease him with a seductive taunt or an extra sway in my hips while walking away from him. Then glance at him over my shoulder. An invitation to follow. Within seconds, he'd be chasing after me.

Once, I didn't even make it up the staircase before he caught me, tugged down my shorts with one hand, undoing his jeans with the other, and slammed into me without any foreplay.

The extra touch wasn't necessary. I'd already been so wet, so needy, so gone for him.

He fucked me on the stairs with my knees digging into the hardwood step. One of his arms was braced on the next highest riser, the other hand between my thighs. And all the while, he whispered sweet things in my ears.

You drive me wild.

Always so wet for me.

Take me like you own me.

A neglected part of me clenches, and I force myself to ignore the deep crater of loneliness inside me. The channel of desire clashes with the hint of attraction to my ex-husband.

No, I want to scream, like I can stop the magnetism with a simple command.

Hastily, I close the door, shutting out the memory and the sight of him.

Damn Dart Rivers for still making my body tingle and my thoughts race.

Damn those wild, whiskey eyes and the curl of his lips like he can read my mind, my memories.

Like he was thinking about the exact same one I was and wanted to re-enact it.

With me.

7

[Trinity]

My mother's advice had been to nap when Mirabelle napped. Contact naps, especially, were vital in helping build a bond between mother and child. With Mirabelle in my arms, I lean into the corner of the couch, legs outstretched toward the opposite end, and stamp a kiss against her sweet head. Her awake time hadn't been more than an hour before she was dozing again.

Snuggling her in my arms, I stare down at her, cataloging all her features. Her round cheeks, skin softer than anything I've ever felt. Her eyes closed, barely-there eyelashes. The faint hint of an angel kiss between her tiny brows. Her lips move in that instinctual motion, sucking even in her dreams. Her nose is like a button.

Gently, I swipe down the little nub, then stroke over her head. The soft spot is still present beneath the downy dust of hair. Her hands are tucked beneath her chin. Her toes are covered in the onesie pajamas she wears. I've counted them endlessly. Ten fingers. Ten toes.

I lean forward and inhale her sweet, milky, baby scent.

My throat clogs with emotion. The reality of being her mother hasn't set in yet. I'm still afraid she could be taken away at any minute. Fear settles next to awe, and the love I already feel for her.

Love, that strange desire to keep her close. Adore her. Protect her.

The emotions are confusing and wonderful.

What had me additionally puzzled, though, was the sudden reappearance of Dart. In Rogue River. In my house.

What was he doing here? Why did he suddenly care about the roof? How could his eyes express concern for me? After three years, an itch irritated my chest, one I didn't want to acknowledge. The spot had already scabbed, nearly healed, and I knew better than to claw at the wound again.

Yet, here I sit, my mind lost in memories. The purchase of this house. The endless list of things done to improve it. The money suck. The drain on our finances and our energy, and eventually a source of discontent when there weren't any babies to fill the three extra bedrooms.

I should have sold the place after Dart left, but I didn't have the heart. I loved this old house, especially after all the renovations. The new kitchen. The updated bathrooms. The refinished hardwood floors. This was my home, and the one thing I'd been grateful for in our divorce was Dart allowing me to keep it.

He gave it to me.

Over time, I made the rooms more my own. The Georgia O'Keeffe poster in the front hallway. The velvety soft, pink couch I lounge on. Throw pillows on my bed with ruffles on the edges. Little touches. Feminine pinches that made this house more mine than ours.

He had no right to say the roof still belonged to him.

The soft swirl of the lock on the front door interrupts my

thoughts and brings Dart into the entryway, like my irritation conjured him to appear. He tiptoes down the hallway with two grocery sacks in one hand.

"What are you doing?" I ask, keeping my voice low.

He jolts, not having noticed me.

"Hey," he whispers, his gaze falling to Mirabelle on my chest.

I swing my legs off the couch and slowly attempt to stand, which prompts Dart to rush forward, setting the grocery bags on the low table and extending his hands to assist me.

"I'm good," I snap, not wanting his help, his touch.

The crackling sensation that rippled down my arm last night reminded me of how long it's been since someone else has touched me, and how it shouldn't be him who ignites such a flare on my flesh.

He stills his hands, suspended in the air. His eyes are contrite. "I didn't mean to wake you."

"I wasn't sleeping anyway," I admit, a sigh of exhaustion follows. "I should probably set her down and make myself something to eat."

Dart lowers his hands, rubbing them against his thighs while his brows pinch. "Why isn't her dad here, helping you?"

"I don't know her father." The truth is the truth, but he isn't privy to it yet.

Dart's mouth falls open, and he takes a step back. Air escapes his body like he's been punched in the gut. Then, he clamps his lips and narrows his eyes. "What do you mean you don't know her father?"

"I mean . . . I don't know who her father is."

His hands curl into fists at his side. "Jesus fuck." He swipes a hand through his hair and spins away from me, exhaling deeply again. He sets both hands on the nape of his neck and tips his head back, blowing out another breath. Then he pivots, causing me to flinch at how quickly we face one another again.

"Just rip the bandage off, Trinity. How many guys have you slept with?" The depth of pain mingled with his question sounds as if I've shaved off a pound of his flesh.

My mouth gapes, lower lip hung in disbelief. He has no right to ask. No right to be hurt.

"What the hell? It's none of your business who I've slept with or how many," I argue, not knowing why I'm even suggesting there has been anyone else in three years. Three long, drought-filled years of no physical contact with another man. No emotional connection either, even with a handful of worthless dates and one failed kiss.

He's probably had tons of women in his absence, and the backs of my eyes burn with a thought I've tried *so* hard not to consider. The pit lizards who'd love a swipe at someone as delectable as him. The casual female acquaintances within the crew. The worst was the idea of someone random and meaningless.

My stomach twisted in knots.

It had taken a long time to rid my imagination of him with someone else, even when his original messages tried to assure me there was no one.

Only me. In his heart. In his thoughts.

That time turned to years of vacancy, and Dart was a sexual man. Touch was his love language. He craved it, he gave it. Once upon a time, he acted as if he needed it for confirmation that I was present. I was physically there with him, beside him.

Until . . . he left.

An action that so stunned me, based on his past and *his* fears.

As he glares at me, something etched in the lines around his eyes emphasizes them. Makes the burnt-orange and gold streaks flare like a flame.

Was he jealous?

"Her father should be here," he fumes, angered on her

behalf. As if he has a right to care about Mirabelle. Care about me.

My tongue wants to lash at him. My teeth hold back an accusation: *Her father left me*. But Dart has no claim to Mirabelle.

I push a different topic. "What are *you* doing here?"

"I thought you could use some lunch." He glances at the bags on the low table, running his hands nervously over his thighs again before slipping them into his pockets.

"I mean in Rogue River." Exasperation cannot be contained. "In this house. How did you even get in here in the first place?" *Let alone the second time.*

"The code is our wedding anniversary." The corner of his mouth tweaks upward. A sheepish smile on the way to smugness.

"In reverse," I snip, shocked he remembers the date.

Then again, flowers arrive each year as a painful reminder of what had been lost. The bouquet was the same one I'd carried on our wedding day. The bundle of daisies with a yellow ribbon around the stems should have meant love and patience. The arrangement was not the average collection found in a floral shop. They often looked hand-picked, which would be impossible.

Instead of tossing the gift in the garbage each year, I'd take the flowers to a new mom who was separated from her child in the NICU. Brightening her day when mine had been soured.

Dart didn't need to be so cruel.

"I'll change the code," I mutter, considering how clever he is.

He chuckles, like I'm joking, and reaches for the two sacks. "Let me make you lunch."

"You haven't answered the rest of my questions. Rogue River?" I quip. "My house?"

Dart sighs, lowering his head and shaking it once. “Lunch. And I’ll explain everything.”

“I’m not hungry.” But my stomach betrays me when an obnoxious grumble rolls through my belly.

He gently grins at the rumble in my tummy, reminding me of how his smile was often a reward. He was a playful man, and he made me giggle, but it was rare that I’d make him smile first.

“You’re a terrible liar.” The grin lazily curls deeper, hooking upward higher on one side than the other. His amber eyes sparkle like warm liquid over ice.

“Yeah. The last thing I am is a liar.” My emphasis hits a mark, and his smile fades.

“Yeah,” he counters. “That’s why I’m here. To give you some truths.”

8

[Dart]

I didn't know where to start, so making her lunch was a good distraction.

Wheat bread. Thick turkey. Thin slice of cheese. No mayonnaise for her. I save it for my sandwich.

All the while, my thoughts race around the oval track in my head. Spiraling down the straightaway of jealousy, then looping around the curve, knowing I have no right. I've been gone for three years.

I did what I thought was best for both of us. Giving us space that bled into time. Time that had been too long.

And now, she had a baby with another man. One she didn't know. Or couldn't recall. Or just . . . fuck.

My stomach is as tight as a stubborn lug nut.

Then I consider my own blame in this situation.

The lack of a partner for Trinity.

The absentee father of Mirabelle.

It's everything I never wanted to be and nothing I'd ever want her to experience, and yet here she is.

I'd failed her again, somehow.

Yet nothing was adding up. While Trinity hadn't been a virgin when we eventually got together, she also hadn't been with more than four other guys before me. The idea of her sleeping with numerous men, enough men to be unable to recall which one was the father of her child, didn't make sense. Something was off.

A memory flashes back to me.

Saving yourself for lucky number five, I'd teased her, running my forefinger and thumb up the length of her ring finger. Hoping, one day, she'd wear a ring from me.

I didn't miss how she wasn't wearing that ring anymore. Her left hand empty of the gold band linking us together. The diamond I'd saved for months to buy for her.

My hands begin to tremble, and I clench the knife in my fist, setting it against the counter to steady myself. The bruise across my rib cage aches, and not just from the exertion of scraping shingles off a roof and lifting rolls of roofing paper to be laid before re-shingling. The black and blue lingering on my chest turns red with this new information.

She doesn't know who the father is.

Suddenly, I've lost my appetite and wonder if we should even bother talking.

Maybe I am too late. Back-of-the-pack-late. Maybe there isn't anything left to be said.

Why the fuck didn't my friends warn me about this?

Last night, I laid into Hutch, my anger hard to contain that not one of them thought to tell me, warn me, that Trin had a baby. That she'd moved on in some manner.

"You're an idiot," he'd told me when I was done venting.

He had not been wrong.

I made a decision that I thought we both needed. We needed time to heal, time to work on ourselves.

I really was an idiot, because I thought we'd find our way back to each other. We were still bound together.

With both sandwiches made and cut into triangular halves, I plate them and pour each of us a glass of fresh-made lemonade I find in the fridge.

The scent of that summery drink makes me think of Trinity's mom, and a sharp pang strikes my chest. Memories of being in the Haven home, seeing what a family should look like, act like, feel like. I wanted that for myself, and I thought Trin and I had it, or we were actively working toward it.

How did it all go so wrong? So sideways? Get so backward and turned around?

How did stepping away to give us time turn into three years gone?

How did we end up here, with her having everything she longed for, and me being on the periphery of that joy?

The kitchen doesn't have an eat-in area, so I carry the plates to the dining room where Trinity took a seat after setting the baby in a bassinet by the front window.

The house looks different. Fresh flowers in vases on the kitchen counter and dining room table. That print of a giant pussy hanging in the entry wall. A pink couch in the living room. Pictures in gold frames on the mantel over the fireplace. The built-in bookshelves are original to the house, and yet, even they look different.

This place had been a labor of love and one of my greatest treasures. It was a total dump when we bought it, but it had so much potential. We signed a hefty mortgage and started pouring all our money into the house, draining every paycheck in a rush to finish the rooms for children that never arrived.

I shake my head, unable to go down that path yet, knowing there are other roads to travel first.

I set a plate in front of Trinity, then take a seat on the opposite side of the dining table, recalling when we used to sit near one another. Her at the head, and me to her left so I could hold her hand sometimes while I ate. Toying with that diamond that I'd placed on her finger. Being left-handed, the position worked in my favor.

One thing that had not changed in this room was the antique walnut table. The same one I'd laid her on the day we brought it home, kissing down her chest and unbuttoning her dress. One that had always been my favorite because the buttons went to her waist. I'd hitched up the skirt, slid off her panties, and slipped into her, christening this thing. Our first official purchase after the bed in our room.

I clear my throat to dispel the memory.

"So . . . Mirabelle. Pretty name." Not one we ever picked together.

Trinity hums, turning her head in the direction of the front room, a wistful smile on her face. The love in her eyes for that baby girl is heavy and thick.

Jealousy spikes again, and I race toward the subject still on my ass in the rearview mirror.

"How did you meet Mirabelle's daddy?" Whomever he might be.

Let's just take a tire iron to the bruises across my ribs and get this over with.

"Nope." She shakes her head, bringing her attention back to me. "We aren't talking about me."

"Just curious about your random baby daddy," I continue, pushing a button I shouldn't press.

Her lips pucker, like she tastes the sharp tang of lemonade without sugar to cut the bite. "I don't have a random baby daddy."

And I kind of hate how stinkin' cute she is, even when she's sassy toward me.

Her hair is a lot shorter than it'd been in the past, hanging just above her shoulders. The slight wave means she washed it and let it air-dry. The color is different, too. A little blonder than her original strawberry color. Her eyes are still deep coffee brown, warm and bright.

Until now.

Right now, they say I better start talking.

I swallow hard and rub my hands on my thighs beneath the table. "I'm on a break from the circuit. Probably a permanent one."

"Probably?" Her voice pitches high, question and sass dipping together. She clears her throat. "What does a break even mean?"

"I had an accident." It isn't really that simple, but I don't want to discuss my argument with my manager. How he didn't think I would surpass where I was. Great times, but not excellent. A strong contender, but not one that would ever consistently be driving the winner's lap.

Her eyes widen. "Another one?"

I blink back at her. *Another one*. Did she know about the others? How had she known there'd been others?

Another issue with management. The narrow escapes and occasional collisions. I'd been pulled from more races this season than I'd finished.

But that last accident felt like a sign. Like I'd been tempting fate or something, cutting it close time and time again, until the track decided to take me out.

"Are you okay?"

For half a second, she sounds concerned about me—my safety and physical health—then I remember she's a nurse. Taking care of others is in her nature. Asking such a question is a habit.

"I'm fine," I lie, because mentally I'm still a little messed up. But losing out on my racing career isn't the topic at hand. "A little concussion. Some bruised ribs."

"Dart," she shrieks, then glances toward the sleeping baby.

Lowering her voice, she says, "There's no such thing as a *little* concussion. And bruised ribs. How bruised?"

Sickly black and blue, and a color I don't want her to see on me.

"Easy there, Forever." I smile cheekily, my leg bouncing beneath the table. "That tone sounds a lot like you might still care about me."

Did she? Could she? Could she still love me?

Because I love her. Always have, always will.

"Don't call me that." Back is the barbed-wire sharpness.

My girl used to be playful and feisty, but over the years, we both struggled. The smiles came less often . . . then not at all. I didn't know how to reach her anymore. Didn't know how to navigate us. I felt trapped in my own failures, so she didn't know how to reach me either. I thought changing myself would be a change for us, bring us back together, move us forward.

I'd been so wrong.

"Call you what?" I ask, truly puzzled, as my leg bounces faster.

"That word." Her eyes dip toward the plate in front of her. Neither of us have touched our sandwiches.

"What word?"

She lifts her gaze and we stare at one another for a long minute. One that feels like—

"Forever," I whisper across the table, slapping my hand on my jostling leg to still it. I focus on her gaze. Those typically warm, rich eyes are a little cold, a little distant.

"You are still my forever." My throat clogs, and I swallow tightly.

Trinity looks away.

Beneath the table, I pound my fist against my thigh, knowing I've said the wrong thing.

In a race, there's something called drafting. You want to get close to your opponent and ride their tailwind. It saves fuel and energy. Trin isn't my enemy, but I still need to follow her lead. She's my energy, and expressing deep feelings is exposing too much too soon. I'm not looking to break away and sneak in a pass, a strategic move in racing. I want us coasting together, alongside one another again.

I clear my throat and smooth my hands over the tops of my legs, then push my plate forward and rest my forearms on the tabletop. My hands are stretched toward her but flattened on the cool wooden surface.

I desperately want to hold her hand, feel her fingers against mine. Touching her would make this easier.

"This leads me to your other question. I'm here because this is home. This town. This house. You."

She snorts dismissively before she levels me with another hard stare. "This house is mine. And I am not yours."

Here comes that tire iron to the chest again.

I expel a deep breath.

"Item one. The house. True, it's yours." I drop my gaze for a second, then pop it back up to meet her eyes. "But it's also mine. *Ours*," I correct.

"Dart." My name strangles in her throat, and her lip quivers. "You gave it to me in the divorce."

"Item two. The divorce." I swallow. "About that . . ."

I'd been served the papers at the track during practice laps.

The delivery guy caught me unaware.

"You've been served," he said, handing over the manila envelope.

"Served what?" I'd joked, completely blindsided, even when I knew it might be coming.

Deep down, I couldn't blame her. I'd been the one to step away. I'd wanted her to understand my reasoning, but I couldn't explain myself. Explain how unworthy I felt, and how desperate I was to prove I was still good at something. Thinking if I did something to change who I was, it would change us.

However, she couldn't comprehend what even I didn't know

at the time. And she ignored my calls and didn't respond to my texts, so we couldn't even *try* to talk. Let the distance be the physical break we needed, but allow us to re-open lines of communication.

She'd been my rock, and she was no longer there to steady me. I'd slipped off a boulder and landed on the wrong side of a mountain. I had no idea if she blocked me and my messages went into the abyss, or just filled up her DMs and voicemail. When the silence grew like the miles between us, I anticipated this moment happening while I still foolishly hoped it wouldn't.

"Are you fucking serious?" I'd asked the guy after pulling out the papers and reading the first few lines.

I glared at him, crumbling the packet in my hand.

"Don't shoot the messenger." He held up a hand, contrite, yet doing his job.

He scrambled away from the pit while I tugged off my wedding band in anger and chucked it down the track, lost to the black asphalt that steamed from the heat of the day and the temperature of the cars, one of which raced over the black surface.

When I went to look for the ring, seconds after feeling the nakedness of my finger, it was gone.

Melted into the asphalt? Stuck to the hot tread of a tire? Catapulted to the grassy infield?

Who knew? But my finger was bare, and my heart split in two.

She hadn't asked for anything other than my signature. Not my earnings. Not the Chevy Camaro, or my truck.

She really wanted *nothing* to do with me.

But I'd given her everything. I paid off the mortgage with my first big win and sent her the deed to the house.

My leg begins to bounce again beneath the table, and I clench my hands into fists, hoping it will stop the jostle. It doesn't.

My heart joins the parade of my body's uncontrolled movements, marching harder, making my breathing shallow.

A bead of sweat trickles down my back.

"The thing is . . ."

She tilts her head, eyes narrowing.

"We aren't divorced."

The rush of information rolls out of me like exhaust puffing out a tailpipe. *Poof*, and I feel clear.

I hold up my hand, emphasizing the silicone ring I wear since the original band is gone.

"You and I are still married.

9

[Trinity]

I sputter and cough, although nothing comes out of my mouth. Not one of the complicated questions racing around my head.

How?

Why?

What?

"I sent you the divorce papers," I eventually state, certain I'd had the correct address of the arena where he practiced.

"And I never signed them."

I stare at him, like I didn't hear him correctly. He couldn't possibly be as blasé about the situation as he sounds. My shoulders stiffen, but my heart hammers away, knocking at my rib cage. I can't draw in a breath. He cannot be serious.

"What do you mean *you didn't sign them*?" The disbelief in my voice should say it all, but the clench in my belly knows the simple truth.

He didn't sign them.

For half a second, something a lot like longing and relief

leaps to my throat, but I swallow it down, knowing the emotions are dangerous. The bile is more a warning not to trust him than to believe him.

"When I called you Forever, I meant it." His whiskey eyes turn to flames. Devotion in the flicker. Dedication in his words. He wasn't letting me go. He never really had.

Slow your roll, sister.

He already left you. You shouldn't believe him. You can't trust him.

"You left," I remind him.

"And I asked you to come with me," he tosses back, the volley serrated like the edge of a key.

He *had* asked. Practically begged. He thought a change for him would bring a change for us.

Maybe it would have.

But I was still me. Not that having a baby was all about me. He never felt that way. *We* wanted to fill those upper bedrooms, but I had become a woman crazed. One determined to make it happen.

Sex was scheduled. Temperatures taken. Failure not acceptable. We could do this. The physical connection so prevalent in our marriage had taken a back seat to function and mechanics.

Mentally, I was psyching myself out, almost repelling the thing I desired most.

Biologically, it just wasn't happening.

Dart started turning down sex, rejection that stung soul deep. Like my gut literally twisted because he wouldn't touch me, didn't want me. The last miscarriage pushed him over the edge. He believed he'd lose me permanently.

Then, he sprang on me the idea of joining a race team, moving, and making a fresh start.

I knew he'd been back at the local canyon, racing in circles to let off steam, but I never thought it'd go as far as it went. And I hadn't wanted any part of it.

Because he appeared to have moved on to a new dream, a new goal, for him, and I . . . felt like I had nothing.

As the silence drags between us, Dart finally clears his throat. There is no sense in rehashing an old argument.

The one where he asked me to go with him, and I refused to leave.

"I'm not leaving again." He drives that determination into the vacant lot of my heart. Braking a second, he lifts his head and levels me with conviction. "This is our house. *You* are my home."

He jabs at the dining table to emphasize his point.

"Why gift me the house then?" I counter. The mortgage was marked paid. The deed titled in my name.

He falls back in his chair and lowers his gaze, dragging his fingertips along the edge of the tabletop.

"In case I died on the track. I wanted you to be taken care of. I wanted you to be secure with the house."

My heart plummets to my stomach. He thought he'd die? I didn't want him to die. I wanted him to love me. I *had* wanted him to love me.

When he finally glances back at me, a deep-seated fear dulls the flame in his sharp eyes. He hadn't been afraid of death. His fear was something else.

Dart was afraid of homelessness.

His mother had him too young. His father was never present. Eventually, his mother disappeared, lost to drugs. She'd left Dart with his grandparents, whom I'd never met. He was especially close to his grandmother, who died when he was in middle school, leaving him with an ornery, abusive grandfather who passed away when Dart was seventeen.

He told Dart he would never amount to anything.

Dart had been too young to live on his own. Too old for foster care. Instead, he became transient, moving from friend's house to friend's house, until finally staying at my house his and Tate's senior year. For some reason, my dad took to Dart and told him to stop couch surfing. With Cortland away at college, Dart was set up in Tate's room.

Clint had his own space.

I was only thirteen at the time.

Dart was strikingly handsome as a teenager, but annoying, like my older brothers, and I ignored him. His teasing. His winks. His sharp smile made my newly-teenage belly flutter.

When he was eighteen, he moved out.

You'll always have a home with us, I'd heard my mom tell Dart before he left.

He wanted to make something of himself. Be someone, he'd told my dad.

He didn't go off to college like his friends but started work in construction.

Years later, after we were married, Dart told me how a house of his own was something he craved. When we bought this place, he actually cried. Not a full-on sob but a few tears to mark his accomplishment.

And he did become someone. To me. He was my best friend, my lover, my husband.

His fear of homelessness now included me. He didn't want *me* without a home, even if the place was missing him.

I stare at his face. His eyes are sad, but the laugh lines are still present. We shared so much joy when we purchased this place, had so many hopes and plans. He worked so hard to give me everything I wanted. Not just finished hardwood floors and a new kitchen layout, but a space that was ours. A roof over our heads and a fire in the hearth to keep us warm in the winter. We'd been house poor with simple dinners, but we had one another to nourish our hearts. Our souls.

My brows pinch with the memory, the depth of our connection and desires.

It's all such a confusing battle. The beauty of the past mingled with the hurt of the present.

"Tell me you don't love me anymore." He interrupts my thoughts. "And I'll walk back out that door. You'll never need to see me again if you can look me in the eyes and mean it."

I lower my lids, glaring at him across the table. The ringing in my ears distracts me. My pulse rushing, memories like chaos firing in all directions inside my head.

"I hate you." My voice is quiet, rough like loose gravel in my throat, because the truth is rocky. I am caught in the crossfire between anger and love. What hurts the most is the disappointment.

Promises unkept.

I sigh, turning my head away from his assessing gaze. The fear that he might read in my eyes the truth. A truth even I'm not able to put into words.

"That's what I thought." The corner of his mouth tips upward. He's not gloating, but he is a bit smug. He heard the lack of heat in my declaration, the absence of conviction.

I *could* still love him. Maybe, possibly, but right now, I don't like him.

His expression sobers a bit. He swallows thickly. "I'm sorry, Trin. I know the words are not enough, but I'm just sorry."

He sounds contrite, but his actions . . . they always speak differently.

"And I want to come home." He blinks hard and drops his gaze.

Time seems to freeze as I process what he's asking.

"You aren't suggesting you stay here, are you?" I finally state, my voice trembling. My emotional state matches the quiver.

"I'm not suggesting it, I'm stating a fact. I'm here to stay. I'm home."

His forearms flex on the table surface. Forearms I do not

need to distract me, with their ink and their raised veins, and their overall strength.

Why the hell are his forearms so attractive?

Those arms that once held me. Looped over my shoulder as we sat somewhere or circled around my back when we danced. He'd drape his arm over my waist when we slept and brace himself on those arms when he was over me, entering me, moving in time with my heartbeat.

And dammit . . . I do not want to think about those arms.

"Absolutely not," I counter, unable to pull my gaze from his forearms.

"Absolutely." His smile grows larger, catching me staring at his arms. He makes fists, forcing the strength in them to pop just the slightest bit.

Our eyes lock on one another, and the tension between us heightens, like a thick fog, heavy and blinding.

I should be afraid of what I can't see, and yet, an electric current exists within me. A pull to give in, to push through the opaque veil and seek the sunshine behind it.

I clench my thighs beneath the table, squirming a little bit. Like my body recognizes something I don't. I cross my legs to stop the sudden pulse, but the position only heightens the thumping rhythm. I clutch at the sides of my seat, mentally willing my body to stop responding to Dart's gaze. A gaze where he quirks one eyebrow, like his body reads mine. He senses my unease, and the lion in him is ready to pounce.

A sharp squawk turns both our heads.

Mirabelle.

Through the mesh sides around the bassinet, I see her legs move. A synchronized lift within the swaddling blanket around them. She lets out a second squeak, announcing she's awake and needs me, and I'm so grateful for the distraction.

Shoving off my chair, I watch Dart move just as quickly, beating me to the bassinet.

He gazes down at Mirabelle, and I pause for some reason, giving him a minute to admire her.

Does he see what I see in her? Love. Hope. A future.

Hesitantly, he reaches into the bassinet, running the thick pad of his finger over her clenched knuckles. Mirabelle opens her fist, and Dart slips his finger into her tiny palm.

She wraps her fingers around his single one. The response is natural. An instinct to grasp. And yet the way Mirabelle appears to focus on Dart, matching the surprised stare he gives back to her, something in my chest cracks.

"She's so beautiful," he whispers, his voice rough with awe. "Just like her momma."

I swallow thickly, licking my lips as well, knowing she'll never look like me. Maybe she'll have similar features one day, but she'll always have her own special, unique beauty.

"Can I hold her?" His tone is still thick, his eyes fixed on her, like he can't look away.

I reach into the bassinet, causing him to step aside, and I pick her up, but then hand her to him.

"Hold her head," I gently warn.

Dart cups the back of her tiny head, using his other hand to hold her butt. Mirabelle continues to watch him, blindly trusting that he won't drop her. He'll keep her safe.

Slowly, he lifts her and presses a kiss to her forehead, closing his eyes a second before springing them open and glancing at me.

The well of those whiskey eyes is so deep, I don't have a clue what he's thinking or feeling. Only that he swallows hard once more and tugs her to his shoulder, like he's seen me hold her.

The gallop of my heart is so strong, I swear he can hear it racing.

Mirabelle is so tiny in his hands, and he's holding her like she's the most precious thing he's ever held.

It's too much. It's just too much. My eyes begin to burn again, and I blink repeatedly.

"Why don't you let me hold her so you can eat?" Dart says quietly, offering me a moment. Not just for lunch but for my thoughts.

"I don't think I could eat," I admit, my stomach twisting once more.

"Just try," he says in a hushed tone.

There is so much more in that simple request. More than I dare consider.

Like a second chance at loving him.

A second chance for both of us.

10

[Trinity]

To my dismay, Dart remains.

After lunch, he said he was going to work on stripping more of the roof, and I decided I needed to get away from the house I'd learned was still his, despite only my name being on the title.

I go to my mom's, whom I tell I need a nap. "Just an hour break."

Despite Dart's sweet display with Mirabelle and half a sandwich for sustenance, my anger returns in a flash.

How dare he keep from me that we are still married? How dare he not sign those divorce papers? The sheer audacity that he'd kept this from me.

Not to mention, I could have unintentionally cheated. Not that I'd had any real interest in anyone else, but still . . . it could have happened.

He was unbelievable. Irresponsible. Downright deceptive even.

I've done years of personal work trying to heal myself.

Grieve the ache of not having children. Mourn the loss of my marriage and Dart's disappearance. I'm in a better place than I once was because of these past three years, and now this blast of information.

I can practically feel the anger bubbling in my veins. He had no right.

And in many ways, I feel betrayed once again. Disappointed. Let down. Alone.

Dammit, Dart.

As I lie awake on the double bed in my childhood room, I stare up at the ceiling, flipping through the stages of my life.

I'm not that thirteen-year-old girl anymore with Dart Rivers living down the hall.

I'm not the seventeen-year-old young lady who witnessed a friend have a miscarriage in a high school bathroom and decided right then and there I wanted to be a nurse.

That seventeen-year-old who finally took notice of Dart, my older brother's best friend. Felt the way my belly stirred when I looked at him.

But I had big plans for me.

I went to nursing school, and after two years at another hospital, I took a job with County General and returned to my hometown for a while.

Dart Rivers was still here. Still friends with Tate. Working with Clint. A favorite of Dad's.

When a much younger Dart left our house, he moved into a trailer outside of town for a few years, raising trouble that worried my parents he'd head down a similar path as *his* parents.

But somewhere along the way, he changed direction.

He moved out of the trailer park and into an apartment with a friend. He'd taken a job working for another construction company with Clint. He seemed focused, determined to be better than who he could have been.

And he was a huge flirt.

He'd been relentless.

"Do I look like I'm that easy?" I'd said to him one night, when we'd both been drinking too much, and I was hanging out with friends at Milton Roadhouse while he was there with his crew.

"You look like forever."

I faked a gag, pointing my fingers toward my open mouth and rolling my throat in a choking sound.

"Does that line work on anyone?"

"Only need it to work on one person." He winked at me. So damn smooth. And yet, he never left my side that night. Didn't dance with other girls. Didn't go home with someone else, which I hadn't known until years later.

I resisted him for six weeks before tequila talked too loudly.

When we finally kissed, I felt like I'd wrapped my hands around a live wire. Like one of those cartoon characters you see with their hair squiggled and their limbs extended, teeth chattering.

Kissing Dart was a need I couldn't satiate, and we were suddenly sneaking off every chance we got to bring our lips together and grind against one another.

But I don't want to think about the passion Dart and I once shared.

I'm still pissed.

Deciding sleep isn't going to be found, I fling my legs off the side of the bed and sit upright, scrubbing at my face. I'm too tired to even cry over this news.

I'm still married to Dart Rivers.

Perhaps I'm just numb to the idea.

When I head downstairs, I move toward the kitchen, where Ruby James is sitting at the table, swinging her little legs beneath it. Clint lost another nanny, and Mom has been helping him out by babysitting the precious six-year-old.

"Aunt Trinity, want to have a cookie with me?" Her little legs swing faster as she eats the creamy center of the sandwich cookie first.

"Sure, sweetheart." I pull out a chair and sit opposite her while Mom stands, swaying side-to-side, Mirabelle curled against her chest.

"How is she doing?" I ask.

"She's an angel." Mom smiles. Her dark eyes dance with love. We're all falling hard and fast for this new blessing in our lives. "But the bigger question is how are *you* doing?"

"I don't know what you mean?" I counter, already knowing she knows something.

"Ruby James, if you promise to be neat as a pin, how about I set you up on the couch to watch a few minutes of *Frozen*?" Mom offers to remove Ruby James, so we can chat.

"I got her," I say, standing back up and settling Ruby James on the couch with her favorite movie on the large screen television the boys bought Mom.

They said she needed a bigger screen for her failing eyesight. Mom has 20/20 vision.

The real reason they gifted her the television was so they could watch sports when the family gathered. Although more often than not, we come together for breakfast.

"All set?" I give Ruby James a thumbs up. A small lap tray rests over her outstretched legs, two sandwich cookies on a paper plate shaped like a Zebra's head, and milk in a covered cup with a straw.

She smiles without looking at me as the movie begins.

Returning to the kitchen, I offer to take Mirabelle from Mom, who has taken a seat in a kitchen chair.

"Not yet," she says. "I'm soaking up the Mimi snuggles."

Mom had grandchildren in spurts. Cort's son Josh is twenty-three and has a child of his own. Clint had Ruby James only six years ago. And now, Mirabelle.

I have concerns about attachment. Me. Mom. Anyone in my

family growing too close to Mirabelle before legal matters are finalized.

Still, none of us can help loving such a sweet, easy baby.

Running her hand up Mirabelle's back, Mom gives her a kiss on the head before playfully narrowing her eyes at me.

"Now, what's this I hear about Dart being back?"

"How the hell did you hear that?" I shriek quietly, like that rumor couldn't possibly be true.

"The Babbling Bean, of course."

My mother loves to bake, and in her forties, she opened a coffee shop that serves a small selection of her favorite items, along with fresh brew. The uniqueness of her coffee counter is that it is also a bookstore, heavy on romance selections.

"He only got here yesterday." Surprise laces my voice at how quickly the news has traveled. Drawing a looping design with my fingertip on the table, I avoid looking directly at my mom.

"And how are you doing with that?"

I toss myself back in the chair. "How the hell am I supposed to be doing?" I glance at Mirabelle in my mother's arms, holding onto the truth of the situation for some reason.

How am I supposed to feel about my ex-husband not being my ex?

And how was I going to tell my mother my husband is still my husband?

My parents adored Dart.

Dad never had any reservations about Dart asking me to be his wife, even though Dart had been concerned Dad would not give his blessing.

Mom said she already considered Dart one of the family.

Which meant Mom had been crushed when Dart left. Thankfully, Dad had not been alive. He suffered a heart attack years before Dart took off. Dart never wanted to disappoint Russell Haven, who certainly would have been upset if he'd known what Dart did to us.

"Heard he's staying at the house."

My mouth falls open because that decision was only made an hour ago, and not willingly on my part. However, I didn't have the heart to kick him out.

Whether that made me selfless or a fool was still to be determined.

His reason for gifting it to me comes back to me. His fears about homelessness and death.

Those fears make my stomach tighten.

I am angry with Dart. Pissed even, but I do not wish him to die. And I didn't want him to feel homeless.

Images of him crushed against a cement wall, flipping a car, or burning in flames bursting from a crashed vehicle make me physically ill.

The thought of such torture causes me to shiver.

"I guess it's his home, too," I whisper, avoiding the knowing gaze of my mom. She's aware that he gave me the house as part of the divorce settlement. Or so I thought.

Not as a protection plan in case of sudden death. Not because he was afraid for me and wanted to make certain I was taken care of.

I place my hand over my belly, gurgling with acid at the thought.

"What do you mean . . . you guess?" Her brows pinch, concern in that divot.

I shake my head, unable to answer, as I'm still processing everything myself.

Mom slowly nods once. "Okay then. Do you think that's a good idea? Letting him stay with you?"

Something in the way she asks, almost like *she* thinks it's a good idea but wants to know my opinion, has me tilting my head.

I don't think it's a good idea that he stays, because I have other concerns.

"He'll leave," I mutter, turning my head, looking toward the kitchen cabinets, while not really focusing on them. "Eventually."

I still hadn't forgotten that nugget of information about his racing career. How it was *probably* over, but definitely on a break.

"And what if he doesn't?" Mom counters, not letting the issue rest. Her questions are asked out of love and concern for me.

"Guess I'll cross that bridge if it gets built."

I would have never pegged Dart as someone who would run from problems. Never pegged him as someone who might lie to me either, like keeping our non-existent divorce from me.

But I also recall that Dart did ask me to come with him. He might have wanted to run away, but he wanted me to go with him.

And I'd said no.

Our separation *had* done me some good. Mentally, I was in a better space. Without the pressure of trying to get pregnant, I had to refocus my attention. I took it inward. I looked at me. Where I'd gone wrong in our marriage. How I could have done things differently. Who I should have been and who I wanted to be. And I'd done it all for me.

Because Dart was gone.

Like the namesake of this town, he would go rogue again despite what he initially promised.

For better or worse.

And my heart was not up for drowning in him a second time.

11

[Dart]

Trinity didn't return home from wherever she went until the summer sky was turning dark. By then, I'd scraped off all the old shingles on the roof. Tomorrow, I'll start rolling out the roofing paper needed before I can lay new shingles. Thankfully, rain is not in the forecast.

Re-roofing the house on my own was a daunting process, but something that needed to be done. While I didn't want to return to construction work, it felt good to be productive. To accomplish something, even if I was sore from the exertion.

My ribs ache. My head has a low hum of pain in it.

I take a shower in the guest bathroom on the second floor, discovering the showerhead needs to be replaced. The water pressure sucks.

While Trinity was perfectly capable of taking care of certain things on her own—she could tackle replacing a showerhead herself—I'd always been the handyman around here. I took pride in the little touches. The wainscoting panels. The chair rail detail. The tile job in the bathroom.

My hands made these improvements. *Our* vision was a home, not just a house.

The overall appearance of this place is immaculately clean, minus the sudden explosion of baby apparatus. Trinity made some changes in my absence, and the space feels more feminine, reminding me of her first apartment.

That place was small but cozy. She had all these damn pillows on the couch and affirmations on the wall, and a giant poster that looked like a pussy that she swore were flower petals.

I'd never lived anywhere so nice, other than her parents' house, which was why I loved to spend the night at her place. She had sturdy coffee mugs, and her silverware matched. Stuff I didn't give a shit about other than when I was near her.

Eventually, she'd turned this dump of a house into a beautiful home, and I loved this place. Loved every crooked wall and refinished plank of wood on the floor.

But home improvement wasn't a one-and-done deal, and it was a good metaphor for our marriage.

We changed. The loss of three babies can do that to a couple. We couldn't just put a fresh coat of paint over old wounds. We couldn't caulk the cracks in our marriage. We needed to renovate ourselves.

Trin was different, closed off and sad. And I got lost in my head, thinking I wasn't enough for her. Old comments came back to me, haunting me. I didn't know *how* to be enough for her. But I never stopped loving her, wanting her. Wanting what this home represented. Us.

After Trin and I hooked up that first time, there was no turning back for me. I went to Russell Haven, wanting him to know my intentions regarding his daughter.

"I'd like to marry Trinity one day," I'd openly admitted, cocky while still concerned the man I admired most would see me as not good enough for his girl.

"Son, I've known that since she was seventeen."

I didn't know how he knew that when I hadn't known it back then. When I was twenty, and she was too young for me. But Russell always saw something in me I didn't.

Potential, he'd once said. He said I somehow reminded him of himself. And he knew that potential could tip one way or another.

"Make certain it always leans in the right direction." He glanced at his daughter when he said it.

He would have been so disappointed in me. The way I'd hurt Trinity. The way I tore us apart.

Now all I wanted was to put us back together again.

Which I could not do if she avoided me by staying out late.

Exiting the guest bathroom in frustration, wearing only a towel and scrubbing at the back of my wet hair, I almost plow into Trinity, hustling down the hallway.

"Dart." She shrieks like she'd forgotten I was staying here, albeit in the second bedroom. A room intended for guests.

I watch as her gaze lands on my belly. Her eyes blow wide, and she repeats my name on an anguished whisper.

The black and blue marks on my midsection are making their way to a nasty yellowish-green color.

To my surprise, Trinity steps closer. While I'm the one who just showered, I catch a whiff of her sunshine and fresh meadows scent. A fragrance that haunts me.

Her gaze never leaves my waist, and I stand taller, letting her have her fill. Those brilliant dark eyes soften. Her hand comes forward, fingers shaky, as she reaches for my ribs, then she catches herself just an inch away from making contact with my skin and jerks her hand back, leaving me feeling empty and deprived.

Instead, she wraps her hand around her throat and swallows. "The accident?"

"The accident." The one that could have taken my life.

Her eyes don't leave my bare chest, and my heart rate accelerates. I hold my breath as her gaze roams upward to my throat and then straight back down my middle to the line of hair leading south. She might as well have skimmed my flesh with her fingertips because that slow gaze makes my skin pebble.

She clears her throat and glances to the left. "You probably shouldn't be on the roof."

I probably shouldn't. Her brothers could have taken care of that repair, but I want to do it.

"Nah. Don't you worry about me." I was terrible at sitting still, which is where racing came in. I loved the speed. Zero to one hundred in a matter of seconds. A sharp curve. A smooth straightaway. I loved the attempt to control something so fast, so reckless.

And it was killing me that I didn't know how to go slow with Trin. With my wife.

I wasn't certain it'd sunk in for her yet. We are still married. Even if we felt like separate individuals, we are technically still a couple.

Stepping closer to her, I pinch a section of her hair, sliding my fingers down the short length. The outside of my thumb brushes her cheek.

"You cut your hair. I like it." My voice is quiet, rough, almost raw. She's different in so many ways, and yet, she looks exactly the same as the day I opened my eyes to her.

Beautiful.

Back then, she was seventeen and too young for me. She had a bright future ahead of her, and I wasn't where I needed to be. Yet. But knowing someday I wanted to bask in her sunshine.

"Yeah, well, things have changed," she states, stepping back. "*I've* changed."

That step away reminds me of the great divide between us. The length of time I've been gone, trying to work on myself while giving her space.

I curl my hand like I can hold onto the briefness of touching her hair. Our gazes click together, and my tongue locks in place. I have so much to say and yet can't find a single word to begin.

"Trin, I—"

Mirabelle lets out a cry from somewhere on the lower level.

When Trinity pulls her attention from me, she blinks rapidly like she's been under a spell.

"Don't touch me," she whispers, her voice shaky and weak when she glances back at me.

Those dark eyes shift to midnight, and she shuts me out by turning away from me, rushing for the stairs.

I grip the railing that surrounds the stairwell, watching her disappear down the steps, and curse myself.

Patience, you dipstick. Patience.

The list of things to be fixed around here kept growing. The showerhead. The roof.

My wife's broken heart.

12

[Trinity]

Two weeks have passed since Mirabelle arrived on my doorstep, and I canceled attending book club.

Which means it's been more than a week since Dart's arrival. A week where we've circled one another.

Despite my protests that he should leave the house, he settled in an extra bedroom. Since then, it's been like a video game of avoidance, but Dart seems to be everywhere.

The hallway without a shirt on.

The bathroom project, his jeans dipping low as he worked on the plumbing.

And most recently, the backyard, measuring space outside the back door.

He'd catch me looking out the window at him, our eyes locking on one another for a brief second, before I'd spin away from the glass, feeling a hitch in my breath.

I'd catch him looking at me as well, when I'd be pacing with Mirabelle or playfully pressing kisses on her. His focus is intense, but his eyes are always soft. Possibly thinking the same things I do about Mirabelle. She is such a blessing.

Then again, I didn't know what Dart was thinking, or what he was doing by tackling all these projects around the house.

I simply knew he was here, hovering when I made dinner or did the dishes. His presence wasn't so much ghost-like as we'd been in the past, but an awareness. I sensed his nearness, felt it tickle my skin and rattle my thoughts, and I even sipped a little comfort from it. Especially when he offered to hold Mirabelle or gave her a bottle or simply murmured something to her.

Which further unsettled me because I did not want to get used to him being present, or near me, or smelling like mountain pine with an undertone of fresh asphalt.

Dart would leave again. It was only a matter of time, I told myself.

Thankfully, we didn't talk. He didn't ask for more details about Mirabelle or her unknown father. We didn't bring up the past. We just . . . circled one another.

It was frustrating as hell.

ONE NIGHT, a knock rattled my front door. Answering it, I'm met with the best surprise. Vale Sylver and Halle Reynolds, now Sylver, stand on my doorstep along with Mavis and Genie, also now Sylvers.

I have officially missed several book club meetings in a row, which is so unlike me, but the girls knew my situation. Mirabelle.

That first night, I'd sent a simple text in our group chat to say that something had come up. But by the next day, I'd shared more details about the crazy circumstances of finding a baby on my doorstep with permission to adopt her.

Of course, news traveled fast between Sterling Falls and Rogue River as neighboring small towns, especially when the sheriff is a member of their family.

"Surprise!" Vale announces, waving a bottle of wine and jazz hands at me after I open the door. "We brought book club to you."

Vale is currently dating my older brother, Cortland. Cort and Stone Sylver were once inseparable friends, but they had a falling out. As Vale and I are the only sisters in either family, and both members of the Sterlets, we called a truce when the rest of the families had already pulled apart.

Now, this cornstalk-blond spitfire is going to be my sister-in-law, because I sense an engagement coming soon. Stone and Cort might not be best friends again, but they've formed their own truce because of Vale.

Vale helps herself to enter my house.

"Hey," Halle offers next, holding out her arms for a welcome hug.

Halle is a lithe red-haired beauty and was my best friend in high school. She returned to Sterling Falls a few years ago as a newly divorced single mom and reunited with her high school sweetheart, Knox Sylver. The rest was a rocky road to happily ever after.

"Actually," Halle drawls, holding up several gift bags that are obviously for a baby girl. "We're throwing you an impromptu baby shower. Congratulations, lady."

These women know my story. How much I've longed for a baby. How hard I worked to make it happen. And how much I lost.

While my throat grows thick, I'm too busy smiling at them, grateful for their presence. It's been too long since I've had adult interaction outside of my own family.

Mavis follows Halle, holding another bottle of wine and offering me a hug as well. Her tan skin and elegant bone structure enhance her dark features, which include deep eyes and long, midnight-colored hair with streaks of gray woven in it. She's tall like Halle, and married to Clay, the second eldest in the Sylver family. As Clay and Knox work together in their family business, Halle and Mavis are close. Mavis is also a nurse and works at County General like me, but in a different department. She's quieter than the rest of us and an excellent listener.

"Yes," Genie Sylver announces, bringing up the rear, with a baby carrier in her hands. "Nolan will be asking Mirabelle to prom."

Genie is the newest friend in the mix. Married to Judd Sylver, who is the chief financial officer for Sylver Seed & Soil, she's a new nursing mom, so baby Nolan is with her. She has a short, wavy bob with stripes of blonde and brown in a style that seems to match her bubbly personality.

I laugh at Genie's comment. "You haven't even seen Mirabelle yet."

"Don't need to see her to approve." Genie winks at me. "I already know she's perfect."

Perfect. That's exactly what I think of Mirabelle, and these amazing friends of mine. We're going to continue to grow older together, especially Genie and me, with babies roughly the same age.

Only a few months old, Nolan is so much bigger than Mirabelle, but perfect in his own right with a shock of dark hair and blue eyes, which are presently wide-open.

I need mom friends, something I haven't thought about until this exact moment. Especially friends going through this experience at the same time as me. Not that Vale or Halle or Mavis have forgotten the baby stage with their children, but Mirabelle will need playdates. *I* need my friends, and gratitude swells inside me.

"And whose fault is it that we haven't met her?" Vale teases loudly over the others as they rush toward my living room, surrounding the bassinet where Mirabelle sleeps through the commotion.

I've been a little preoccupied and overwhelmed with Mirabelle's arrival and . . . Dart's.

Soft murmurs follow Vale's playful chastising, keeping me in the present.

"She's so sweet."

"Look at her little nose."

"What a precious angel kiss," Mavis says about the harmless red birthmark near Mirabelle's eyebrows.

"Putting it in my calendar now," Genie says with a laugh. She's a calendar creator. "Future prom dates."

Vale chuckles. "On that note, wine and then presents." She heads toward my kitchen, helping herself to the glasses while the other women continue gushing over Mirabelle until a masculine throat clears.

All heads turn sharply in his direction.

"Sorry to interrupt," Dart says, glancing around the group of women he doesn't know.

He probably doesn't remember Halle, as she graduated high school with me, making her years younger than him.

Genie is roughly my age as well, but was not part of my friend group back in high school.

And Mavis is a transplant, moving in, then out of Sterling Falls, before settling here again, all in the span of Dart's absence.

My ex-not-really-ex-husband looks freshly showered despite wearing black joggers that hang loose on his hips and a baseball-style shirt that hugs his chest. The ink on his arms is on full display.

My friends ping gazes from Dart to me and back to him. I can almost hear the questions suddenly in each of their heads.

Who is that? Mavis would ask.

You didn't mention you had a man in your life. Halle would tease.

Yes, yes, yes. The last being Genie in all her enthusiasm.

But it isn't until Vale re-enters the room, laughter in her voice while she juggles wine glasses. "Okay, let's get this party started right with— Dart?"

She stalls out behind the back of the couch, blinking at Dart like she can't believe he's standing there.

I still can't believe he's here.

"With darts?" Genie says, confused, glancing from Vale to Dart.

"No." Vale's clarification is said low and long before she looks at me, compassion and fear mingled in her eyes.

"What is he doing here?" she asks, like Dart isn't present.

"Everyone," I begin, clearing my throat before casually waving toward him. "This is Dart. Dart Rivers. And it appears he was just leaving."

I glare at him because I do not want him to crash my impromptu baby shower, especially since it just morphed into a truth-sharing session with friends.

Because they are going to have questions, and unfortunately, I still don't have all the answers.

"Right." He smiles with enough wattage to set all the lightbulbs buzzing. "I'm headed out to a baseball game."

Baseball? Whose team? He can't possibly mean Tate's team? My older brother plays in an adult, men over thirty-five league during the summer months with some of the guys he's been friends with since high school. The star gang, I used to call the five guys tight as brothers.

Only three remained in the area.

And I wasn't aware Dart had been in contact with Tate.

"Looks like a party," he keeps his voice light, while his gaze roams from friend to friend.

No one speaks, perhaps too stunned to find a man in my house.

After an awkward beat, Dart crosses the room to Mirabelle, rubs his hand over her little head, giving her a soft glance before stepping closer to me.

He leans in like he's going to kiss my cheek. Like he's forgotten my don't-touch-me rule. Or maybe he's acting out of some long-gone habit.

He always kissed me before he went somewhere.

He stops himself just shy of my cheek, slips his hands into his jogger pockets, and says, "Behave yourself, Forever."

I absolutely hate the chill that ripples down my center at the soft brush of his breath and the heat of his nearness.

He must have showered because the pine over asphalt fragrance lingers when he pulls further away.

"I'll be home around eleven," he states, like he owes me his time, or I even care when he'll be back. Then again, he could simply be warning me: *he'll be back.*

When he steps away from me, he grabs a ball cap I hadn't noticed on the antique coat stand in the hallway and tugs it on his head before giving me one last look and a wink before disappearing out the front door.

Halle and Genie rush to the front window, like they can't help themselves from watching him walk away.

Vale remains behind the couch, still too stunned to move. Woman frozen with wine glasses in hand, a painting of her might read.

But Mavis gives me a concerned look, causing my knees to give out, and I fold down to the edge of the couch.

"Who the hell was that?" Genie finally asks, spinning to face me with a big grin. Like she's proud of me for having a man in my house, thinking I'm getting something I'm not.

"Dart Rivers," Vale answers for me, only she says it with grit, like dirt on her tongue, incredulous that he's in my house. Most days, I still can't believe it either.

"The man who broke your heart," Mavis states quietly, perceptively, while she continues to watch me.

Halle finally swings her head in my direction and takes a seat in a chair opposite the couch. "Oh no. That's Dart?"

"That's Dart." I sigh.

"Who's Dart?" Genie asks, her hair flying around her head as she glances around the room.

"Trinity's ex-husband," Vale offers.

While three of the four present know I've been married, I don't talk about it much. The occasional too-many-glasses-of-wine at book club can bring out lingering pain, but for the most part, I keep Dart locked away inside me.

"You were married?" Genie asks, her voice rising at the sudden information. She finally takes a seat in the second chair.

"Apparently . . ." I swallow hard and glance at Mavis for some reason. "I still am."

"What the fuck?" Vale grinds out.

"Are you serious?" Halle's eyes bug wide.

"Oh, sweetheart." Mavis takes a seat beside me and cups my hand.

"Wait, what does that mean?" Genie asks, glancing from Vale, still behind the couch, to me, perched on the edge of it.

"It means Momma needs a drink. Then, she has some explaining to do," Vale states, rounding the couch and setting down the multiple wine glasses in her hand.

Once seated, Vale pops the cork on a wine bottle and hands me the entire thing. No glass.

"Drink. And start talking."

While my friends know the basics about how Mirabelle came to be with me, I back up and fill in all the details about Dart's return.

"And now he thinks he can live with me. In my house."

"Which is definitely not okay," Vale argues.

"In your house . . . collectively," Mavis corrects, her eyes full of compassion. "Are you afraid of him?"

Knowing Mavis's history, I shake my head. "Only afraid he'll break my heart again." I pause, sitting straighter. "Which can't happen, because I'm not giving it to him a second time."

"That's my girl," Vale cheers.

"Best laid plans, though," Halle mumbles, her smile slow and sympathetic. While she didn't want to reunite with Knox when she first returned to town, their history is vastly different from Dart's and mine.

"Do you still have feelings for him?" Genie asks, the question sympathetic.

"I—" I don't know how to answer. "I have a lot of feelings toward him. Disappointment. Upset. Anger. I'm pissed."

"You have a right to all those feelings," Halle adds. "Be mad."

"I kind of hate him, a little bit," I admit.

But the real question Genie is asking is if I still care about him, love him. Despite those negative emotions, is there something positive beneath the dirt and rubble?

In many ways, I will always love Dart. How could I not? I'd been married to him for twelve years. We'd been happy together, good for one another. Our falling apart feels like a force outside of who we were.

A dream denied over and over again, taking a toll on both of us.

My gaze falls to Mirabelle, who remains asleep in the bassinet despite the commotion in the room. Because this room is also filled with love and support. My friends want to help me sort out my feelings.

"Hate is valid," Mavis says, still assessing me. "But love and hate also walk a fine line, and holding onto hatred takes a lot of energy. Energy you need to focus elsewhere."

She glances at Mirabelle as well.

Mavis is right. Hate is a strong emotion, and even though Dart left me, I never hated him. Not truly. I'd been hurt. I'd been confused. And most of all, I'd been alone, without my best friend, my husband, to talk about all the conflicting emotions.

It also took energy to hate someone, concerted energy that I didn't have to focus on Dart when I wanted to focus on myself instead. I needed a reset, and perhaps, him ripping out my heart, recharged me.

I took giant leaps through grief and loss, anger and disbelief, and then, I just woke up one day and told myself to move on. One step forward at a time.

"He might be good-looking, but I'm willing to collect shovels if we need them," Halle teases, especially as her shovel collection would come from Sylver Seed & Soil.

"I know a guy or two who could help," Mavis suggests, a small hint to her past, which she rarely mentions.

I snort, knowing both women are joking.

"He obviously still loves you," Genie states. "The way he looked at you before he left." Genie dramatically sighs and fans her face. "My ovaries exploded and I just had Nolan. Luckily, Judd and I have the all clear to—"

"La, la, la, la," Vale sings. "Brother talk, remember."

Once upon a time, Vale and I made an agreement. Never discuss our brothers. Their decisions did not dictate our friendship. Vale now demands that none of her sisters-in-law share their sexcapades with her because . . . brothers.

Halle chuckles. Mavis smiles.

Vale breathes out a heavy exhale. "I hate to agree that he's still a tall drink of water."

"Question is, how thirsty are you?" Halle asks, knowing how vocal I can be about my sexuality.

Single. Individual. Independent.

I've bragged for years that a woman only needs herself for pleasure. I take care of my needs. With the help of some tools sold during our book club meetups.

I've probably been Meredith's best customer over the past three years.

Mavis squeezes my hand. "She looks absolutely thirst-deprived." As the subtle one among us, her comment surprises me.

"Like she needs hydration," Genie adds. "Bet he's willing to moisten whatever you want."

Halle snorts, holding up her palm toward Genie, who smacks it back.

"Still want a sip of that water?" Vale asks, hesitantly.

"I don't know," I admit, as tears fill my eyes.

I just don't know.

13

[Dart]

I mentally spiral as I drive to the baseball field.

I'm watching Trinity struggle to eat. Watching her barely sleep. Watching her parent alone. I've been trying to do small things to help without overstepping.

And every time I look at Mirabelle, that little pink bundle of joy, I struggle, knowing she belongs to Trin and someone who isn't me. She slept with someone else. Possibly even multiple men.

I'm not only jealous, I'm devastated. And I'm disappointed that I lost her so completely. She's built a life without me. Hell, she even has new friends, minus Vale Sylver.

When I pull up beside the chunk of land just east of downtown Rogue River, there is a tremor in my hands as I set the truck in park. I make a fist and tap the side of it against the steering wheel, trying to calm my nerves.

But the second I reach the field, I explode. "You're all assholes."

I haven't seen any of them since I went to The Ferryman's

Rest more than a week ago, but there have been dribbles of chat in our group text. Hutch invited me to join their team, the One-Eyed Snakes, which is a thirty-five-and-over, men's baseball league. Their logo looks like a braided penis, with a split tongue coming out the tip.

"Yeah, and fuck you, too," Tate grumbles at my outburst.

"I'm serious." I glance at Hutch, Marshall, and Petty, ignoring Tate. "Not one of you guys told me Trinity had another man."

"Uhm . . ." Marshall glances at Tate.

"What the fuck, man?" Tate stands taller, squaring off at me, although it's difficult to take him seriously with a giant dick on his shirt.

"Don't what the fuck me, *man*," I snap. "I know I hurt your sister, and you're fucking pissed at me, but someone could have told me she moved on. Had another man. Or many."

Tate charges me faster than I'd expect and only narrowly misses clocking me in the face before Hutch catches him around the waist, and Petty yanks the back of my shirt to get me away from the punch.

"Easy," Petty warns, his tone sharp near my ear.

I know. *I know* I'm in the wrong, and my accusation is unfair, but my chest feels like it's been cracked open. Like someone took a bat to my already damaged ribs and slammed straight into my heart.

"She fucking slept around." My voice cracks with thick emotion.

My wife, my beautiful wife, had a baby with another man, and no one told me.

And she's had multiple lovers.

The kicker is, the guy is gone, abandoning her, leaving her a single mom and that precious baby without a father. A position I'd never want for Trinity. To be alone. To parent on her own. Without a partner. Without me.

My own guilt socks me in the gut. Maybe Tate should punch me.

"I'm going to kill you," Tate vows, struggling to rush toward me again.

Hutch wrestles him back.

"Enough," Marshall hollers, holding out his hands to separate Tate and me. "Don't talk about Trinity like she's trash."

Someone might as well have taken another bat to my gut, because that is not what I intended.

"She's my wife," I counter, devastation causing my voice to crack.

She thought we were divorced. And whose fault was that?

She had the right to do what she wanted with whomever she wanted, but it still fucking hurts to consider there's not only been one man touching her soft skin and tasting her sweetness, but enough men that she can't remember who the father of her child is.

I shrug Petty off me and bend at the waist. I've been worked up for days, but my thoughts spew like poison out of me, which pitches me forward. I'm going to be sick.

"Funny way of showing it," Tate hisses. "And not like you didn't sleep around with all those pit lizards."

I stand so abruptly that Tate flinches, although he's more than a foot away from me. "I didn't." The words squeak, emphasizing the truth.

I haven't slept with anyone other than my wife.

Hutch and I meet eye-to-eye. He knows the truth. Marshall's head swings in my direction, meeting my eyes next, before Petty claps my back so I will look at him.

"Right," he teases, wiggling one brow higher than the other.

"I might not have been the best husband, but I've been one-hundred percent faithful." I snap my attention back to Tate. "I'm practically a virgin again."

Tate stares at me, disbelief in his eyes.

"Despite what it might look like . . ." I pause, glancing from Petty to Marshall to Hutch before falling to Tate. "I love my wife."

"*Ex* wife." Tate scoffs.

Marshall hangs his head. Hutch shakes his.

"Not ex-wife." I whip my left hand upright, flipping it like I did the other night. The silicone ring dark and prominent.

Tate is not the smartest one in the group, and he clearly wasn't paying attention when the other guys put things together.

Trinity and I are still married.

"Fuck," Tate growls, as if finally realizing the truth.

I drop my hand and stand taller, thinking of Mirabelle. "And one thing I would never have done is leave my kid behind."

These guys know this. For all the ways I've been left behind, I'd never do that to a child. Never.

"Only your wife," Tate counters, spit forming in the corners of his mouth.

I deserve that. I've done Trinity wrong. I've done wrong by both of us, but Tate also isn't perfect. His faults are many, and he shouldn't be casting stones. I realize he might have had to draw a line, his sister or me, but he's also a guy. He's human. And we all fucking make mistakes.

"*Man*," I mock him. "You don't know anything."

How I asked her to come with me, and how she refused. How broken we both were by the last miscarriage. I almost lost her forever. I was desperate to make a fresh start for us, somewhere away from all the reminders. The empty bedrooms and the packed-up baby clothes.

But I also needed to prove something to myself. I thought I needed to reinvent myself.

"Well, whoever that guy is . . . the baby daddy . . . he's a dick." I glance at each of them as if they know who he is, or where he is. Another slice of information no one is willing to share with me.

I'll kill the guy for leaving Trinity and Mirabelle behind, and I realize that makes me the pot calling the kettle black.

At least, I'm wearing my shame, owning up to it. I made a fucking mistake.

"Hasn't she told you anything?" Marshall asks, additional questions etched in the creases near his eyes.

Again, I sense they all know something I don't. And that sensation of things not adding up comes back to me. It just didn't seem like Trin to suddenly run out and hook up with a handful of men.

As for my friends, I could argue that I thought we were tight, told each other everything. But our friendship has a red flag, and it is Trinity.

Glancing over Tate's shoulder at Hutch, I beg. "Tell me what I'm missing."

He purses his lips and shakes his head. "That's between you and her."

I meet Marshall's eyes next, imploring him.

He tips his head back and lowers his shoulders. "Look, I don't want to be a dick, but we have a game to play." He looks back at me. "You in, or you out?"

He nods toward the field where the other team has been warming up, but several of them are watching our party of five. The tension is still heightened between us.

I glare back at Tate. "I'm in. One-hundred *and ten* percent."

As our gazes lock on one another, Hutch asks a deeper question. "For the long haul or only the season?"

Their baseball season? The summer months? The racing circuit?

"I'm back. For good." I don't think I realized it until the words are finally shared.

I'd told Trinity my racing career was probably over, and in

many ways, it is. I'm out for the season, and I might not be able to return. But I already know one thing for certain, I'm not going back to racing without her. I won't leave her behind again.

I'm here for my wife, and I'll do whatever groveling I need to do to make things right between us. Between her and me.

Our marriage is a race I refuse to lose again.

When the game is over, which we won, I drink one beer at the field and head home. As much as it felt good to be part of a team again, and among my friends, their quiet still haunts me.

What if . . . I'm missing something big. Like . . . Trinity didn't sleep with multiple men. Like she didn't sleep with any man.

Could she have adopted Mirabelle?

It wasn't like adoption hadn't been an option. We'd discussed it, but Trinity was determined to have a baby from her body. We'd already lost three, though, and the last one nearly killed her.

I refused to take the risk of losing my wife. It scared me. The thought of her not in this world made me physically sick.

Then, I did the exact opposite of what I should have done. Instead of holding her closer, I pulled away. I was almost afraid to have sex with her. Afraid she'd get pregnant again. Afraid I would lose her permanently.

Instead, I lost my wife slowly over time.

I threw myself into the distraction of racing. I could control the speed, manipulate a machine, make it move the way I wanted. The adrenaline rush was fueled by intense focus. The ability to push limits and take a different risk, and win, when everything else in my life felt like I'd lost.

My wife. Our dream. My motivation.

I'd worked in construction since I was seventeen, when Russell Haven hooked me up with a family friend.

Clint Haven eventually worked for a different construction group, and I switched jobs to work with him.

My ties to the Havens tightened.

I worked with Clint. I was best friends with Tate. And I had a crush on their sister.

When their football-playing brother came home, Clint and Cort started their own business. I transferred once again.

I'd been happy for a while. Happy for them. I was a hard worker and dedicated, especially because they were family. But eventually, I felt expendable. I didn't feel seen as a devoted part of the family, but just a member of their crew. It hurt. I didn't need special favors. I just longed to be noticed. I was blending in, instead of standing out, and I hated the insignificance.

Russell Haven once told me I had so much potential and to use that potential wisely. I didn't think I had been. I'd been failing at giving his daughter a baby, and I wasn't good enough for two of his sons to bring into their fold.

I needed to rewrite the script about me. Racing became my medium.

The Chevy Camaro I'd been working on in the detached garage had been a steal. A toy for someday. I'd put racing on hold for a while, not having as much time during my new marriage and home renovation era. Plus, Trin and I wanted a family.

I didn't think hanging at the canyon was a wise idea anymore.

But after years of tinkering with that Camaro, I got her to purr, and I wanted to test her out.

I took her to the old coal mine property, which housed a dirt track, and gave her a spin. Then another one, then another one. The drives were freeing. The disappointments disappeared for a little while.

I was my own person. Not a husband. Not a construction worker. Not a man on a sex schedule.

I was just me, and everything changed after those first few spins around the track.

Sitting in my truck staring at the empty garage, I let the memories roll through my head.

Meeting Max Larsen. Running a time trial for *people he knew*. Getting signed with Velocity.

At the time, it had been worth it, but it also had been empty without Trinity at my side.

I thought the escape would bring healing. Instead, it did more harm to both of us.

Shoving open the driver's door of my pickup, I hop out and slowly saunter up to the dark house. The impromptu party is evidently over.

Fuck. Vale Sylver's face was stricken when she saw me. Like she didn't know whether to toss a wine glass at me or tackle Trinity, intending to protect her from a bomb threat.

Me. I was the threat.

The other women looked equally shell-shocked to see me standing at the edge of the living room.

Like they'd never heard about me, before or presently. Like they didn't know she'd ever had a husband. Like they were shocked to see a man, period, in Trinity's home.

Has Trinity been as lonely as I've been? Has she missed the touch of my hands like I've missed hers? Has she held herself back from getting involved with anyone? Does she still honor our vows?

Then again, she thought we were divorced and misunderstood when I paid the mortgage and signed over the deed to the house.

She *could* have done as she pleased with someone else. But did she?

After I quietly unlock the front door, noting that Trinity has not changed the code like she threatened, I double-check the locks on the windows and back door before heading upstairs.

Where I hear a tiny squawk.

The door to Trinity's bedroom is open, and a little bundle shifts in the bassinet at the end of the bed. I pause a second, waiting on Trinity to stir, but she doesn't, even as Mirabelle begins to cry louder.

Taking a step into the room, I stare down at the swaddled baby. Even crying, her face all scrunched up, that angel kiss near her brow accentuated, she's the most precious thing I've ever seen.

My hands look clumsy and large as I wrap one underneath her head and the other beneath her bottom and lift her.

"What's the matter, baby girl?" I whisper as I bring her to my chest, head tucked near my shoulder, like Trinity holds her.

I've held babies before. Trinity always said I looked like a natural when I didn't know the first thing about kids.

Holding Mirabelle feels different. Like some instinct I didn't know I had clicked into place. She felt nice in my arms, good against my chest, right where she should be. My heart ballooned, feeling too large to be contained behind my ribcage.

I press a kiss to her downy hair and inhale the sweet scent of baby wash . . . and something not so sweet.

"Woo-wee, baby girl." I chuckle quietly.

While Mirabelle is staying in Trinity's room, a half-assembled room down the hall will be Mirabelle's future bedroom. I'm a little surprised the paint hasn't been updated or a crib put together. Only a changing table stands in the room, along with a dresser that belonged to Trinity as a child.

"Here we go, Mirabelle." I set her on the changing table, which instantly stops her cries, and change the first diaper I've ever changed.

Peeling back the full diaper, I gag at the odor. How could something so little produce such a stench? I make quick work of getting her clean and into a fresh diaper, thankfully labeled FRONT and BACK with images for where to set the tape. Tucked back into a sleep sack, I lift her again, bringing her to my chest, and tighten my hold on her when I turn toward the door.

"Jesus," I hiss, flinching when I find Trinity standing in the doorway. "You scared the frick out of me."

"Frick?" Trinity weakly smiles at my fright before letting her gaze fall to the baby. "I didn't hear her cry." Her forehead furrows.

"You need your sleep," I state. I'm typically a sound sleeper but knowing both these girls are close has made my sleep lighter, and I've heard the baby crying over the past few nights.

"I still should have woken up." Trinity enters the room, giving me a better glimpse of what she's wearing. A silky-looking nightdress with thick straps over her shoulders and a deep V between her breasts that accentuates them. Her nipples are hard.

I swallow thickly and chew at my lower lip before dragging my gaze away from the outline of her body in something I've never seen her wear to bed before.

"I don't mind helping." I want to help. I want to take the burden off her shoulders for a while. Not that Mirabelle is a burden, but having a baby brings lots of change. I've seen it among the guys who have kids. The exhaustion can be soul deep at times.

"Why don't you go back to bed?" I offer. "Mirabelle and I can hang out for a bit."

"The middle of the night shouldn't be awake time." She scowls.

"We'll just dance for a while," I say, swaying a little with Mirabelle nestled against me. I hum near her head, feeling her settle into me.

Trinity leans against the changing table and crosses her

arms, watching me. The room is dark except for a nightlight plugged into an outlet.

The low light further outlines Trin's body and that silky nightdress hugging her breasts and hips.

"Go back to bed. I got her." I nod toward the hallway, trying to dispel thoughts of what I'd like to do to her in that flimsy gown.

We need to talk, but now still isn't the time. She's tired, and I . . . I just want to soak in this moment representing all that could have been.

Wishing that I was Mirabelle's dad.

Wishing that Trinity still loved me.

Wishing that I'd made all our dreams come true.

14

[Trinity]

I hesitate. A boulder on my chest while looking at Dart with Mirabelle.

The way he holds her with confidence, like he's a natural at being a dad. His large hands cup her head. His forearm creates a ledge for her bottom. She tucks into him. Her head rests near his heartbeat. Maybe she senses his strength. Maybe she's thinking, *I'm safe here.*

He presses a soft kiss to her downy hair, murmuring something so quietly I don't hear it despite the silence around us. His eyes briefly close as if the kiss is an instinct. A reassurance she *is* safe with him.

Looking at them is a twisty-turny reminder of all we wanted together and all we never had. The longing for something so precious as Mirabelle.

And here she is.

Earlier, I almost didn't feel worthy of the impromptu shower from my friends, realizing I haven't shared Mirabelle with others because I can't shake the sliver of fear that she'll be taken from me. That her appearance is all a dream.

But watching Dart hold Mirabelle, like he'd chase away nightmares and battle any demons, I can't help picturing him in her future. In our future.

That boulder presses harder.

This right here is the forever we could have had, should have had.

And he looks so good with his backward baseball cap on his head and the low-slung fit of his sweatpants, which accentuate his—

"Trin." He whispers my name in a way I've heard a thousand times. Low and deep, seductive and rich even when he's not trying to seduce me. "Just go, baby."

My mouth opens, intending to argue, but something in the way he runs his bristly cheek against Mirabelle's head gives me pause. Like he needs this moment with her, even if I don't want him forming any ideas. Mirabelle is mine.

Would he like to share her with me?

The thought has me standing straighter and shaking my head. I will not allow myself to get ideas either. That picture of our future dissipates.

"I guess I could use a little more rest," I admit over the grogginess in my throat from lack of sleep. A dull ache weighs down my limbs.

He nods, closing his eyes as he sways with Mirabelle, humming a tune near her ear.

I slip through the door and return to my bed, only to find I can't sleep. Not with images of him cuddling Mirabelle. Singing to her. Soothing her.

He would have been the best father. He'd been such a good man, until . . .

My eyes cloud, and I blink away the tears.

Let's just give ourselves a break.

He might have meant a break from baby making. I took it as he wanted a break from us. Sex had turned mechanical. Functional instead of intimate. His resentment was present in the way he performed. And I hated how I felt like I was using him.

We'd lost the thunder between us. The strike of lightning. The merest spark was gone by the time he left.

Yet a new flame flickers inside me when I watch him holding Mirabelle.

A candle in a window as a sign of longing, of waiting, of hope.

I don't dare hope for more from Dart, other than giving me an hour of rest.

One I don't get thanks to the visions in my head of him dancing with Mirabelle, acting like he'd be the perfect dad.

THREE DAYS LATER, Dart is in the kitchen. The strong scent of bacon sizzling in a pan fills the air.

For the past three nights, he's collected Mirabelle in the middle of the night, allowing me to catch up on some sleep. With the much-needed rest, I feel clearer lately, more sensible.

No more visions of Dart being Mirabelle's dad. I'm grateful for his help, but I'm back to thinking he'll be gone like the wind soon enough.

Still, I can't seem to help admire the strength in his back as he stands shirtless, another pair of sweats dangling on his hips, and Mirabelle in his arms.

Just . . . *fuck* . . . those black sweatpants *and* a baby in his arms. He's got hot dad vibes happening here, and I quickly glance away from him before he spins to face me.

"Good morning," he says. Then, he takes Mirabelle's little arm and waves it at me.

"Morning." I chuckle before asking him the same question

I've asked each night over the weekend. "Did you get any sleep?"

Mirabelle should sleep in a bassinet near the foot of my bed, but during the middle of the night wakeups, Dart takes her out of the room. Sometimes, she's back in the bassinet by morning. Other times, I hear Dart take her downstairs or down the hall to his room.

"Did you?" he counters. His eyes look tired but bright and wild. The man can exist on coffee and four hours of sleep.

"Yeah," I whisper with gratitude. "Thanks again for that." He doesn't have to keep waking in the middle of the night to feed Mirabelle or comfort her, but I truly am grateful for his help right now.

"Did she eat?" I keep a chart on the refrigerator, neurotically marking each time she takes a bottle and how much she drinks.

"Fed her at three a.m. Marked it on the schedule."

For a second, I'm reminded of a different schedule we kept. A calendar of sorts. Penciling in sex with him. My stomach pitches at the reminder of how hard I pressed him, knowing he'd give me anything I wanted. How the moments I tried to seduce him became *un*seductive. How *less* intimate every attempt to get pregnant became.

I stare at his scribbled handwriting that fills a line on the chart.

"Here," he says. "I need to flip the bacon." He steps closer to me, almost charging into my space, and while I'm eager to take Mirabelle from him, I'm also hyper aware of his closeness.

The scent of pine and asphalt rushes up my nostrils. His bare skin overwhelming and present.

With Mirabelle in her scrunched body position, like a ball of bliss, Dart tips toward me, and I reach out for her, slipping my hand between Mirabelle and him.

Only, the back of my hand brushes over that firm chest, and sparks crackle and burn up my skin.

I glance up at Dart. His face is close. His eyes wide and focused on mine.

Slipping Mirabelle from him, it feels like I'm moving in slow motion as I bring her to my chest, but don't step away from him. Her little body is the only thing separating us.

I'm very aware that I'm still wearing my nightgown. The silky chemise, one of three, that I bought myself long after Dart left as a reminder that I'm sexy on my own. I not only deserve underwear that empowers me, like a matching set of lacy panties and bra, but I can have nightwear that makes me feel bold and strong, even though I sleep alone.

And right now, that silky material feels almost too warm, too sensitive against my skin.

Dart's gaze drops to my lips, and I press mine to Mirabelle's head without breaking eye contact with him. The instinct to kiss her is too great. The need to tuck her close to me, almost as a shield . . . against him.

"She's so good," Dart says, his voice full of awe while he stares back at me.

I inhale Mirabelle, attempting to right my senses with her baby-fresh wash, but find she smells like him. From being pressed against that bare chest, near his heartbeat, held in his arms, and—

A hard knock comes to my front door.

Both Dart's and my eyes widen, startled out of the moment, and then sinking into the surprise of a visitor.

"Expecting someone?" Dart arches a brow.

"No." My gaze remains on him. "Are you?" I have no idea who knows he's here with me. Obviously, my mother and my friends, and the guys on his baseball team.

The other night, I received a text from Tate.

We need to talk.

Admittedly, Tate and I aren't close. He's always been a wild card in the family. But every once in a while, he'll play protective older brother. Dart is one area of concern where Tate steps up. He knows how much I loved his best friend and how much it crushed me that Dart left. The thing about Tate is he's loyal to the people *he* loves. That shovel joke Halle mentioned, Tate would do the same and not even blink.

Stepping away from Dart, I check the doorbell monitor I keep on the kitchen counter. Then, I glance back at Dart, wide-eyed and a bit panic-stricken.

"What?" he whispers, leaning toward me, with concern. His hands come to my bare arms, but I don't have time to register the touch.

"Put a shirt on," I whisper, a tremor in my voice, like the person outside the door can hear us, despite the wood barrier being yards away. "I'll get the door."

With Mirabelle in my arms, I brush past Dart and head for the front door, opening it to the social worker assigned to my adoption case. Stone Sylver, in his sheriff's uniform, is beside her.

My heart plummets to the floor. I've had nightmares of them coming to reclaim Mirabelle, telling me there's been a mistake, and her biological mother wants her back.

However, Cassidy Lane is smiling at me while Stone offers his own stoic smirk.

"Mornin'," he greets me.

"Good morning. It's early for a visit, Sheriff," I tease, despite the tension in my shoulders. I hold Mirabelle even tighter, like they're going to reach out and snatch her from me.

"Spot check," Cassidy states, adding a warm smile. "And some news."

The relief in those words doesn't register just yet. My heart is racing too hard.

I step back, waving them both inside, when Dart suddenly appears wearing a white T-shirt that looks like sin on him.

Stone's brows lift. His head turns from Dart to me and back. "Dart?"

"Hey." Dart steps forward, offering a hand to Stone. Growing up, Stone's brother Judd attended school with Dart, Tate, and the rest of the star gang, but Judd was never friends with them. He was quiet and reserved back then and hung mostly by himself.

I have a theory about why Tate and Judd never got along, but discussing our brothers is not the reason Stone and Cassidy are present.

"Can I get you anything? Water? Coffee?" I offer, leading them into the living room, attempting to keep my voice steady despite the quiver in my limbs.

As if knowing I need stability, Dart's hand comes to my lower back. The heat of it seeps through my silky nightgown. I should probably have changed before I came downstairs. I should go change now, but I don't want to relinquish Mirabelle. I'm afraid to let her go.

Dart gently nudges me forward as Cassidy takes a seat. Stone remains standing. His large presence doesn't reassure me in the least.

"We won't stay long." Cassidy narrows her eyes at Dart when he sits beside me. His knee pressed against mine like a reminder that he's here. He seems almost as stiff as I am.

"I wasn't aware there was a man in your life," Cassidy says, her voice still kind, but hesitant.

The statement is a question. An implication that the situation might be an issue. Dart isn't vetted like I am. Background check on file. Education and experience to back up my good standing as a potential parent. I've been concerned I'd have to apply as a foster parent first before I could adopt Mirabelle.

Previously, Cassidy assured me she didn't think that would be necessary.

Dart glances at me before giving Cassidy a blinding smile. "I'm her husband." His left hand comes to my thigh, showing off the silicone ring on his finger.

He shouldn't be touching me, acting almost possessive of me, and I'm torn between telling him to buzz off or accepting what appears like a display of support. He's here for me; we are in this together.

Stone's brows couldn't possibly rise any higher. Cassidy has a look of surprise on her face as well.

"Well, this is good news," she says, her tone light, almost giddy.

"Why?" I snap, the defensive sharpness unnecessary, but still, I don't understand how Dart would have anything to do with their sudden visit.

"A couple adopting a child looks much better than a single mother."

If Dart is surprised at the news, he doesn't react other than the sudden tightening of his fingers on my thigh. Like he's gripping me to give him strength.

I've leaned into the misconception that I had Mirabelle with someone else because I was hurt. He's probably been with countless other women, even though he keeps flashing that silicone wedding band on his finger. And childishly, I wanted him to hurt in return.

This isn't how I wanted him to learn the truth.

We remain still, stiff beside one another. I continue to cling to Mirabelle.

Clearing my throat, I know I need to come clean to the authorities. To the people who can either help me or hurt my chances of keeping Mirabelle with me.

"We—"

The sudden wrap of Dart's arm around my shoulder freezes my explanation. The physical display is too much, and I'm torn again, wondering what he's playing at by acting like the doting husband.

"I've been away for a while, but now, I'm back."

Stone narrows his knowing eyes and fixates on me. He's well aware Dart has been gone for years.

Despite my stiffness, I lean toward Dart, further presenting the illusion of a united front.

"Good. This is so good." Cassidy beams, brightening with hope, shifting her attention from us to Stone and back. "This could expedite your case."

"Really?" The hope in me springs forth, echoed in the squeak of my voice. I nearly melt against Dart. Anything to move things along.

"Where are we with everything?" I ask, inhaling after asking, as if I'd been holding my breath. But I'm very conscious of the way my heart hammers and my lungs work.

"It's rather cut and dry," Stone states, hitching his fingers into his gun belt. "I found the girl. She admits she gave Mirabelle to the former nanny with instructions to do as she did. Leave Mirabelle with you. She's fully consenting to the adoption."

He offers a rare smile. "Mirabelle will soon be yours."

Releasing another shaky breath, I glance at Dart, as if Stone just told me Mirabelle will be *ours*.

A baby. All that we'd hoped and longed for. She's here. Actually here in my arms and almost ours.

Met by a shaky smile from him, I look away. I won't drag Dart into this situation. Parenting. Responsibility. Longevity.

Mirabelle is a gift for me.

Dart squeezes my shoulder, arm firm and steady around me. "This is wonderful." Laying it on extra thick, he presses a kiss to my temple.

The action takes me by surprise, and I glance at Stone, who is watching us with hawk-like interest.

"Can I have a word with you? Alone." Stone asks, nodding toward the kitchen.

He's an officer of the law and a man I respect, but I know the gist of what he'll ask me. Do I feel threatened, coerced, or in danger? All valid questions if I felt endangered in any way. But Dart would never physically hurt me. He's not a threat. Not like Stone thinks.

Stone is an investigator by nature and protective to a fault, both things I adore about him. So, I want to assure him without a lengthy discussion that I'm safe.

"I'm fine."

Holding my gaze on Stone, I will him to read my thoughts. I'm not under distress. Maybe a little confused by the husband-who-I-thought-was-my-ex, but I'm not afraid of him. A bit baffled by this outward display of affection, but not in fear of Dart. Not physically.

Stone tips his chin to accept my answer. "Okay, then. Just wanted to pass along the good news in person." He glances at Cassidy. "And apparently this new development . . . Dart . . . will help speed things up."

"Should be rather easy to mitigate," Cassidy states, offering Stone a confident smile before giving me another one. Her gaze dips toward Dart, pleased by this *new development* as Stone called him.

"Of course, we'll need to run a background check on you as well, Mr. . . ."

"Rivers," Dart offers, sitting up straighter like he's being called on in a classroom. "Run all the checks you need."

"Wonderful. I'd predict three months and Mirabelle will be all yours."

"Three months," I repeat, a whisper full of both shock and

relief. I hadn't expected things to happen so quickly. I'd been braced for a year at best, but this . . . three months . . .

I glance down at Mirabelle. Her eyes open and staring back at me. Awe in those little eyes, watching me, observing.

Are You My Mother? It's a famous children's book about a little bird looking for his parent. Without even knowing the term mother, I hope Mirabelle senses who I am. Who I want to be.

I might not have grown her inside me, tucked beneath my heartbeat for nine months. But my heart does beat for her. From the moment I held her in my arms, and the reality of the situation hit, I knew there was nothing I wouldn't do for this child. No fight I wouldn't fight to keep her with me.

I'm reminded of the moment I first found her, uncertain who she was and who she belonged to, but once I read that letter, and re-read it, and then this same social worker sat across from me, Stone at her side, and my mother at mine, I knew . . . Mirabelle belonged to me. And I belonged to her.

Yes, whispers through my head at her, like she can read my thoughts. *I am your mother*.

And everything will be legal and binding, and official in three months.

That calendar date and formal papers only make it certifiable.

In my heart, in my soul, where it really matters most, I already am Mirabelle's mom.

I glance back at Cassidy, blink at the sudden well of tears in my eyes.

"Wonderful," I parrot her, a breathless wisp of relief shoving aside the surprise.

Cassidy abruptly stands, holding open her arms, and I step into them, still a little stiff with shock, but also appreciating her hug.

"Congratulations." In a rare show of affection, Stone wraps an arm around me as well and tugs me to his side.

"You okay?" he whispers out of the corner of his mouth, eyes still aimed at Dart.

"I'm . . . amazing," I answer, because I'm still a bit stunned at the incredible turn of events.

As for Dart, well, that's still to be determined.

But as they exit, and Dart gives them a final wave before closing the front door, I realize that the adoption timeline might not have zipped forward without his presence.

A couple adopting a child always looks better than a single mom.

No shade to single women or single parenting, just that studies have proven two parents can be better than one.

The second the door is shut and the lock twirls, my heart skips for a new reason.

Dart doesn't hold back from jumping in, staring at me with the deepest expression of pain I think I've ever seen on his face.

"Why didn't you tell me you were adopting?"

The casual shrug feels like a reflex. A brush off of the uncertainty, when the real answer is I was being petty. I wanted him to hurt in some way, like he'd hurt me.

I knew the conclusion he'd drawn. He thought I'd been with someone else. A true blow to his ego and our marriage. The one I didn't know we still had. I should be equally pissed at him. Turn his previous upset around on him, but the gash of hurt across his face stops me.

And it makes me realize how devastatingly ruined I'd be if the tables had been turned. If he'd been with someone else. If he got someone else pregnant.

I don't have the energy to lash out at him. Not when I'm on this emotional rollercoaster, riding up with the high of the amazing news about Mirabelle, knowing I'm about to drop down the other side with the discussion we need to have about her.

"I'm sorry," I whisper, my remorse sincere, although the apology isn't enough of an explanation.

Dart rushes toward me, closing the distance between the entry hall and the living room where I stand.

"Look." He blows out a struggling breath and swipes a hand through his hair. "I've been sick at the thought of Mirabelle without a father." His gaze drops to where I hold her in my arms. "Sick that you might have slept with someone to . . ." He pauses, swallowing thickly. "That you . . ." He can't even form the words.

That I got pregnant without him. Is that what he wants to say?

He exhales a second time, as if blowing away what he can't say.

"Let me be here for her." He waves toward me. "Let me be here for you."

I shake my head, squeezing Mirabelle tighter. "I can't do that," I admit. "I will not make Mirabelle the glue between us."

A child is never a reason to stick together. And there is no us.

He sighs, glancing toward the front window. Stone and Cassidy are both gone.

"You heard what she said, though. It looks better that a couple wants to adopt a child." He slaps his hand against his chest. "We're already married, and I'm not asking for any right to her."

His voice cracks like he's saying the opposite of what he wants. If Dart were to be a dad, he'd never relinquish his rights. He grew up with an unstable family. He learned from them what he never wanted to be.

Everything in me believes he would be present and supportive of a child if he had one.

"But we aren't a couple," I whisper, reminding him that although we are married, we haven't been a couple for three years.

"Then let's learn to be." His hand slips from his chest. He lifts his head, standing taller.

I don't know if we can. I don't know if *I* can.

"How?" The word pops out before I can stop it, but I'm quick to clarify. "I'm not saying I agree, I'm just asking."

He turns toward the window again, brows deeply creased, before he gazes back at me. "Date me?"

"Date my husband." I laugh without humor.

"Get to know me again." He waves toward me once more. "Let me get to know you."

I tilt my head, not sure how I feel about this idea. "But in the end, we aren't together."

Dart sighs, frustration on his shoulders. "Let's not talk about an end yet, Trin." He steps closer to me, and I hold my ground.

"She said you have three months before the adoption is final. Give me those three months."

"Why?" The question is breathless, and I inhale, hoping to draw in more oxygen. My chest constricts, accentuating the rapid hammering of my heart.

"Forever," he groans, quiet and rough, emphasizing both the nickname and the reason he wants this.

"And what do I get out of this?"

He tips his head.

"You said give you these three months, but what do I get?" I realize it might sound like getting to know him, and him getting to know me, might not be enough, because I'm not certain it is. There's still a lot of unspoken pain between us.

"At the end of three months, you'll have Mirabelle." He glances at her, though his eyes are sad and his expression tight. "She'll be yours."

Because we're a couple, or at least, we'll look like one. Two people living in a house together.

With a baby.

"I want to be here for you." His voice grows in strength. "For anything you need. Roof repairs. Meals. And the baby's room. It needs to be painted."

His smile shifts from sober to soft, his eyes still on Mirabelle.

We had so many plans. Pink for a girl, or maybe yellow. Green for a boy. Maybe racecar décor when he was older.

"I haven't had the time," I admit about her bedroom. "Mirabelle was quite the surprise."

"Yeah?" His brows lift. "Think you could tell me about it over breakfast?"

Breakfast. I'd completely forgotten about the bacon cooking earlier.

"Okay." I nod toward the kitchen, and Dart waves out his arm, so I'll lead the way. I feel him behind me, close but not as close as his hand on my thigh, or knee against mine, when we sat on the couch. I could question all that affection, but I understand now. Dart was reading the room, thinking he was helping. Showing off for the case worker.

Disappointment pinches at my chest, but I quickly ignore it. Instead, I set Mirabelle in the bouncy seat on the island counter, and Dart returns to the bacon, turning the pan back on and pulling eggs from a carton on the counter.

While he works, I explain how I found Mirabelle on the back step.

Dart whisks eggs for scrambling so hard that some splashes out of the bowl onto his shirt. He ignores the mess, staring at me, wide-eyed with surprise.

"She was just left out there?" He glances toward the back door, incredulous at the possibility.

"Yes." But I smile. "It was purposeful. And now, she belongs to me." I reach for her little covered toes and jiggle her leg, causing the seat to bounce and Mirabelle's eyes to widen.

I'm still in awe of the adoption. And maybe a little afraid.

Her biological mother could change her mind, want her sweet baby back. But in my heart, Mirabelle is mine, like I just said. And I am afraid of that feeling too. The ferocity of that love, and that it could be taken from me.

I glance at Dart quickly, then back at Mirabelle. She's been staring at the overhead lights like they are the most fascinating thing in the world. Her sense of color is still developing. For now, she might only see in black and white, maybe shades of gray.

I gaze back at Dart, realizing nothing is black and white between us.

We are shades of gray.

"She's lucky you were here." Dart glances at Mirabelle, then back to the stove. The pan sizzles when he pours the eggs into it, sweeping a spatula back and forth with more force than necessary once again.

Even through his t-shirt, I can sense the tightness in his shoulders. The stiffness in his back.

He hates how Mirabelle came to me. Abandonment.

And yet, I can't look at it like that.

She was a gift. A blessing. Given to me because the universe knew I'd take care of her.

When the eggs are done, Dart plates them with the bacon and sets the dish in front of me on the slim island. He stands on the opposite side, a plate of his own in front of him.

He pokes at the eggs. "So, when you said you didn't know who the father was, you meant you really didn't know." He slowly lifts his head, both fear and hope in his eyes. "You hadn't slept with someone else."

What he's really confirming is that I hadn't gotten pregnant *by* someone else.

"I haven't slept with someone else," I state, holding my head high, clarifying the truth.

The admission feels like a confession. One he doesn't

deserve, but he still should know, as he now knows how Mirabelle came to me, and I'm going to adopt her.

Bodily fluids with another human being have not been exchanged.

If ever I wondered what relief looked like on a human being, I witness it on Dart. His shoulders fall. His chest rises. And his eyes are the brightest I've ever seen.

"Really?" His voice cracks. His hand stills, fork pinning scrambled eggs on his plate.

"Really," I whisper, my own heartbeat suddenly slowing, questioning if I want to know if the same is true for him.

He sets his fork down and blows out a breath, gripping the edge of the island between us.

"I haven't been with anyone else either."

"Why not?" I exhale in disbelief, like it can't be possible that he's been faithful. That this gorgeous hunk of a man wasn't tempted by another. Or maybe it's relief that he has been loyal. A strange rush of gratitude that his love language wasn't spoken to someone else.

"Forever," he moans, staring at me, hard and convicted.

For the rest of my life, he'd told me when he playfully proposed to me in bed. He only ever wanted to have sex with me. Forever.

I don't know why I act coy or bashful, cheeks heating as I glance down at my own eggs, pushing them around with my fork.

"I'm sure there were tons of women interested in you, though." Maybe he'd even been interested in them.

"If they were, I didn't notice." He leans forward, his mouth curling in a playful tease.

"Liar." I choke around a quiet burst of laughter. *I mean, look at him*. All these years later, and he's still the hottest man I've ever seen. Tight white tee. Those damn black sweatpants.

Like Vale called him, a tall glass of water. I have been thirst-deprived. And I'm suddenly so thirsty.

His expression sobers a bit. "Trin, I made you a promise, and I might have broken a few of them, but the big ones have always held true. I have been faithful to you. There has only ever been you."

I lower my head, unable to fight a smile, unable to look at him.

"There has only ever been you, too," I admit soggily.

"Trin." He blows out a breath again, and I slowly glance up at him. "Let me hold you. Just one hug. Please."

The depth of the plea has me nodding. I could use a hug right now, too. A familiar one.

He moves so quickly, I forget to set down my fork. Instead, I drop it, causing it to clang against my plate.

Mirabelle lets out a cry, but Dart has his arms around me, and I'm pinned in place against his chest. His nose is near my ear, and his breath is warm on my neck. Slowly, I slide my hands around his middle despite Mirabelle's frightened cry.

She'll be okay for thirty seconds.

Thirty seconds, that's all I need.

I slip my hands up his back, feeling the tension in his muscles. He only tightens his arms around me. I breathe him in. Sturdy mountain pine, a whiff of asphalt. I close my eyes.

He always gave the best hugs.

Until he stopped hugging me.

I didn't want to get lost in the past. I just wanted to breathe in these few seconds.

Pretend.

Pretend it all happened as we planned. Him and me and a baby.

Mirabelle continues to cry, and I pull back, breaking the embrace I wasn't ready to release.

When I turn toward Mirabelle, I swipe at my eyes, realizing too late that they were wet. Dart remains close, his hand still on my lower back, as I lift Mirabelle from the seat. Then, he pulls us back to his chest. Wrapping his arm around both Mirabelle and me.

He presses a kiss to her head, closing his eyes so I can't see. Tears of his own swam in his.

15

[Trinity]

I don't know why I was so agitated. Perhaps I was just tired. Another long week has passed since Cassidy and Stone's arrival, but it still feels a little surreal.

I'm going to be Mirabelle's mom.

And Dart is still here.

Maybe I'm still a little nervous, waiting for the shoe to drop. Or Dart to hit the gas pedal.

He isn't working. Just puttering around the house finding odd jobs. He mentioned building a deck out back.

But he hasn't talked about racing. That *probably* still hangs in my head like his hats on my coat rack.

He's *probably* done with his career in racing. And if he's done, what's next for him?

It's not really my concern and all thoughts vanish when I spin from the counter, full glass of wine in hand, and smack into the man himself.

Red wine splashes everywhere and I drop the glass in my surprise, causing it to shatter on the hardwood in the kitchen.

"Dammit!" I bend down to pick up the larger chunks of glass. Red wine pools beneath it.

"Careful," Dart says, lowering to his haunches and picking up pieces as well.

"Don't tell me what to do," I hiss beneath my breath.

"Whoa," he chuckles, despite my tone. "Trin?"

I lift my head, already shaking it. I don't know what's wrong with me. Tears fill my eyes. Maybe I'm just on emotional overwhelm *because* I'm going to be Mirabelle's mom, and Dart is still here.

Even though he's been helping me at night with Mirabelle, I'm still not sleeping well.

"Baby," he whispers. "You need a break."

I don't. This is what I've always wanted. A baby. Mirabelle. But it's been every second of every day, and most nights, and I just . . . yeah, I think I need a little breathing room.

"I've got it," I snap again, looking downward for glass shards and filling my hand with them.

Dart catches my hand as I reach for another long piece. Then, he cups my other hand holding the broken collection, and he slowly forces me to stand.

He aims my hand with the glass toward the sink and twists it to dump the mess.

"Why would you do that?" The trash is behind me.

I'm also barefoot, and before I know what's happening, Dart scoops me upward. He's wearing his boots as he's been outside, and glass crunches beneath his feet.

He spins toward the hallway.

"You're going to drag glass everywhere," I warn, despite my arms wrapping around his neck, holding onto him.

"I'll clean it up. But you . . . you're headed for the tub."

"I can't take a bath." I don't know why I'm protesting. A bath sounds heavenly. That glass of wine was going to be heaven as well.

Mirabelle is finally asleep after a long, cranky day for her. I'm worried she might be sick, have something I can't detect. She sounded a little congested earlier, and I toyed with calling the pediatrician. Then, I argued with myself that I was overreacting. I'm a medical professional, so I know how to make a diagnosis. My gut says it is nothing, but my mom instincts raged to make a call.

I'm a mess.

The red wine stain on my T-shirt and the fact I'm in my ex-not-ex-husband's arms proves it.

Dart takes me right into the bathroom and sets me down beside the tub. Then he turns on the hot water and plugs the drain. He finds a jar of bath salts on the back of the toilet and drops in a hearty amount. He tests the water, adds some cold, and turns for the door. He stops just before leaving, lights a candle, and then reaches for the doorknob.

"Try to relax, baby." He turns off the light and leaves me in only the dim glow of the candle.

With shaky hands, I remove my ruined shirt and fumble off my shorts, knocking my knee on the edge of the tub.

I'm clearly having a moment, but I sink into the growing depth of the perfect temperature water and sigh. Closing my eyes, I inhale the fresh scent that matches my favorite lotion, reminding me of sunshine and fresh meadows.

Within minutes, the tub is full enough, and I stretch my toes, thinking I can turn off the faucet with them. Instead, I kick over my shampoo bottle, and it lands outside the tub with a loud thud on the tile floor.

I lean forward, turn off the faucet, and retrieve the shampoo, when suddenly, there's a knock at the door.

"Trin? You okay in there? I heard a thud."

I quickly cover my breasts, as if he can see me through the door.

"Yep. I'm good." My voice squeaks. I sound guilty of something. However, I'm simply conscious that I'm naked. Very naked, in the bathtub, and my husband is on the other side of the door.

He's seen me naked thousands of times. He can't even see me right now, but I'm still sitting here, hands tucked in my armpits, hardly covering my boobs, with my knees pulled upward to shield another part of me.

"Trin?" Through the slim light beneath the door, I can almost see his feet. He's taken off those boots I worried would drag glass through the house.

"Yeah?" For some reason, I can't pull my eyes from the door, staring at the outline of his toes in the sliver of light.

Silence continues, before there's a shift. A sound like he's knocked his head against the door.

"Can you hear me?"

"Yeah." My brows pinch, and I lean on the edge of the tub, crossing my arms on the cool porcelain and resting my chin on my forearm.

"You know, when I left, this is kind of how I thought we'd communicate." He chuckles softly.

"Through a door?" I lift my head, my voice rising as well, followed by a weak chuckle. What a silly thought.

"No." The word is muffled, and he repeats it louder, stronger. "No. I thought we'd talk on the phone, like we used to do."

Those nights before we were married, when I worked late but he asked me to call him when I got home. We'd talk until I was nearly asleep. The phone on my pillow. His voice in my head.

"What would we have talked about?" I lay my cheek on my forearms, wondering what he thinks we'd say after he left.

"Maybe we'd just talk about all that happened."

"Instead of facing each other." My voice is tight, almost

muffled against my skin, and I don't think he has heard me because he doesn't speak for several seconds.

"Just thought it might be easier. Easier not to look into each other's sad eyes and say some truths."

He isn't blaming me for the sadness. He knows why it existed. He never faulted me.

Or did he?

"Like what?" I ask, turning my face back toward the door. Curious, despite my position. Naked. In the tub.

"Like I missed you. Like I loved you no matter what."

Back then, he'd said the same thing. Baby or not, he was still going to love me. I'd been the one who grew determined, obsessed almost. It had to work.

Just one more time, I begged, although I'd nearly died. I'd had some kind of seizure. A drop in blood pressure.

No more, he said. There had been fear in his voice, although I wasn't listening at the time. That fear didn't register until after he left, when I was questioning everything.

Presently, I don't respond to him, but my heart screams that I missed him, too.

"Like I was sorry it hadn't worked like we planned," he continues. "And how I wanted to write us a new plan."

"By racing," I answer. Because that had been his proposal. A change of scenery, as if moving away would erase all the pain in my heart and disappointment in my head.

"Well," he chuckles, but it sounds bitter. "That had been part of the thought."

But I didn't race. Racing wasn't about me. I would have had to give up the home that I loved and the nearness of my family. I didn't want to move away.

He clears his throat. "But I realize now that racing was more about me. I thought if I reinvented myself, maybe I'd be good enough for you in other ways."

This has me sitting up, the water sloshing around me.

"Dart." I choke on his name. "You were never *not* good enough."

"But I wasn't, was I? I didn't provide you with the one thing I'd promised to give you."

I pause a second, realizing he thought all his worth was tied up in having a baby.

"You gave me lots of things, Dart." I glance around the bathroom, full of every feature I wanted. Subway tiles and a soaker tub. The double vanity and pretty tiles.

But he'd also given me so much more than a bathroom. He'd given me a home. A place we called our own. A place we worked together to renovate, providing us a space to rejuvenate at the end of a long week and take joy in during the holidays. He'd also given me his devotion. He was as dedicated to having a baby as I was.

He loved me. I had no doubt about that. He loved me when he was here.

"Did I push you away?" I ask, the question nearly choking me. However, I know the answer before he tells me the truth. I pushed.

"I think we both *pulled* away, baby." A soft thud hits the door again, and I imagine him tapping his head against it once more. "And I'm sorry I did that to us."

"I don't think you did it alone," I admit. We both pulled away as he said. When I grew so dissatisfied with myself and turned toward work as a place to hide. A place to feel capable. And he disappeared at the track, racing in circles, chasing I don't know what.

For the longest time, I worried he had a death wish. It scared me. I didn't believe he'd really be that reckless, but I was still afraid.

And he'd been afraid when I had the last miscarriage.

And instead of pulling together, we went in opposite directions.

"I'm sorry, too," I whisper, but I'm not certain he hears me. My throat is suddenly too tight.

I'm sorry because I've missed him. I wish *I'd* been better for him. He needed me as much as I'd needed him, and we simply failed each other.

I have further confirmation that he might not have heard me when he knocks harder on the door, just once, and says, "Well, I better get back to cleaning up."

"Okay," I say, a little louder this time.

"I've got a baseball game tonight, but—"

"No, go. You should take a break, too." I don't say it bitterly. He's done so much as well. Dinners. Even laundry. And all the handyman jobs.

"I could stay home, though," he finishes his thought. His voice sounds hopeful.

"No, go see your friends. I'll be out in a little bit." The water is already starting to cool. The bath hadn't been as relaxing as intended, but it had been refreshing in a different way.

We talked, and I had a few things to think about.

Like whether he knew how truly sorry I was for my part in our separation.

Like if he still loved me.

16

[Dart]

I hated to leave her.

I'd hoped to give her a few minutes to herself, but then, selfishly interrupted her bath. Without planning to, I intruded upon that precious time, and then she sent me out with my friends. I should have stuck around, but maybe it was best to give us more space. I'd already revealed too much.

I didn't want to hide behind a screen, suggesting that we'd talk on the phone better than we might talk in person, but I did believe that not looking at each other might have helped. Without the sadness in her eyes and the pain I was certain she'd see in mine, maybe we'd be a little more open with each other. Tell each other things we couldn't face. If we faced the other, I worried we couldn't, or wouldn't, voice our concerns.

Then again, what did I know? I'd walked away after begging her to come with me and her telling me no. I got the message. It only took me six months of rejected phone calls and unanswered text messages to finally get the hint.

However, rather than sign those divorce papers I was served, I doused them in gasoline and struck a match.

I'm still trying to wrap my head around the news about Mirabelle.

Adoption. It'd been something I wanted us to do. While I could harbor hurt that we hadn't gone that route together, I'm just too stinking happy that Trinity is accepting that option now.

She will have Mirabelle in a few short months.

And I try not to think about where that leaves me.

Part of their life? Or not?

Either way, I'm not going anywhere. I'm here to support Trinity *and* Mirabelle in any way Trin will let me.

As for what I really want, I want to be the dad Mirabelle doesn't currently have.

I forgive Trin for lying to me, or rather playing that game, making me think she'd slept with someone else. I hadn't really given her the chance to explain herself or Mirabelle when I first crashed here, and the fault falls on me. I'd been too shocked by a baby in her arms and the despair of being kicked out to be rational. To stay calm.

I'm also so fucking relieved she hasn't been with someone else, which eases the ability to forgive her for allowing me to think otherwise.

No one else has touched her sacred parts. No one else has climbed into her heart.

She is still mine in some manner.

The relief almost makes me giddy.

After cleaning up the wine mess, I pour her another glass and leave it on her nightstand next to her reading tablet. I stamp a sticky note to the top like I used to do when we'd go more than a day without seeing each other due to her shifts at the hospital and my construction schedule.

Just a simple heart. No extra words needed.

A sign that I loved her. That I'd miss her. That I'd be thinking about her.

All things I did when I was gone for three years.

~

A FEW NIGHTS LATER, I find Trinity set up on the pink velvet couch with the television on. It's positioned at ninety degrees to the set when we originally had a couch that faced the fireplace with the set above it. The new arrangement looks formal, but Trin also didn't watch television as much as I did.

Still, she's settled in tonight. Mirabelle has started sleeping longer stretches in the night, and although it's still early, Trin will get a few hours reprieve before a feeding close to midnight.

"Mind if I sit with you?"

She already has the screen pulled up to a historical romance prepped for her to click start.

"Sure. Okay." She clicks the remote back to the guide screen.

"Don't sound over enthusiastic," I tease.

She chuckles softly. "It's just that I've been waiting to watch this one, but I'll find something else."

I don't want her changing her mind because of me. "Keep it. Let's watch it." I'm not opposed to watching this kind of movie. We've watched them together before.

She hesitates another minute before clicking back to the original title. "This falls in the middle of the series. I already watched the first half when it came out."

"Go for it. I'll catch up." How hard can it be?

It doesn't take long to see the pining of the man for a woman beneath his economic status, and it reminds me a little bit of Trin and me. Not the financial part, but the way the female lead believes she isn't good enough for him, and the way he wants her anyway.

He's wrecked by her. For her.

Because Trin sits beside me but angled toward the screen, I have both an appreciation for the fictional man in the series and a view of Trin's neck. The back of it with fine hairs from the shorter cut. The spot where the column of her throat curves toward her shoulder. A spot I used to nip just to weaken her knees. My fingers twitch to trace along that line of skin. To inhale her scent. To kiss her there.

I clear my throat, and Trin shifts, twisting her body so her side is more open to me while her head still turns toward the television.

The position is almost worse. Her breasts are perfectly on display in a fitted tee. Her arms bare. Her hands on her belly before something happens on the screen and she drops them to her sides, resting them next to her thighs. She's wearing jeans that hug her curves and flare near her ankles.

Her feet are bare, exposing said ankles and I feel like I'm living in this period piece. Trin once explained to me how exposed ankles were almost like flashing someone your breasts. Sexual and scandalous.

I scrub a hand down my face, feeling ridiculous for getting hot over my wife's feet.

My wife.

Trinity is still mine, but a divide remains between us.

I shift, repositioning myself to mirror Trinity's position. I hike my feet up on the low table and set my hands next to my legs, smoothing my palms over the velvety material of the couch.

Which causes my pinky to brush against hers.

Trinity immediately glances down, scowling.

"Sorry," I mutter, dragging my hand back toward my thigh and tucking the tips beneath my leg as if that will prevent me from touching her. From wanting her.

Because the more the tension builds on the screen, the more the tension rises in this room.

She's so close and yet so far away from me. Inches yet miles.

I try to concentrate on this poor sap trying to come up with a way to be with the woman he loves.

Until I feel something brush the side of my hand. Glancing down, Trin's pinky flicks against the side of mine.

At first, I think she's done it unintentionally. But I continue to watch the space between us long enough to learn she purposely moved her hand closer to mine.

When her finger brushes mine again, my breath hitches.

"What?" She turns her head sharply toward me.

"Nothing." I hold still and glance back at the show. "He's really aching for her."

Trinity hums and returns her attention to the screen, but her finger slides over mine until I trap it between my pinky and ring finger. The silicone ring digs into her pinky. Maybe reminding her that we're still married.

She glances down at where I've caged her finger.

"What happened to your ring?"

I hesitate to admit the truth but decide there is no point in holding it back. "I lost it. Tossed it down the track the day I was served divorce papers."

She struggles to remove her finger, but I grip it harder between my own.

"The moment I did it, I regretted it."

She'd bought me that ring. A black titanium band I wore with pride.

She nods and turns back toward the television, keeping her finger looped over mine.

"Where are your rings?" I hesitantly ask. If she says she was as careless with hers as I'd been with mine, I'll be crushed. I should have never tossed mine in anger.

"Upstairs. In a drawer."

I could joke that she could have pawned them or sold them through a resale market, but I can't muster such a tease. I hate the thought and foolishly find relief that she has the set.

One day, I'd like to give her a new one.

We return to watching the show, moving from one episode to another. Trinity takes a bathroom break and comes back with popcorn in a large bowl and two water bottles.

"Thank you, baby," I easily say to her when she hands me a bottle and sets the bowl in her lap.

This may be even worse than brushing fingers. Our hands meet every few seconds in the shared bowl.

I scoot closer to her, and she glances at me over her shoulder, her brows pinched.

"You're too far away. Popcorn stretch." I exaggerate how I had to reach *so far* for a dip in that bowl on her lap.

She shakes her head but doesn't say more, returning her attention to the show, while I'm hyper aware that her shoulder is next to my arm and her thigh is a mere centimeter from mine.

While the couple on the screen are supposed to be staying away from one another, the lady has just slipped into the man's bedroom. My heart rate jacks up, hoping this doesn't lead where I think it's going to go.

But suddenly, they are kissing, and he's taking off her dress . . . and *oh, fuck no*.

I swipe the popcorn bowl off Trinity's lap and set it on mine because I can't watch that without thinking about doing the same thing to the woman next to me.

And then, there's a whole fucking montage. Him on top of her. Him behind her.

I lean forward, setting the bowl on the table, and swipe down my face with both hands.

Trinity's breathing becomes shallower. My heart races

faster. I feel like I'm watching a horror film, fingers over my lips, prepared to cover my eyes at the soft porn on the screen.

Finally, the scene ends.

"Well," I choke, knowing we have *not* watched something like that before. Or at least, not something I remember being so hot.

Trinity rolls her head toward me. Her eyes blown wide and bright brown. I've seen that look before. I know that look, and I cannot have her looking at me like that unless . . .

Suddenly, I'm pressed back into the couch, and she's on my lap, her fingers fisted in my shirt.

I'm so startled that my hands lay limp beside her calves for a second.

"Dart," she whispers, staring right at my mouth, not even trying to disguise what she's looking at, while I try to meet her eyes. Try to guess what she's thinking.

Fuck it.

"What are you thinking?" I whisper, holding my breath. Holding as still as I can, though I'm certain she can feel my arousal through my jeans. I'm not hard from watching someone else get what they want, but because I kept imagining us.

The positions we experienced. Me over her. Me behind her. Her on top of me, like right now.

My hands lift to her hips, a will of their own.

"I'm not thinking," she whispers, her voice almost hollow only seconds before her mouth crashes against mine.

The shock is hard. Her mouth tight. But after my brain catches up to what's happening, which is my wife is trying to kiss me, I run my tongue along the seam of her lips.

And suddenly, I feel like that guy on the screen, frantic for more of Trin. Desperate to pull her closer.

I grip her ass and drag her forward, feeling her settle over where I'm hard. Letting where she's soft know what she does to me.

She moans into my mouth as we move together in a way as familiar as my name, and yet everything about this kiss feels different.

Charged.

I know this woman. My wife. I recognize her kiss, and yet I don't. There's something almost electric between us.

We kiss like we did all those years ago, and yet, with all the years between us.

I slip my hand up her back and dig my fingers into her hair, cupping the back of her head. She moves to my jaw, and I shift to her neck, taking a bite right where I wanted to earlier.

She groans as my teeth gently sink into that soft pressure point right below the surface. Her body melts against mine. Her center hot over where I'm hard. Her breasts brushing my chest.

Screw the actors on a television. This is so much more.

Because my wife is kissing me again. She's letting me kiss her.

I tug at her hair and bring her mouth back to mine, needing more of her, needing confirmation this is really happening. I'm not dreaming.

She's in my lap. Her lips on mine. Her hands on my shoulders. And—

A sharp squawk comes through the baby monitor on Trinity's phone.

Abruptly, she pulls back, glancing over her shoulder at the device on the table near my feet. Slowly, she turns back to me. Eyes dazed. Lips swollen. Neck slightly red from where I bit her.

Shaky fingers cover her lips, and I feel her retreating before she actually does.

"Trin?" Panic lands in my chest.

She scrambles off my lap, struggling to stand on her feet.

Her legs actually buckle, and I reach for her. But she holds out a trembling hand. The other comes to her lips again.

"That shouldn't have happened."

It should have. It definitely should have. We need to get back to who we were. Two kids in their twenties, insatiable for each other. A newly married couple who couldn't have sex often enough.

But that isn't who we are anymore, is it?

Those twenty-somethings turned to thirty-year-olds struggling to have a baby and build a home.

Then forty hit, and I had a bit of a crisis moment.

But dammit, I want my wife back.

Unfortunately, she is already swiping up her phone and racing for the staircase.

Scrubbing both hands over my face, I fall back on the couch and glance up at the screen.

The episode has ended, leaving me in suspense.

Does the hero ever really get a second chance with the girl of his dreams?

I suppose if he didn't, it wouldn't be much of a plot.

But is it possible to fuck up the second chance once you finally get it?

I'm about to find out.

17

[Trinity]

What was I thinking?

I shouldn't have kissed him like that.

I could blame Benedict Bridgerton, but it wasn't the fault of a fictional character. Dart Rivers was to blame. His closeness. The subtle brush of our fingers. The press of his shoulder against my arm. Him eating freakin' popcorn.

I was so wound up. I don't know if I wanted to punish Dart, feeling like I deserved a kiss from him. Or longed for him, after his apology the other night.

Either way, I hid in my room the remainder of the night.

Thank you, Mirabelle.

But even while using her as a distraction, my mind raced.

I haven't been kissed in three years. The last one was sad, pathetic even.

Dart tried to kiss me at the end of our argument. The one where he asked me to go with him and I refused.

Let's just give ourselves a break.

He'd leaned in to kiss me. I turned my head.

He was gone in the morning.

I was angry. I was hurt. I was alone. But the break gave me perspective.

Maybe I leaned on Dart too much. Like he said the other night, we *pulled* apart. He needed space, and I needed it as well.

I realize that now. We needed time to come to terms with reality. I wasn't going to produce a baby. *I* needed time to accept myself, without Dart. And he needed to do the same.

The biggest surprise the other night had been Dart admitting he didn't feel he was good enough for me.

Maybe I kissed him to let him know he was. Or he had been.

I shouldn't have said the kiss shouldn't have happened. A kiss was inevitable. We needed to experience at least one to see if that spark could be rekindled. But I'm kidding myself if I thought I was no longer attracted to Dart. If a flame didn't exist beneath the surface.

And that kiss felt like promises made long ago. Even though promises were broken, the kiss still felt . . . right, even if I couldn't explain yet why that was.

IN THE MORNING, I head to the store, hoping to give Dart and me further separation. My mind is still reeling from that kiss. My lips as well, because I still taste him. Salt and butter from the popcorn and all male. Not to mention, the feel of him beneath me. How hard he was. How he fit against where I'm soft, as he always has.

I might pride myself on being the queen of self-love. Might feel like an expert on taking care of me. But that doesn't mean I didn't need an active imagination to get what I needed, and

Dart starred in many of those fantasies. Fantasies that were more like memories.

But my memory has clearly played a trick on me, because Dart felt different beneath me.

Maybe it was simply that I haven't been with a man since him, and even then, we were more mechanical than intimate.

Maybe it was the passion of last night. Climbing over him, taking what I wanted, and the way he eagerly gave it back to me.

Or maybe, it's as I said to him more than a week ago, it's only ever been him who can make my belly flutter and my heart skip.

When I return from the store, Marshall and Hutch are in a truck, pulling out of the driveway, and offer me a quick wave. With all Dart's home improvement projects, it hasn't been unusual to see an extra truck in the yard, but his friends haven't paid a visit. At least, not that I know of.

As I enter the house with Mirabelle in the car seat over one arm and two sacks of groceries over the other, I hear something heavy being dragged or shifted against the floor upstairs.

"Dart?" I call out.

"In Mirabelle's room."

I set the groceries down in the kitchen but leave Mirabelle in her car seat because she's sleeping.

Lugging the car seat up the stairs, I find Dart where he said.

In the past week, he has tackled painting Mirabelle's room. He'd picked out a bunch of color samples before he ever knew about the adoption. His favorite was daisy yellow, but the choice was mine.

I approved.

The room is sweet with that bright shade of yellow. A white crib is assembled. The changing table was already in here, along with a white dresser that had been mine as a child. Dart found butterfly and daisy decals to decorate one wall, giving it the appearance of a summer meadow.

And presently, he stands in front of a soft-green padded chair. I set Mirabelle's car seat down on the floor.

"Happy Mother's Day." Dart waves toward the seat.

"Dart," I whisper, my throat thick as my belly flips. I stare at the piece of furniture.

"I picked it out a few days after I got here, but the delivery was delayed."

"It's . . . it's beautiful." I continue to stare at the simple gift. A chair.

"And it rocks." He steps closer to the chair and pushes the back, causing it to tip back and forth. "It also reclines. Try it out."

He sets his hands on my upper arms and guides me to take a seat. I practically fall into the plush cushion, then glide backward and melt in the comfort. The material is as soft as the color, which complements the meadow theme.

"This was so thoughtful of you," I admit, tipping my head back and staring up at him. "You didn't need to do this."

"I missed Mother's Day."

"To be fair, I didn't know I was going to be a mother." I chuckle while I glance at the miracle that Mirabelle is. Her little head is tilted awkwardly in the car seat, but she's sound asleep.

"Still, I'd hoped it would arrive sooner."

I glance back at Dart and run my palms over the padded armrests. "This was so sweet of you. Thank you."

Dart lowers to a knee in front of me. "You deserve it, Trinity. You deserve her, and she's so lucky to have you as her mother."

"Dart," I whisper as tears well in my eyes.

"I don't know how you feel," he continues. "Because we never had one of our own. But Mirabelle is yours," he reiterates.

"The love you feel for her is no different than if she came from your body or not."

I choke on his name again, a tear slipping free.

"And she loves you. She knows who you are to her. Her mother."

Another tear falls, but a choked giggle escapes as well. "I'm so lucky," I whisper.

"She's lucky, too." He glances over his shoulder, smiling affectionately at the little bundle scrunched up in the car seat.

Then he gazes back at me. "I don't want you to ever have regrets, Trin. Not about anything." His whiskey eyes are darker today. Sober and still.

Has he thought about that kiss as much as I have?

"You mean about that kiss last night?" I sheepishly ask and lower my head.

"No, I don't want you to regret marrying me. About still being married to me."

My head lifts.

"I don't want you to be angry at the process because look where it got you." He twists his upper half, glancing at Mirabelle again. "And look at who you are now."

He spins back toward me. "Strong as ever. Maybe even stronger. With or without me, you're one of the strongest people I've ever known."

I scoot forward in the chair, bringing our faces closer. "You're strong, too. Stronger than you know." I drop my gaze from his face to his hands, clutching that one raised knee. "For the longest time, I thought you were a coward for walking away."

He lowers his head, nodding.

"But I also think there was strength in breaking us apart. We were a mess, Dart. Both of us. And we would have continued to spiral if someone didn't leave. If someone didn't give us space. I would have preferred that we worked through everything together, but maybe . . . maybe we just couldn't. We needed that time apart."

He nods, keeping his head down.

"I'm not a marriage counselor, and I'm certainly not going to say I'm a marriage expert, but I think . . ." I swallow hard again and lick my lips. "I think it was too painful to look at you because *I* felt like such a failure."

His head pops up. "Baby, no. Never."

I tip my head, balancing my forearms on my thighs. "My body failed me."

"It wasn't your fault." His eyes are wide, his tone adamant.

"I know. But I also think I took the separation between us, before you ever left, as blame. Shame even."

Dart scoots closer to me. "There was nothing to ever be ashamed of. It just happens."

There were so many ways others try to console someone after a miscarriage. A blessing in disguise. Something was already *wrong*. But the painful truth is even science doesn't fully know why some pregnancies take and others don't, and it is not a reflection of my body, or habits, or thoughts, or religion, or my soul.

It just happens.

Dart tried to understand, but it wasn't his body. The miscarriages were not a physical loss to him. A confusing, frightening loss.

Dart's fingers lightly brush mine. He stares down at where he tickles the tips down my knuckles. I glance down as well.

We haven't talked like this in a long time. I'm not certain we ever really talked so openly. We didn't ever really fight. It was just all . . . frustration and tension.

"I don't know if you heard me the other night, so I wanted to tell you again how sorry I am."

"For what?" His brows lift as he slips his palm underneath mine. His hand is warm. His touch tender.

"For everything, at this point." For pushing him away. Or pulling apart. For falling to pieces.

"You don't owe me an apology." He slowly smiles, glancing up at me while he continues to rub his hand underneath mine. "But thank you."

I chuckle. "I also owe you a thank you."

He shakes his head, laughing quietly, while looking back down at our hands. Mine smaller than his. Our palms still rubbing over each other's.

"Nothing to thank me for."

"You've been working hard around here. The roof. The bathroom. Mirabelle's room. And you've cooked dinners and done laundry. And this chair." I sink back into it, pulling my hand from his.

He smiles a little wider and bends his raised knee, so both are on the floor. Then he sets his hands on the armrests, lifting his upper body taller. He leans over me. My knees brush his belly.

He lifts one hand and pinches his fingers. "Might be a teeny tiny bit selfish, in hindsight, about this seat. Lying on that couch at night isn't easy." He grins wide and teasing, while setting his hand back on the armrest, continuing to cage me in. "But I'll do anything for my girls."

His eyes lock on mine.

His girls. Me *and* Mirabelle.

I should warn him not to love her. We haven't discussed what Dart's role is with Mirabelle. We haven't discussed where we are headed, as a still-married couple.

But I'm tired of the heavy stuff.

So, I simply smile back at him, letting his claim wash over me.

His girls.

Mirabelle and me.

18

[Trinity]

It's a beautiful day, and Mirabelle and I could use some fresh air. I decide to take a walk around downtown Rogue River.

The historic commercial district is best described as T-shaped, with the main road, Dock Street, dead-ending into an old, covered dock, freshly restored about ten years ago. The landing was once used by ferrymen who ferried people and products from one side of the wide river to the other. A bridge over the water has since been built outside of town, a few miles away.

Parallel to the river is River Street, where a large grassy strip runs the length of the road and river combination. It's a public space with a white gazebo near a small boat launch and marina. The area is used for celebrations, such as the upcoming RiverFest.

The main area of town is full of fun restaurants, quaint boutiques, and one coffee-slash-romance bookshop.

My first destination is The Babbling Bean. The interior is a rich emerald green with one wall full of bookshelves. Mom only stocks romance novels. The front window is a boxy bay and has a long, cushioned bench with three small café tables and wrought-iron chairs, like something from a patisserie in Paris. A rectangular wooden table fills the center, allowing a party of eight or individuals to share the space. The coffee counter, as well as a countertop display case, frame the back wall. A chalkboard menu behind the counter displays the daily specials.

Mom is the only one working today, and her only customer is presently sitting on the outdoor patio in the late May sunshine.

"Hi, honey," she greets me, but beelines for Mirabelle in the stroller, leaning in to pepper her cheeks with kisses.

"How are my girls?" she says, standing upright and wrapping her arm around me.

"We're doing okay," I admit. Mom and I have already talked about how hard, yet rewarding, motherhood can be. She knows I'm tired. I don't need to tell her. But something else weighs heavier on me this week.

Or rather, someone.

"Just okay?" she asks, arching a brow before stepping behind the counter and setting to work on a coffee concoction.

"I kissed Dart." I didn't plan for that nugget of information to blurt out of me. I definitely didn't foresee telling my mother. But I needed to tell someone.

She spins to face me. "Really?" Her brow arches higher along with the tone of her voice. "And how did that happen?"

My face heats. I'm not about to tell my mother how I practically forced myself on Dart, climbing into his lap and pulling him to me.

"It just happened." I shrug.

Mom chuckles like she knows better. She finishes making a very red drink and hands it to me.

"What's this?" I haven't even ordered.

"I like to call it after-the-kiss glow." She smiles.

I laugh. "Somehow I don't think that's really the name."

She waves toward the rectangular table, and I adjust the stroller to take a seat. Mom sits opposite me.

"Does this mean you're back together?" Her eyes are warm, encouraging. She'll listen to whatever I want to share. She'll accept any decision I make.

"We're . . . talking."

Mom leans forward, stretching her hands across the table to pat one of mine. "That's good, honey. That's so good."

I hum and lift my drink, taking a sip of something lemony and sweet, refreshing even. "Hibiscus?"

"My secret." She winks, neither confirming nor denying her ingredients. Then she sits up straighter, "You know, honey. Having reservations is totally understandable. You've had a lot happen in just a few short weeks. Mirabelle arriving. Dart returning. Finding out you are still married."

She pauses and glances at my hands around the clear plastic cup. "It would also be understandable to have walls up. To protect yourself." She makes a soft fist and taps at her chest. "But don't let those walls be so thick that someone can't get in. See how beautiful you are. How much love you have to offer."

I nod, glancing down at the plastic straw standing out of my cup.

"Dart and you . . . you remind me so much of your father and me."

My eyes burn at the mention of my dad. Dart was close to him. Dad always had a soft spot for Dart.

"A little bit of the bad boy trying to be good," she says.

I chuckle, never having that impression of my parents.

"And we both knew Dart loves you. He needed someone

like you to love him back." She catches my gaze. "Strong. Stable. Driven."

"But did I drive too hard?" I lower my voice, fidgeting with the straw. "I think I might have pushed him away."

Mom sighs. "I think what might matter more is that he's back. Is he planning to stay?"

That word *probably* comes back to me. His racing career is *probably* over. I still didn't know what that meant.

"I don't know."

She smiles in her motherly way. I wonder if I'll wear the same expression with Mirabelle one day. If I'll impart wisdom and offer advice to her with patience like Mom.

"Only way to know is to ask. Or maybe what you need to do is keep enjoying one another as you are. Kiss the toad again, see how much of a prince he can be."

"Mom." I laugh.

"Keep talking to each other. But don't forget to step back and allow a little fun in between." She wiggles her brows before pressing up from the table and rounding it for the bookshelves at my back.

She's become quite the expert on romantic affairs, or so she thinks, with her collection of novels for sale. She dispenses the books like dating advice. Or couples' therapy, apparently.

"Here. Take this one." She hands me a book with a pretty cover. A couple in a mountain setting.

"What's it about?" I hesitate, although I almost always take my mother's suggestions for romance reads.

"Second chances. Reunited lovers." She wiggles her brows. "And falling in love again."

"Mom," I groan.

"Stranger things have happened. But there is nothing *better* than love." She squeezes my shoulder.

The bell over her door tings, and our discussion is cut short as she steps behind the counter, while the customer steps forward.

"Love you, Mom," I call out, holding up my drink. I lift the book next. "Thanks for the book." I stand and situate the stroller. Mirabelle is awake but staring at the toy dangling from the handle.

"Love you, too, baby. Both my baby girls."

19

[Trinity]

I'm in the kitchen, putting a pre-made bottle in the fridge. The room is dark except for a light over the stove. Dart is out at another baseball game. It's been almost a week since our kiss. I've had a lot to think about lately. The things Dart and I have revealed and shared. The advice Mom gave me the other day.

Don't let my walls be so thick someone can't get through them. Or love can't get out.

While I've worked hard to keep emotions in, it might be time to set them free. Not just the anger and disappointment, but forgiveness. Real forgiveness. And as mom said, maybe allow a little fun. See if Dart and I can be who we once were. Or even better.

With this thought in mind, I close the refrigerator door and shriek.

"Jesus," I hiss, flattening my hand over my chest, glaring at Dart, who stands near the corner of the fridge, originally blocked from view by the previously open door.

"Nope." He smiles, wide and lazy. "Just me." He's wearing a backward ball cap and smells like summer evenings and baseball diamonds.

"I didn't hear you come in." I swallow thickly, my heart still racing. "Did you have fun tonight?"

He shrugs and leans against the corner of the fridge. "Eh. Hit a double. Struck out once. Was hit in another time."

I smile. I'm glad he's reconnecting with his friends. Friends are important, which reminds me I haven't been to book club in weeks. Other than the impromptu baby shower and our active group text, I hadn't been out with my friends in a while.

Dart doesn't move, still leaning casually against the edge of the fridge.

"How are Hutch and Marshall?" I ask.

"Good. Petty is back."

"Petty?" How have I missed that? Another prodigal son, though Petty has been much more wayward than Dart.

I chuckle with surprise. "How is the rambling musician?"

"I'd rather talk about you." He pauses, his eyes glowing from the light behind me over the stove. "I feel like you've been avoiding me."

"Avoiding you?" I laugh nervously. He's practically everywhere I am. Giving Mirabelle a bath, Dart is there, hand on my lower back, cooing at her in the kitchen sink. Feeding Mirabelle a bottle at night, Dart is beside me on the couch, arm against my arm.

I feel like I couldn't get away from Dart if I tried, and I'm not certain I want to. Be away from him, that is.

Still, I'm afraid to make another move.

Somehow, I've twisted so my back is against the fridge, and Dart is in front of me, arm raised so he can clutch the top of the appliance.

"Avoiding me," he repeats.

His eyes are so bright despite the dim room. And laser-focused on me. My eyes. Like he wants to read all my thoughts. If only he could.

"What do you need?" he whispers, dropping his gaze to my mouth.

"Uhm. What do I need for what?" I'm making no sense because he's suddenly invading all my senses. That outdoor scent. The gleam in his eyes. How close he is.

"What do you need from me? To help us move forward."

"Oh." I clear my throat. "I . . . I haven't really thought about it."

But I have. I need him to promise not to hurt me again. Not to leave me. But I can't make him give me promises he can't guarantee to keep. I can't ask him to stay.

"You haven't?" His brows lift, his chest rises, but he doesn't shift from caging me in against the fridge. The coolness from the stainless-steel seeps into my back.

My mom's advice comes back to me again.

"Okay. I need you to be open with me. Honest. If you feel me pushing you away or find yourself pulling back, we need to talk."

He nods, blinking a few times before settling his gaze on my mouth again. "I can do that."

"And what about from me?" My voice sounds small, quiet in the already quiet space. The hum of the fridge behind me. The slowness of Dart's breath.

I lick my lips, nervous but almost giddy from our position.

Dart tracks the quick movement of my tongue before meeting my eyes. "I need the same. I need you to force my attention when you think I'm not listening. Tell me if I hurt you." Pain slashes through his eyes, knowing he'd never intentionally do such a thing, but it happens. A sharp comment. A terse retort.

We weren't perfect. But we were . . . ours.

"I need you to not push me away but pull me closer. When you need me."

The truth could be read two ways. Emotionally. But also, physically.

My hands are tucked behind my butt, palms flat on the fridge, like magnets holding photos against the appliance's surface.

We just stare at one another.

Amber eyes reflecting the darkness of mine.

"Remember our first kiss?" Dart's voice lowers, his gaze dropping to my mouth again.

How could I forget?

"You were out with girls from the hospital," he begins.

"And you somehow ended up at the same bar with your friends."

"That might have been intentional."

I laugh quietly. "Liar."

His eyes dance, the truth in them. "I gave you a ride home."

And I remember being caged in, like my current position.

He'd opened my door like a gentleman, helping me out of his truck, and I stumbled, falling back against the side of the bed.

We just stared at one another for the longest minute of my life.

Like we are doing right now, both privately recalling the memory.

"You were terrifying." His mouth slowly curls, and he reaches for my hair, slipping his pinched fingers down the short length. Watching as he caresses the strand.

"Me?" I chuckle harder. "You were frightening." My brother's best friend. A known flirt. And yet he was so focused on me, always teasing me by calling me Forever.

"Meant it when I said it," he whispers, as if reading my

thoughts while running the back of his fingers along the side of my throat, watching once again where he touches me.

"Forever." The word ghosts between us. Louder, he says, "Knew I'd never be perfect, but I'd be better with you by my side."

"Dart," I whisper, overwhelmed by the honesty.

He sets his fingertip gently on my clavicle, in that little dip between the bones, then drags it up my neck, causing me to tip back my head and glance up at him. He still watches his finger, painting a line over my skin until he reaches my chin.

He gently pinches me there, tipping my head down, catching his gaze on my lips again.

"Still want to be by your side," he says. "Want you to let me try again."

I swallow hard, uncertain how to answer him.

"I think we just need more time." Like Mom said, a lot has happened so quickly.

Dart nods, still looking at my mouth.

"Think we'll ever kiss like that again?" The question is rough, vulnerable.

"Like the first time?" I arch a brow. "I think there's only one first time."

He shakes his head. "Agree to disagree. Because we had so many firsts. First time beside my truck. First time in your bed." His smile curls, pulling up another memory. "First time as my wife."

His grin grows larger. "First time in this house."

I can't seem to help myself. I smile back at him with every reminder of other first kisses.

"And first time on that pink couch." The pitch of his voice has dropped even further, like soft gravel on a sandlot. "That's my new favorite."

I snort, quiet and choppy, while my cheeks heat. "I wasn't exactly graceful." I practically ambushed him.

He shakes his head, slowly, eyes on mine again. “Don’t need you to be graceful. Or even careful with me, Trin. Just need you to be you.”

I lick my lips once more. “Okay.” Breathless thanks to the flutters exploding in my belly, I wonder if he’ll kiss me right now.

First time kissing against this fridge. Although we probably did that sometime before. We must have at one point or another. But some memories just mingle with the mundane, not standing out as significant when they should.

Another memory comes to me. “Remember our second kiss?”

Dart smiles again, one corner of his mouth tipping up higher than the other. He shakes his head.

My mouth falls open, like I’m a little aghast and a lot offended. “You sent me a text. Asked me when I had a break at the hospital.”

“Ah,” he nods, but I’m not certain he really remembers.

“You showed up with a single daisy.”

His lips spread. “Saw it on the roadside and stopped to pick it.”

“And then you kissed me by your truck again,” I remind him, enjoying this game of finishing each other’s thoughts. Filling in the memory together.

“Wanted to know if the second time was as good as the first.”

He’d said something similar on that day as well.

“And?” I arch a brow, like I don’t already know the second one was just as good as the first one.

“Might have been even better.” His gaze drops to my lips again.

“Really?”

“Yep. Because you gave me a second chance.”

Our eyes lock.

First kisses are important, special even, but so are the second ones. It meant one more time to experience something that already felt kind of perfect. And then, make it better.

Maybe have a third, and a fourth . . .

I can't make the first move here, so I squeeze my thighs and clench my fists behind me, while willing him to kiss me like he once did. First time or last time or anytime in between.

Because as much as I've proudly proclaimed my sexual independence, the one thing I can't do is kiss myself. And I want Dart to kiss me.

He lowers his head, and my mouth waters. I hold perfectly still as he runs his nose along the side of mine. I tip back my head and our eyes meet, too close to really focus on each other.

Then he pulls back, a sly smirk on that seductive mouth.

"You hold all the flags here, Trin. And I'm still in the yellow zone."

Caution. I know this much about racing.

"When you're ready to give me the green, I'm all in."

He stares at me a second longer, then pushes off the fridge. He runs the tip of his finger along my lower lip, and he might as well have kissed me, because his touch lingers long after he walks out of the kitchen.

As I remain plastered to the fridge, my heart wildly hammering, and my breath shallow.

And my mouth missing his.

20

[Dart]

A week has passed since I nearly kissed my wife against the refrigerator. I'd come home from a baseball game, a little amped up from hanging with the guys and talking to Hutch. He knew I wanted my wife to date me, and he also knew I didn't know how to make that happen.

He also reminded me just talking to her and being honest would help.

So I asked her what she needed. And then I told her how I felt.

I'm all in when she's ready to wave the green flag.

I'm already all in the race, but I'm just keeping a steady pace, not looking to rush or pass her. I'm just fucking thankful she's keeping me on the track somewhere near her, which is why I couldn't kiss her the other night. I didn't want to pressure her. And while she'd made the first move by kissing me a few weeks ago during movie night, I wasn't going to be the one to make a second move. At least not physically.

Reminiscing about our first kiss—and the second one—was

fun. And I'm hoping it pulled forward more positive memories for Trin. Not that they all needed to center on kissing or sex.

I just wanted her to remember us. The good times. The flirty ones. The reasons we were so attracted to one another.

Then again, I worried she might still hold onto the reason we fell apart, even if we're being more open with one another.

Like I said, she is the pace car in this race. I am following her lead.

So, I'm surprised when she enters the kitchen, dressed in a flirty summer dress that accentuates her breasts and tips off her shoulders. She's wearing flat sandals and has the front of her hair clipped back.

"You look pretty," I tell her, because I can't help myself. Like that image of her on my phone smelling a daisy, she looks like a summer flower.

"It's RiverFest," she reminds me about the local festival to celebrate the start of summer. There will be a crowd on the green space near the river. Music in the gazebo. Restaurants and craft vendors offering their wares. And an all-around excitement about the next season.

Eventually, the river will be more active with boaters, and a summer market will fill the green area every weekend.

I hadn't planned to attend the fest. The guys each had their own plans for the day. Hutch had his boys, and I didn't want to intrude on his dad time. Marshall was working the alcohol tent. Petty had something arranged by the mayor. And Tate . . . well, Tate and I were still hardly speaking other than in baseball terms during the games.

As Trinity stands across from me, fluffing the dress she has Mirabelle in, one that matches the color of Trin's pink one, she says, "I thought we could go together."

What? I press off the island that I'd been leaning on and stare at her, certain I hadn't heard her correctly. My heart leapt a mountain, and my breath seems to choke me.

"What?" finally staggers out of me.

"I thought we could go together. You, me, and Mirabelle."

Like a family. It shouldn't be my first thought, but I've been thinking so much about Trin and me. And Mirabelle. About how I want to be Mirabelle's dad. I want to raise her alongside Trinity.

My heart races wildly, and I repeat my disbelief, "Really?"

"Unless you have other plans." Trin's voice drops a decibel, vulnerable even. Like it took a lot for her to ask me, and she shouldn't be so hopeful.

"Yes. I mean, no." I fumble, rushing around the corner of the island. "I mean, no, I don't have plans. And yes, I'd love to go with you and Mirabelle to RiverFest." I cup the back of Mirabelle's head.

She's grown so much since I've returned. Since she arrived. She's nine weeks old and every day brings some new development. Some little change that feels so big, and I don't want to miss any of it. I don't want to miss her first word or first step. When she can sit up and eat her first food.

I still want to rock her at night, feel her snuggle into my chest, keep her safe from nightmares, and make all her daydreams come true.

Startled by this sudden invitation, I'm still not moving. Not saying anything. Just staring at Mirabelle before I look up at Trin. Her eyes bright and brown, and so warm, so inviting.

"Thank you," I blow out, catching the emotion in my throat. "Let me just change. You look so nice." I scan down her outfit again.

She smiles and chews on her lower lip. "Thank you."

"Thank you," I say again, running my hand over her shoulder before rushing past her to change into fresh jeans and a crisp tee. RiverFest isn't anything formal, but this will be my first appearance in public with Trinity. And the baby.

I don't give a flying fuck what people think of me, but I care about Trin. What people might have thought on her behalf. How they've treated her.

Rogue River is a small town. Certainly, news has traveled about how Mirabelle came to be and how I've returned.

And I intend to hold my head high and stand by Trinity's side, taking any lashing I know I've earned.

TRIN HAS me drive her sporty SUV because of the car seat. Parking is a struggle in the overcrowded town. Other than my visits to the ballfield and The Ferryman's Rest, I haven't been in town.

This little area comes alive for a festival, and RiverFest is no different.

"You excited?" I ask, once we park.

"A little nervous for some reason," she admits.

My heart plummets to my belly. "Worried about being seen with me?" I try to keep it light. Almost a joke, but I'm concerned she's suddenly having second thoughts about the three of us being out together.

"No." She smiles warmly, reaching over to grab my wrist and giving it a squeeze before releasing me too quickly.

When Trin and I first started getting together, we were a secret. Sneaking off to make out at bars and eventually hooking up at her place, although it was never as casual as hooking up for me. When I pressed that I wanted to go public with our relationship, she hesitated, and I panicked.

"You don't want to be seen with me?" I knew I would never be good enough, but her hesitation stung.

"Just want to keep you for myself a little longer." It wasn't a line. Wasn't said in some cheesy way to appease me. She'd turned bright red and ducked her head, like *she* was embarrassed she'd admitted that to me.

"Why?" I'd been truly baffled back then.

She shrugged. *"Just don't want to share you yet."*

She never had to worry. She wasn't sharing me with anyone. I was proud to have her under my arm and at my side. I was all in with *her*.

This time, I wasn't certain what the hesitation might be, but I decided not to dwell. She invited me to attend RiverFest with her. We'd be surrounded by friends and family, and a community that loved her, despite what they might think of me.

I reach for Trin's hand and pull it to my lips. "It's going to be a great day."

"Yeah," she whispers, a little more confidently.

I pop open my door and round the SUV to open Trinity's door. While she takes Mirabelle out of the car seat, I open the hatch to remove the stroller. The thing is quite the contraption, but opens easily and gives Mirabelle a space to be upright and shaded, and facing Trinity.

Mirabelle smiles up at Trinity as she smiles down on her. Smiling is a new thing, and my heart nearly explodes every time Mirabelle gives me that little lopsided grin. Her cheeks are so round and her eyes so vibrant yet dark. Maybe she'll even look a little like Trin when she gets older. Same strawberry blonde hair. Brown eyes. It could happen.

As we walk down the street, Trin pushing the stroller, I set my hand on her lower back, helping guide her path, while also disguising the sudden tremor in mine.

Being here with Trin feels like a huge victory. One I will not take lightly. We're making a debut of sorts. A reunited couple. That's how I view us, but I need Trin to confirm that status.

To say yes to us.

As we reach the town's green space, cramped with visitors on blankets and picnic benches, our first stop is The Babbling Bean's booth.

"Well, Dart Rivers. It's about time I saw you." Mary Haven says, laying her hand against her chest.

Trin goes over to her mom's house more than Mary has been to ours since I've returned.

The matriarch of the family exits her booth and hugs me so tightly, I nearly stop breathing. Mary gives some of the best hugs, second only to her daughter's. She's been the mother I never had, welcoming me into her home, and giving me her blessing to marry Trin.

She's always been good to me, and I did her wrong.

Her hug says many things, but one of the biggest is acceptance.

The prodigal *husband* has returned.

"Mary." I'm stiff at first, overwhelmed by her easy embrace, her forgiveness of sorts. Eventually, I hug her back.

When Mary pulls away, she cups my face. "Come by the house soon." A clear invitation and indication that I owe her some answers.

She steps over to Trinity next and hugs her before leaning into the stroller to give Mirabelle a bundle of kisses.

"So precious," she whispers to Mirabelle before standing upright and reentering her booth.

She rattles off a variety of specialty drinks plus her latest bakery creations. Trin and I both order an iced coffee concoction and then argue with Mary about payment. She wants to give us the family-is-free discount. Trinity wants to pay her mother, like any other customer.

"Did you read the book I gave you yet?" Mary asks Trinity. "The one where the couple is DTF." She winks.

I've just taken a drink of cold caffeine goodness and sputter at Mary's use of a common acronym for Down To Fuck. Coffee sprays everywhere.

"Mom," Trinity groans, like an embarrassed teen, side-eyeing me.

"What?" Mary says innocently, clutching at non-existent pearls while speaking about fucking. "Did I use that term incorrectly?"

I chuckle, dabbing at the coffee dribble on my T-shirt. "Always a pleasure, Mary."

"You use that pleasure elsewhere," she says, nodding toward her daughter.

"Mom!" Trinity shrieks loud enough that Mirabelle jolts in the stroller. Her little lips pout.

"And that's our cue to move on."

Trinity sets her drink in a cup holder on the stroller handle before she places both hands on it and pushes it forward.

We walk past another booth or two before Trinity suddenly clutches my wrist. She turns her body toward me, her face drained of color, like she'd like to hide behind me but can't move because of the stroller.

"What?" I ask, suddenly concerned before following the direction of her gaze.

"I'm so sorry," she says under her breath, like she's prefacing something with the apology.

Spencer Reid. *What is that fucker doing here?* Spencer is one of those guys who thought he was better than everyone in Rogue River. He went off to college like the rest of my friends, and I wasn't aware he was back in the area. Then again, tons of people return for RiverFest.

Thinking Spencer is stepping toward us to address me, I'm confused when his attention is on Trin.

"Trinity." His voice is syrupy-smooth while his gaze glides down her body, ignoring the stroller in front of her. "I haven't seen you in a while."

Cocky confidence oozes from this guy with hair slick as a Ken doll. Trinity leans toward me and I instinctively slip my arm around her back.

"Oh, uhm, well, a lot has happened since I saw you last."

She glances down at Mirabelle with a soft smile, but Spencer still doesn't acknowledge the baby.

"You still owe me that second drink."

"What?" I snap, unable to contain myself.

Spencer glances in my direction, blinking once like he hadn't noticed me standing there, my arm so obviously around *my wife*.

"Spencer," Trinity murmurs, side-eyeing me before meeting his gaze head-on. "I don't think that will happen anytime soon."

Damn right, it won't.

Spencer looks back at me, tips up his nose, and glances at Trinity again. "You still have my number. If you need me."

If she needs him? For what? Fuck no. Not happening.

I shift around Trinity, intending to get on her other side, but she catches my arm before I can kiss this guy's face with my fist.

"It was nice to see you again, Spencer," she says, before pushing the stroller forward. I knock into his shoulder when I pass him. Childish, but sending a clear message. *Fuck off.*

He chuckles, like he knows something I don't.

"Spencer Reid." I huff, my heart pounding a million miles a minute. "Just what the fuck was that, Trinity?"

She shrugs, but I stop us by placing my hand on her forearm. She grips the stroller tighter but twists to face me.

"I went on a date with him." Her voice is quiet, embarrassed, apologetic. She further emphasizes her discomfort with an apology. "I'm so sorry."

"Why?" *Why that guy?*

"You were gone." She shrugs and lowers her eyes. "And he asked."

The explanation sounds simple enough, but Trin knows there is no love lost between Spencer and me. And the idea of Trinity trying to find someone to replace me in her life makes me ill.

A date. What did that involve? Dinner. Conversation. A goodnight—

"Did you kiss him?" Unbelievable. I don't really want to know that answer, however, I couldn't help but ask. She didn't sleep around like I initially thought. Hasn't been with anyone else since I left. But a date could mean a kiss.

Trinity keeps her head lowered.

Fuck. I swipe both hands through my hair and blow out a sharp breath.

"You don't need to act jealous," she whispers, eventually looking back at me.

"I'm not acting." My voice rises before I lower it and lean toward her. "I *am* jealous. Always going to be." Always going to know I put this large blip in our marriage.

"Look, this might not be the time or place for us to discuss our relationship status, but we're still married." I lift my hand. She might have wanted a divorce. But I hadn't given it to her. "Do you want to . . . not be?" I can't even say the word.

She shakes her head, keeping her gaze aimed at her hands. "But you're right, I think we should talk about this later."

Unable to stop myself, I reach for both her hands, tugging them free of the stroller handle. I step closer to her. Close enough to touch my forehead to hers. "Trin, right now, I want to kiss you like you deserve to be kissed and wipe that fucker's goodnight kiss off your lips."

No one gets her mouth again except me.

I kiss her brow, lingering there, squeezing her hands because I'm afraid to let go. Afraid if I step back, she'll step away.

"You don't need to do that," she whispers, and I pull back, needing her eyes. Needing to understand. She doesn't want me to kiss her. Again? Ever?

"You've already erased it." She smiles sheepishly, reminding me of our too-brief kiss on the couch.

"Damn right, I did." I scoop my arm around her. *And I want to do it again.*

But she's the pace car.

We stand still for another second. My arm around her. Her leaning against my chest. My heart is still racing. We're going to have these moments. Incidents that have happened while I've been gone.

"Just tell me now, Trin. Are there others?" More dates. More kisses.

"No." She shakes her head adamantly. "Only a few dates. No kisses."

"Okay." I breathe out. I can handle poor dates. I can. I wasn't here. She misunderstood. The dates didn't go anywhere.

And I'm fucking here now. I'm back. For good.

"Shall we keep walking?" Trinity eventually asks, sensing I'm still a little wound up but maybe moving will help for the moment.

"Sure." I point toward another booth, and we step closer to bundles of flowers and displays of soap and lotion.

"Hey, Dart." Savannah Grant is ten years younger than her brother, Marshall, but a raven-haired beauty with sharp blue eyes like her sibling. Over the past decade, she's been working to turn a portion of the family farm into lavender fields, and her booth represents her success.

"You haven't placed your flower order yet." She smiles warmly, knowing my ritual.

Fuck.

"What order?" Trinity gives me a sharp look.

Savannah glances from me to Trinity and back. Her face drains of all color before flushing a deep pink.

"Uh. Nothing." Savannah waves dismissively and immediately jumps into a sales pitch. "Can I get you anything today?" She gestures toward the array of homemade body products.

Trinity gives me another questioning stare before offering Savannah a tight smile.

"I'll take the Daisy Delight. You know it's my favorite." Trinity points at the lotion that smells like sunshine and fresh meadows in a jar. Her signature scent.

Savannah glances at me before picking up the container and ringing up Trinity's order.

My friend's little sister knows a few of my secrets, like an annual purchase of my wife's favorite fragrance.

Once I pay for the lotion selection, I set my hand on Trinity's lower back again. We've barely stepped away from the booth when we come face to face with Tate and Marshall.

Marshall greets Trinity with a hug, while Tate watches me, taking note that my hand hardly leaves his sister's back. When Marshall releases her, Tate crosses his arms and glances at his sister.

"I told you we needed to talk." His tone is too sharp for my liking, and I'm opening my mouth when Trin speaks.

"And since when do I listen to you?"

Tate and Trinity have one of those push-pull relationships. He wasn't always the best brother when they were younger, but he's protective of her. Like it was okay for him to torture her, but he'd torture anyone else who tried to harm her.

If I didn't know Tate better, I'd question if that was hurt in his eyes at Trinity's strong retort. But Tate only glares back at his sister.

He's more pissed at me than at her.

Tipping up his head, he must see something out of the corner of his eye, and he turns in that direction.

"Pete," he calls out, walking away from us without another word. I watch as the two men shake hands and pat backs.

"I see I've been replaced," I mutter.

Marshall slaps my shoulder. "He'll come around." He

addresses Trinity with a short, "Trin." Then, steps around us to chat with his sister.

I stare at Tate and Pete Gallagher. Pete's a good guy, but I don't know him well. He's a college friend of Tate's who hung out with us when he visited Rogue River.

"I didn't know Peter Gallagher was in town," I state.

"He moved here shortly after . . ."

You left lingers unspoken between us.

"Anyway," Trinity clears her throat.

"Isn't he married?" I squint in their direction.

"Moved with his wife and kids. His sister, Prudence, works with Tate."

Prudence. I couldn't place the name.

"And you aren't being replaced," she clarifies, bumping my arm with her shoulder. "He's just hurt." Her gaze follows mine, watching Tate and Pete speak animatedly with one another.

"Yeah." I gulp down the lie about replacement and accept the sting. While Marshall, Hutch, and Petty all offered sympathetic ears and listened to me, Tate has refused to talk to me. That hurt *me*.

I wanted my friend to understand that my leaving wasn't about his sister. Not directly. It was about me, but then again, I don't think Tate can understand. He came from a loving family. He had a place in it. Despite his own trials, living in the shadow of Cortland's success, Tate was important in his own right.

I'd failed all of them.

As we wander from booth to booth, making our way toward the end of River Street, where a giant grill is set up outside Dockside, a bar and restaurant on the corner of River and Dock, we encounter the rest of Trinity's family.

Cortland Haven is tall and solid like Tate. He's also graying at the temples and in his beard, and he has his arm slung over Vale Sylver's shoulder.

Clint stands near the couple. His hair still has a light auburn cast, cut short and stylish, making him look younger than he is. He swings hands with a little girl who has bright red curls.

Ruby James. How did she get so big?

"Hey, guys," Trinity greets everyone.

Vale steps forward first to hug Trinity while I stand there wondering when Vale and Cortland happened. The last I knew, Cortland was the *ex*-best friend of Vale's older brother. The story behind their friendship split is messy, yet Vale and Trin have a truce despite the Haven and Sylver families drifting apart. Cortland and Vale are clearly a new development.

After Cort and Clint each hug Trinity, they shake my hand, questions in both of their eyes.

"How you been?" Clint asks.

"You're back," Cort states, not so much a question but confirmation.

"Good. Yeah." Not the most elaborate answers.

I glance at Trinity, who offers me a concerned smile. We knew these moments would happen. Seeing Mary and Tate, Cortland and Clint, still, the awkwardness is more than I anticipated. These men had been my bosses, my brothers, and I don't know what more to say to them.

"Are you just on a break from the circuit, or . . ." Clint hesitates, glancing from his older brother to his sister before looking at me.

"I'm retired." Is that what I am? Officially retired from racing cars? A driver with one of the shortest careers ever?

Trinity's breath hitches, surprised at first, but then her jaw tightens.

She hasn't asked me much about the circuit, and I haven't offered. We have more important things to discuss.

"Plus, we have this little one to consider." I nod toward Mirabelle as I slide my hand up Trinity's back. I've been touching her all day, but she suddenly stiffens under the scrutiny of her family. I remove my hand and cup the back of my own neck.

"How is she?" Vale coos, stepping closer to the stroller to peek at Mirabelle.

Cortland eyes me suspiciously. "Are you working?"

The question shocks me, and I don't immediately respond.

"You'll always have a job with us," Clint states.

"Thanks, man." My appreciation sounds half-hearted, as I'm too quick to respond. But if I read deeper into the offering, this is acceptance. They'll take me back into the fold. The job would mean stability and inclusion. But it would also feel like one more failure. Turning back the clock. I don't want to go back to construction. I want to do my own thing, even if I don't know yet what that is.

"I'll think about it," I offer more cheerfully, slipping my hand into my pocket, knowing I won't need to think about it. But I'm grateful for the suggestion.

Trinity watches me for another second before turning back toward the group, when Vale asks, "Are you guys just getting here?"

"We're headed to Dockside," Trinity explains. "And some of that barbecue chicken that smells amazing." She hums and bounces on her toes before glancing back at me, offering a more genuine smile.

"We're headed to the beer tent," Vale says. "Book club soon?"

"Soon."

The women hug again while the rest of us just stand there, eager for the tension to be released. After exchanging wishes to have a good evening, they wander away, and Trinity lets out a long exhale.

"Well, that went better than I expected."

"That was awkward as fuck," I say at the same time. I snort

as I run my hand over my head and cup the back of my neck again.

But everything in due time, right? I might be saying I'm in a race, but this is more like a marathon. Three hundred miles is a long way to travel. I'm up for the drive.

21

[Trinity]

Once Dart and I have chicken dinners in Styrofoam containers and beers in bottles, we make our way to the grassy section along River Street. Dart spreads out a light blanket I had in the basket of the stroller, and we settle on it, each with our own thoughts at first.

When we saw Spencer Reid earlier, I didn't know how to explain why I went out with him. Maybe deep down inside, I knew it would hurt Dart if he ever found out. That it might sting to know I'd gone out with someone Dart disapproved of. The date was innocent enough. One drink. Which ended with one kiss that was too wet and tasted like too much whiskey.

Spencer Reid is a horrible kisser, and I instantly regretted my actions.

It'd been a good reminder that I wasn't over my ex-husband.

I don't think I'll ever be *over* Dart Rivers.

We've looked like a couple today. A family, maybe. All the back-touching and forehead-kissing. Dart was putting on quite a show, but I didn't think it was an act. He was behaving like he would have behaved had we not fallen apart.

He was always physically attentive, until *we* were not.

And Tate needed to get over himself with the protective attitude. He'd been a constant tormentor when we were children and not much better as an adult, so it was surprising that he'd been upset once he found out Dart and I had been hooking up. He'd warned me about Dart's *manwhore* ways and tried to steer me away from his friend. Equally shocking was how upset Tate had been about Dart leaving me.

Seeing Cort and Clint had been even harder. The hurt in Clint's eyes and the questions in Cort's. Neither understood Dart's sudden decision to leave Haven Exteriors. Dart hadn't only quit our marriage, he'd quit their business even though they considered him family.

Dart was the one who never felt like he was good enough. Then in the next breath, he'd vow to me that he'd spend his entire life trying to be enough.

Love was so complicated. Our current position proves it.

I'm sitting here with my ex-not-ex-husband, who has been gone for three years, but not forgotten by any of us. He's not a blip in my memory, but someone I've felt present every day in one way or another.

Replaced, Dart said about his friendship with Tate.

The heaviness in the word gave me a glimpse of Dart's perspective. Perhaps he felt he was replaceable. With Tate. Within my brothers' company. With me. Which was the farthest thing from the truth.

He'd let people down, but they were still family. *His* family.

"That Ruby James is a cutie," he says, interrupting my thoughts.

"Yeah, she's adorable but can be a spitfire."

Dart arches one brow. "Must run in the family."

I snort. Dart already knows how hard it was when Clint

brought Ruby James home. A daughter he didn't know he had. A child he hadn't ever wanted, but instantly loved, like I love Mirabelle. Still, it'd been hard to look at them. Difficult to appreciate he'd gotten all I ever wanted.

I glance at Mirabelle. We've taken her out of the stroller and laid her on the blanket. She has baby sunglasses over her eyes and a wide-brimmed hat on her head, and she scoots her head like she hates them both.

"How come you told my brother you were retired from racing?"

Dart's brows lift. "Well, I guess I am."

"Are you?" I ask, trying to keep my tone light. Curious but not enthusiastic. It's not like I want Dart to quit something he loves. I just know that it will take him away again. And I shouldn't risk Mirabelle's heart or mine if he's going to leave soon.

"After the accident," he begins, squinting in the sunshine. "I had a huge fight with my manager, Max."

Max Larsen. I vaguely remember the name, but I know he's the one who recruited Dart. Told him he had potential.

"He told me to take a break. Heal. Maybe I could come back next season."

I chew my lip, holding back that the situation is exactly as I thought. *Next season*.

"They thought my head wasn't in the race anymore." He slowly lifts his eyes to meet mine. "Might have been a nice way of saying I was too old."

The irony is that Dart convinced me he wasn't too old when he left. Starting a racing career at forty-one, who does that? He'd had examples. He wanted to do it, try it. He was practically buzzing with excitement, with the possibility, with the change. It wasn't about the money, although it would certainly have been a hit to our dual income. He used the Chevy Camaro he fixed up as collateral.

I'd been resentful. I hadn't expected to be alone in my grief. But, in hindsight, I realize how alone Dart felt as well. How grief affected him.

I glance at Mirabelle.

I hadn't expected to be alone in my happiness either. I always pictured Dart beside me in either scenario.

"Are you too old?" I ask because I am curious. Does his age matter?

He squints toward the river. "I don't think so. I think they just wanted me to take time to figure out what I wanted."

I don't dare ask him what that is. Racing? Or me? It wasn't an ultimatum.

Dart and I weren't on shaky ground, but I wouldn't say we were solid either.

"How long do you have?" I ask, picking at my dress. "Before you need to make a decision."

He chuckles without humor. "I guess I have until the next season. Or at least November, when this one ends."

November is months from now. We'd just graduated into summer. Could I handle getting close to him and then have to watch him leave again? I didn't know.

Dart clears his throat and opens a dinner container, stuffed with barbecue chicken, coleslaw, and a roll.

"So, tell me about this book your mom gave you," he says, changing the subject.

My mom. Bless her.

"You know my mom. She's always handing out books." Like advice. "She's part of her own club now. They call themselves The Blooming Garden. People think it's a garden club, but it's really a group of older women, most of them widowed, who talk about romance and sex. They got the idea from watching *Bridgerton*."

"Ah, *Bridgerton*," Dart says, giving me a knowing glance. His cheeks are pink, and I don't think it's from the sunshine.

He's recalling when I nearly attacked him on the couch weeks ago.

"So, the book is about being DTF, huh?" His mouth curls, his eyes brightening.

I snort. "Yeah, well, that doesn't have to happen." I take a swig of beer. *It's so hot out here all of a sudden.* And our eyes connect.

Dart arches a brow. *Doesn't it?*

My face heats as my mind flits back to our position on the couch. Me over him. Him beneath me. So hard. So eager.

Maybe I just need to get Dart out of my system. Maybe I need one final farewell fuck, and then I can let him go.

Mirabelle fusses on the blanket. The glasses have slid off-kilter. Her hat nearly covers her face.

Dart chuckles and picks her up, tucking her to his chest so she faces me. "You eat first." He nods toward the container he opened.

Then he lifts Mirabelle higher, blowing raspberries on her belly and making her smile at him. I witness pure joy in his eyes. The way they lighten when he looks at her. The way they soften. He loves her. And she loves him.

And it's all so dangerous.

Because I'm pretty certain I can never let Dart go again.

BLOSSOMING summer evenings take longer to shift from day to dusk, but eventually Mirabelle needs to go home. She's had a long afternoon. She needs a bath, and I need a cold shower.

Dart's attention on me and with Mirabelle has just been too much. Or maybe it was the second beer I had that made me all hot and bothered.

It's still earlyish, but I want to maintain the bedtime routine I have established for Mirabelle, so we collect our things and head toward The Babbling Bean's booth. I want to say goodnight to Mom before we leave.

As we're standing by her booth, giving her a minute to finalize a sale, a voice I haven't heard in a long time comes through the speakers in the gazebo.

"Hello, all you gorgeous Rogue River people."

Heads turn. Cheers erupt. Another prodigal son has returned. Jon Pettington. Petty.

Dart told me Petty was back, but I haven't seen the phenom drummer-turned-superstar since his return. Even as he's aging, he still looks like Adonis with a goofy grin and laughter in his throat. He sits on a low stool, casually holding a guitar on his lap while speaking into the microphone.

"It's good to be back in Rogue River," he continues. "And a very persuasive town council member asked me to play a set."

He pauses as people clap their approval.

"I'd like to start the night with a request. Something special for a special couple." He plucks at his guitar.

The initial chords are unfamiliar. I was not aware that Petty could play the guitar or that he could sing. Makes sense because he was in a famous band, but I've only ever known him to play drums.

As he sings the first line, his sultry, deep voice waves over the crowd.

Dart turns towards me, a mischievous smile on his face. "Dance with me."

I'm holding Mirabelle, so I say, "I don't know."

But Mom comes out of nowhere, slipping her arms between me and Mirabelle, and taking her from me.

"Sounds like fun," she mutters before peppering Mirabelle with kisses while she steals her away.

I glance at Dart, who holds out his hand.

"Everyone will be watching us," I state. No one else is dancing right now.

"And see what?" Dart chuckles. "Me dancing with my wife? Let them look." He steps closer to me. "They're all jealous that you're with me."

I laugh, hesitation tickling my throat. "You're so ridiculous."

"And that's what you love about me."

We both freeze. His eyes wide. Mine mirroring his.

"I mean . . ." Dart swipes the hand he extended to me through his hair.

"I know what you meant," I tease, sticking out my hand. "I haven't danced in a long time. I might be rusty."

He takes my hand and tugs me closer. "We can be rusty together."

"Thought race car drivers didn't like rust," I tease again, the joke coming out shaky because I'm suddenly nervous to be in Dart's arms. It isn't that we are in public. It's that I'll be so close to him.

Hand in his. Chest to chest. Hips to hips.

He slides one hand around my back, pressing me even closer. My breasts brush against his warm T-shirt. He bends a knee, forcing me to follow his lead. And our hips move in tandem. The rhythm is familiar. His hold . . . like he'll never let me go.

I'm a little stiff, so Dart takes my hand and sets it around his neck. He slips his now free hand to my hip. We feel even closer. His heart races beneath my other hand. The back of his neck is damp. His forehead is almost against mine.

"Hold onto me, Forever," he whispers, his breath brushing my lips.

"I don't want people to think I'm clinging to you." The words come out in a rush. A river of panic. Not that I care what people think, but I don't want to look like I'm clinging to the man who broke my heart.

Dart stills. He lifts my chin and meets my eyes. "Then let me cling to you."

He scoops his hand around my back again while the other one slips around my nape. We look like we're embracing more than dancing. Dart picks up that subtle sway again and hums in my ear, emphasizing certain words in the tune.

Home. Never leaving. Love.

"Dart," I whisper, finding I've melted against him, becoming one with him.

The bounce of our hips. The jut of our knees. The heat of our chests.

His fingers dig into my short hair, and my nose runs along the collar of his T-shirt.

I lower one hand for a belt loop on his hip. His hand spans my back.

We cling to one another.

Before I know it, the song ends. People whistle and cheer for Petty's performance, but Dart and I are in our own little bubble. The one we used to find even in a bar full of people or among our closest friends.

Just him and me.

It's all I ever wanted.

He tips his forehead against mine, and I close my eyes, breathing in his familiar pine scent mingled with the heat of the day.

The hand on my back runs up my spine. A shiver reverses down it. My flesh pebbles. My limbs feel loose and heavy, relaxed.

Dart cups the sides of my neck, tipping back my head with his thumbs beneath my chin.

My mouth waters, anticipating a kiss like I did the other night against the fridge. My heart is beating so fast, it eclipses the next song Petty sings.

Then a throat clears next to me.

Turning my head, I gasp, "Mom." I pull back from Dart, like we've been caught kissing on the sofa in a dark room after curfew. Only Dart doesn't let me go. His hand still cups the back of my neck.

"Why don't you let me take Mirabelle tonight?" She presses a kiss to Mirabelle's head. "Give yourselves a break."

I blink, the mist of Dart's nearness clearing. "That's probably not a good idea."

I don't dare look at Dart for some reason and continue my argument. "You've worked all day, and you still need to take down your booth."

"Oh, I have help for that. Plus, I need some Mirabelle and Mimi time." She peppers Mirabelle's cheek with more kisses.

"I don't know," I whisper. Of course I trust Mom. She has an extra infant seat in her SUV and a portable crib at her house, plus a stock of diapers and a change of clothes.

Dart makes the decision for me, for us. He steps toward Mom and stamps a kiss on her cheek. "Thank you, Mary."

Mom winks. "Go. Have fun. And breakfast tomorrow." Then she rushes off with Mirabelle in hand, leaving me in a position *I* don't trust.

Being alone with Dart.

22

[Trinity]

On the ride back to the house, Dart has his hand on my thigh. However, he isn't simply resting his palm there. He's gently squeezing my leg, like he's adjusting and re-adjusting his grip. Fingertips kneading my flesh, massaging it. Every press of his fingers sends a shockwave of desire up the inside of my leg and straight to a part of me that's only been touched by me.

For three years.

He doesn't move any higher up my leg, keeping his hand respectfully mid-thigh, but all I can think about is how disrespectful I want him to be.

How I want his hand to slip underneath my dress and his fingers to tickle my skin. How I want him to brush where I'm damp and desperate and feel how much my body responds to his.

I shift only slightly, spreading my legs a little wider but not wide enough. If he senses the hint, he doesn't act. Just keeps toying with my thigh and winding me up until I nearly rocket from my SUV in desperate need of some alone time.

A battery-operated date is required.

Only, when we enter the house, Dart pauses in front of the staircase, blocking the hasty retreat I planned. We stare at one another, the tension between us as tight as his fingers gripping my thigh only moments ago.

"I need a shower," I state as an excuse. Fisting my hands at my sides, like I'm ready to implode from sexual tension.

Everything seems to collide at once. The way he was with Mirabelle. The way he doted on me. All the back-touching and forehead-pressing and the anticipation of another kiss. The way he handled my family. And forgave me for Spencer Reid.

I want to kiss you like you deserve to be kissed.

I wanted that too.

He'd also asked me earlier if I still wanted a divorce. Something I'm not ready to discuss, but I want him. Right now. Right here. I want him again.

And I haven't felt this feeling in years. This buzz beneath my skin. This flutter in my belly.

His nostrils flare as if he senses my desire. His shoulders rise. He looks like a bull ready to charge.

Do I want him to charge? Should I charge him? Could I have sex with him again?

One farewell fuck, I'd thought earlier. One more time to just feel him between my thighs. See if we still fit in the ways we fit for years.

I collapse against the closed front door, almost like I'm blown back by the force of my thoughts. The idea of him inside me again. Touching me where I haven't been touched.

My back meets the wood with a soft thud.

"Tell me what you want." His voice is ragged, sounding as desperate as I suddenly feel. "I'll give you anything."

Anything. He'd always been like this with me. Promising, and coming through on it.

This house. Attempts to have a baby. His love.

His love was always there, underneath it all.

I want him to love me again. I want to love him again.

"Sit," I quietly command.

He steps back, catching his calves on the first riser of the stairs and lowers to take a seat. The same place he once took me when we first moved into this house.

It's exactly where I want him.

Dart keeps eye contact with me the entire time. "Be sure about this, Trin. Because once we go there, I can't go back."

He wasn't setting demands. He was making promises again.

I don't respond, just keep my focus on him.

The strength in his forearms. The span of his chest. The spread of his legs.

He leans back, settling his elbows on the wooden tread, watching me, waiting.

We continue to stare at each other for another long minute before I cautiously step forward. One foot in front of the other until I reach his bent knees. His legs are already spread but he spreads them wider to accommodate me, although I have no intention of standing between them.

Instead, I press his legs together and slide my hands up his sturdy thighs, spreading my legs to climb over his. I hitch up my dress, so my inner thighs meet the denim covering his outer ones. At first, I situate myself near his knees, taking time to run my hands up his lap and along his belt.

His eyes flutter shut until I glide forward, dragging my body over the tops of his.

We don't speak. Nothing needs to be said. This is my moment.

Once I'm settled more firmly in his lap, the hard length of him directly beneath where I'm soft and tender, I rock forward.

Dart hisses. He moves his arms so one hand is plastered to the wall and the other grips the spindle of the railing, like he's holding himself back from taking over, taking control.

I rock again, rubbing my hands up his chest. His T-shirt is warm from the sunshine and heat of his skin beneath the worn cotton. His chest rises and falls with his shaky breaths.

I lean forward.

As if some of the tension in him snaps, he meets me half-way, kissing me hard. His tongue immediately invades, sweeping into my mouth and stealing my breath. He sucks on my lower lip, before popping off it.

"Don't you ever kiss someone else again."

God forgive me, but that command ripples down my middle, exploding in my lower belly.

I could snap at him. Demand he never leave me. Demand *he* never kiss someone else.

Instead, I cup his jaw and bring his mouth to mine again, kissing him back just as hard, thrusting my tongue forward, meeting his again. He cups the back of my head, keeping me attached to him, commandeering this kiss until we fall into a natural rhythm. Tongues twirling. Lips sucking.

And my hips have a mind of their own, as I rock faster and faster as the kissing grows more intense.

This is that first kiss. And the second one. And all the ones in between.

This is Dart and me.

Zero to one-hundred in a blink.

His other hand comes to the small of my back, and he presses on me, holding me in place to grind harder over him.

Eventually, I break free from our mouths, letting out a gasp as my body comes alive like it hasn't in years. In a way I cannot achieve on my own. This only happens with him.

Dart. *My husband*.

He's hard beneath my clit. His length eager to fill me. The

desire between us is so visceral I can feel it through his jeans and my damp panties.

He releases my head and slips his hand to my bare thigh. "Let me touch you."

"Please," I beg as his mouth comes to my chin, my jaw, my neck. I cup his head as I move to allow his hand deeper between my thighs.

He brushes his fingertips over the damp fabric of my underwear, forcing a small whimper from me before he pushes the panel aside and the tip of his finger instantly finds where I need him most.

Like he's never forgotten. As if he remembers every trigger on my body.

At the same time his fingertip teases my clit, he nips at the juncture of my neck and shoulder, and I cry out, melting into him.

"Yes," I moan, as his fingers rub small circles, then dip lower, slipping into me. I groan at the easy glide of the sudden intrusion. He's so familiar with how to work my body.

One finger dips deep before pulling back. A second one immediately joins the first.

Dart adjusts his wrist, so I'm practically in the palm of his hand, riding his fingers until his thumb flicks, catching on the most sensitive spot.

"Dart," I gasp, like I haven't ever been touched like this, when he's already touched me a thousand times. It feels like it's been a thousand years ago.

I flatten my hand on his cheek and tilt his head, needing his mouth again, but I'm terrible at multitasking in this manner. All my concentration goes to where his fingers have entered me and his thumb plays me. I grip his shoulders, mouth agape, and rock faster.

"Dart," I whimper, in shock and awe, and out of control as the orgasm barrels through me like a lightning bolt, striking fast and bright. I cry out one more time, and Dart captures my mouth, breathing in the ecstasy as I break apart over his fingers.

"Forever," he breathes into my mouth.

Hastily, I reach for the buckle of his belt.

Dart gently removes his fingers and glances between us. "Baby, we don't have to—"

"Shush." My fingers shake as I fumble with the buckle and unsnap the button of his jeans.

He chuckles. "Did you just shush me?"

"No talking," I growl.

"Yes, ma'am." His hands land on my hips as I push myself upward so I can pull his jeans and underwear lower.

We're a mix of rushed fingers as he releases me and lifts his hips, shoving down his pants himself, forcing them over his knees. I grip his thick cock.

The touch is like an electric shock. The familiarity of my hand causes his eyes to roll back.

"Trin," he groans, tipping back his head, as I stroke up and down the steel-like length, swiping my thumb over the tip that weeps with desire.

All movements are based on instinct. I know this man. He knows me.

We both hiss when I bring his tip to my entrance.

His head whips forward, eyes bright and blown. "Trinity." Restraint sizzles out of his mouth, mingling with my name.

Slowly, I lower, taking him in, inch by excruciating inch, until I can't hold the base of him anymore. Then I fall. Drawing him the rest of the way into my body.

Dart snaps forward and wraps his arms around me, holding me tight. Pinned to him. His forehead meets my shoulder, and he exhales.

"Never thought I'd be here again."

We're here, but we aren't. This is different. While we might have fucked on these stairs before, that was another time, a different us, and a totally new position.

This time, I'm in control.

"So good," he whispers.

I run my hands around his head and then gently tug his hair, so he tips back. My mouth crashes against him in a kiss that's almost painful at first.

Then I release him and shift, lifting my hips.

Dart falls back again. His elbows land with a thud on the tread. His fingers dig into my hips.

He lets me lead.

And I lose control.

With my hands on his belly, with only the faint dusting of his former bruises present, I nearly bounce up and down on him, drawing him deep and then balance on the tip, threatening to release him. The threat is merely seconds before I fall over him again, bringing him back into me before repeating the motion. Gliding up his length. Dripping down his shaft.

I'm so wet, and the sound of our skin smacking faintly fills the front hallway.

This is what I've missed. This unrestrained feeling. This sense of freedom. The safety of him.

Dart lets me play with his body. Use him, like the song we heard at RiverFest.

"So good," I whimper, riding up and down him. A rush of counteractive motions that result in the most delicious pleasure.

"So good," Dart echoes me, gripping my hips harder and adding to the rhythm by slowly bucking his hips upward.

"So deep." He grunts. "Never—"

I crush my mouth to his again. I don't want to think about the past. Don't want to think about the future.

I just want to be present.

And I am.

Through the spiral winding up my belly.

Through the tingle in my legs and a cramp in my toes.

Through the thundering of my heartbeat.

Until I finally let go.

The release is so sweet. Flower petals raining down on me. The burst of a firework. A wild jump straight into the river.

I'm soaring in a way I've never soared before.

With my fingers digging into Dart's shoulders and my head tipped back, I practically howl.

And Dart follows me.

He lifts his hips faster, tapping into me harder, until he slams me down, pinning me to his lap. He tilts back his head and lets out his own deep sound of pleasure. His eyes close tight. The vein on his neck extends.

Then he flashes me with those amber eyes, and his mouth crashes mine. His fingers pinch my jaw, holding my lips against his. He kisses me as deeply as he did when we first settled on these stairs. Only the kiss is a little kinder. The sweep of his tongue softer. His lips curl into a smile against mine.

"Forever."

The nickname snaps me out of the moment. A rubber band pulled taut then released.

I flinch at the term and pull back, staring at Dart.

So familiar. So far away in the same instance.

What was I thinking? I'll never be over him, and a moment like this only renews the heartache.

Because I'll never be with someone else the way I am with him.

Nothing will feel the way it does when I'm with him.

Never.

23

[Dart]

The second she shuts down, I see it. Her eyes wide, almost panicked. Her mouth slack instead of smiling.

What we just did catches up to her.

I'm still buried inside her. The two of us are slick and breathing heavily, and yet I've lost her.

Trinity scrambles off me, releasing me with a soft suction. A rush of our collective releases trickles down me. She fumbles off my lap and tucks her dress between her legs.

I don't know what to do with my hands. Pull her back to me or let her go.

When she starts up the staircase, wedging herself between me and the railing, I catch her ankle. I don't intend to trip her, I just want her to stop.

"Trinity."

"I . . ." She's practically crawling up the stairs, and she glances at me over her shoulder. Her mouth is swollen from our kisses. Her neck reddened by my scruff. But her eyes . . . they kill me.

"Shower . . ." she mutters. She's pushing me away, pulling back, doing exactly what we said we wouldn't do.

I let her go, collapsing on the stairs for another second to catch my breath. To catch my thoughts.

I want to give her space, but space is all we've had. Too much time. Too much distance.

Am I too late?

I pull up my jeans and press off the stairs to slowly climb the steps.

I hear the shower running in her room.

Stay or go? Steamroll or settle?

There's only one choice.

Her.

I stalk toward the bathroom. Because of the closed door, I knock. "Trin?"

When she doesn't answer me, I risk her wrath and enter. She's in the shower, back to the door, head against the wall.

Spreading my hands wide, I press my forehead to the glass. "Trin. Talk to me."

Her shoulders shake. We've been in this position before. Her silent tears. My broken heart.

I should leave her alone, but that's also what I've done in the past. I'd let her wallow in her emotions instead of addressing them.

Slowly, I peel off my clothes and pop open the glass door.

Trin tilts her head, glancing at me over her shoulder, bewildered, overwhelmed possibly.

Too much happened too fast. I won't deny I loved it. Won't pretend it didn't happen either. I don't regret it one bit, but this . . . the fear in her eyes, I want to dispel.

I run my hands over her shoulders and down her arms, cupping her elbows.

"Talk to me."

She shakes her head. "I'm not certain I can even explain it myself."

I slip my hands down her forearms and then wrap both our arms around her middle, pulling her back to my chest.

"Then we'll just stand here. Together."

We don't need words. We need time. Not the distance behind us, but a slow, steady pace dragging us forward.

I'm not going anywhere.

Still, the silence kills me, and I realize maybe she does want her privacy. Maybe she needs time without me to process what happened. I don't want to crowd her. I don't want to control her.

I press a kiss to her shoulder. "I'll give you space."

Slowly untangling our arms, I slip away and turn for the shower door. I'm just pressing it forward when her arms wrap around my middle. Her cheek rests on my spine. I close my eyes.

"I'm scared," she admits.

It's all I need to know. I spin to her, tucking her into my chest, cupping the back of her head. "I'm scared too."

Scared that I'm too late. Scared that I'll lose her. Scared that I'll lose Mirabelle.

Everything I've ever wanted is right in front of me, and I might be too late to grasp it.

"Can you tell me what you're afraid of?"

"I'm afraid you'll leave. You'll still love me, but you'll go." She pulls back to look into my eyes. Hers reflect liquid pools of darkness, accented by fear and confusion

I did that to her. I put that fear there. I took what I was most afraid of myself and turned it on her. Being left as a child by both my parents. Being unloved by my grandparents. Feeling abandoned most of my life and promising I'd never do that to another person. That I'd never do it to her . . . my person.

And I did.

"Can you ever forgive me, Trin? Am I too far gone from

you?" I cup the sides of her face, the warm water pelting our sides.

"I do. I have." She swallows, lowering her eyes. "But it still hurts." A sob escapes and she quickly covers her mouth with her hand.

Forgive but not forget. Not yet.

I tug her back to me. "No more hiding, Trin. For either of us. You've got to tell me these things. I'm a guy, baby. I need my hand held and my heart explained."

She soggily chuckles, only a sliver of the tension cracked.

"I'm here, Trinity. I'm here." I lower my voice, pressing a kiss to the top of her head. "Forever."

She nods against me, but I'm not certain she firmly believes me.

"I might have been physically away from you, but I was never gone. Never without you." She was always in my thoughts, in my heart.

Her arms tighten around my middle, and I squeeze mine harder around her shoulders.

"We just need time."

In racing, you want the best time. The fastest speed. The lowest number on the clock.

But this . . . there's no rush. We aren't measuring our pace with stopwatches.

"I'm here for all of it." Eternity and beyond, but I need to stop talking. I'm afraid I'm only messing further with her head.

Right now, we need to focus on this moment. "How are you feeling right now? About what we did?"

Does *she* regret it? Did she hate it? Did I hurt her?

She pulls back a little bit, releasing her arms from me. "I feel like it needed to happen."

I softly smile, swiping at the hair clinging to the sides of her face.

"Any regrets?"

She lowers her gaze and shakes her head.

"You were pretty demanding, baby." I hope she picks up on the tease in my voice. "I liked it."

If her cheeks turn pink, I don't know because of the steam in the shower, but the corner of her lip curls.

"But did I hurt you?" We were a little rough and that staircase certainly wasn't a soft bed.

"No." She closes her eyes, shaking her head again. "I liked it."

My smile grows, and I swipe beneath her eyes with my thumbs. When she opens them, they are clearer but still sad.

"Let me take care of you." I reach for the shampoo and pour a healthy dollop into my hands.

Trinity turns to face the wall. I lather up my hands and wash her hair, taking my time with the short length, massaging her scalp.

Eventually, I tip her chin to rinse the suds.

Next, I cover my hands with soap that smells like summertime and fresh meadows. Her scent. I press my fingers into her nape and my palms along her back. I rub her arms and down her legs, picking up her feet to scrub them.

And every time I touch her, she touches me in return. Her fingertips dance up my arms and along my wrists. Her fingers dig into my hair as I bend forward and lower for her legs.

"You always did take the best care of me."

Sorrow still fills her voice. All the heartbreak of the past just beneath the surface.

"Want to take care of you again. You and Mirabelle."

Her eyes widen. We haven't talked about my role with Mirabelle. Whether I'll be given one.

It's a discussion for another day. Right now is about us. Just her and me.

I give my own body a quick rinse as the water turns colder. Then, I turn off the faucets and reach outside the shower for a towel. Wrapping it around her first, I step out and find a towel for me.

Her single towel on the hook is another reminder that I left her alone.

Tonight, and every night that follows, I don't want her to feel alone again.

We each dry off a bit before Trinity reaches for one of those silky nightgowns she's been wearing. They aren't sexy as much as soft-looking, so feminine, so pretty on her.

"Trin. Can I be so bold as to ask if I can sleep with you tonight?"

I don't want to leave her alone. I can't control rambling thoughts or even settle them in one night, but one night is one step, and that's what we need.

"I'd like that," she says, reaching for a spare toothbrush in the vanity drawer.

As we stand side by side, brushing our teeth, the moment might feel mundane to another man. A nightly routine done by rote. A practice that happens out of habit. I might not have ever noted how many times Trin and I went through this process, side by side.

But I'll never forget it again.

This is my chance to make new memories.

I won't squander even the smallest ones.

24

[Dart]

I wake first and take a second to process where I am.

The room is familiar. The layout. The paint color on the wall. And yet everything about this space feels different.

I shift my head, finding Trin still tucked under my arm. Her arm draped over my waist. Her breath against my chest.

A quiet awareness of what we did on the staircase and our interaction in the shower afterward surrounds me.

I tug her a little tighter to me, not hoping to wake, but not willing to let her go yet.

The feeling of holding her again. In this position. In our bed. It's like a dream. Only I have proof it wasn't because she's still here. She didn't disappear last night. The heat of her body seeps into mine. Her skin is so soft when I tickle my fingertips along her shoulder.

Trin wakes with a little start. Her body stiffening beneath mine, perhaps wondering where she is, just like I did. Then slowly she melts into my side and tips up her head.

"Good morning." Her voice is groggy with sleep. One of my favorite sounds from her.

"Morning, baby." I kiss the tip of her nose and continue to stroke my fingertips around her shoulder.

"How did you sleep?" I ask, worried that she was plagued by more fears about us.

"Surprisingly well." She shifts down my arm, getting a better view of my face.

I shift as well to mirror her position, both of us on our side. "Surprisingly well," I tease, meeting her eyes. Eyes that still hold a ghost of concern, and I want to address that issue. I want to address all her worries, but right now I just want to breathe in our position, luxuriate in it.

"Better than I have in years," I admit.

"Me too," she whispers.

I take her hand and bring it to my lips, kissing the ends of each finger. Trinity watches me, a slow smile curling one side of her mouth higher than the other.

"Hi," I whisper, suddenly hyperaware of our body position, while almost shy about it when I've never been shy a day in my life.

"Hi," she says back.

Suddenly, I recall one of our first times in her bed. We were in a position just like we are now. Just staring at one another. For my part, I kept wondering if we were real. If this incredible, beautiful, smart, driven woman was really lying next to me. Had she really let me touch her, enter her, kiss her everywhere?

Presently, Trin reaches forward and traces down my nose.

A subtle reminder that not only did it happen as I thought all those years ago, but it happened again. And again.

A dozen years of marriage to her, and some things were steadfast. She was still incredible and beautiful, and smart and driven. And she did let me touch her and enter her.

I can only hope to kiss her everywhere soon.

For now, I lean forward, breaking our eye contact, and run my nose along the side of hers. Her breath hitches. But her hand comes to the side of my head, stroking her fingers through my hair.

"We should probably get up soon," she whispers.

"Okay," I mutter, still running my nose against hers, breathing her in.

Her summertime and fresh meadow scent is still apparent. A hint of sleeping against me.

We don't move.

Her hand rubs down the side of my neck and over my chest, resting against my sternum. I slide my hand over her hip, feeling the silky material of her nightdress.

"Dart," she whispers, the sound a little breathless more than a warning.

"Yeah, Forever?" I smile, my mouth just centimeters from hers.

"If we don't move, I might attack you again."

I chuckle, low and deep. My chest expands. She didn't attack me. She . . . I don't know what she did to me. Make love is too soft. Fucked me is too hard.

She clung to me.

For all her protests while dancing, she clung to me on those stairs, and I did the same to her.

"Promises, promises," I tease, speaking quietly right near her mouth.

She leans forward and brushes her lips against mine. She isn't kissing me. Not exactly.

"I promise," she says against my mouth, then she pulls free and tosses back the covers, sliding out of bed.

She laughs, knowing what she's done to me. I'm hard and horny . . . for my wife.

~

When we reach Mary Haven's house, the driveway is full of pickup trucks. Saturday morning breakfasts are apparently still a thing around here.

"Hello," Trinity calls out as we enter. The chatter coming from the back of the house signals that is where the majority of her family gathers.

Trinity enters the kitchen first. I stand behind her.

All conversation comes to an abrupt end.

Mary is standing at the stove. Cortland sits at the table. Vale is holding Mirabelle. Clint sips a mug of coffee while his little girl is seated beside Cortland, coloring.

And Tate slowly stands from his chair. "I just lost my appetite."

The flinch in Trinity is subtle. Just a twinge of her shoulders, but it's enough to raise my hackles.

"Tate." My tone is sharp. "Can I have a word with you? Outside."

The tension in the kitchen doubles.

Mary slowly turns, spatula in hand, raised and ready to speak.

"I'm leaving," Tate announces.

"Outside." I snap. "Now." The gauntlet is thrown down. He can either step outside with me or look like an ass in front of his family.

He pushes in his chair, making it thud against the table, and slips out the back door.

Trinity's head turns, her eyes concerned, but I rub my hand up her back and kiss her cheek. "Be right back."

I expect Tate to sneak around the side of the house and disappear. Instead, he stands in the middle of the backyard, a space we've used for parties and family celebrations.

His arms are crossed, eyes aimed at me like arrows. Tate and I are roughly the same height. He might be broader than me, but I could still put up a good fight. And right now, Tate is looking to fight.

"Just what the fuck is the problem?" I stop a few feet in front of him.

"Are you serious?" He glares at me while fisting his fingers at his side.

"Look. I know I left. I know I hurt your sister. I broke my own heart at the same time." I thump my fist against my chest. Tate has never been in love. Not really, and while it used to not bother me, each man to his own, his lack of a true relationship is one reason I never went to him with my issues. Besides those troubles revolving around his sister, I really didn't think Tate would understand.

I love his sister, but it doesn't mean marriage is easy. Relationships take work. Hard work. Tate doesn't get that.

"Yeah, well, not everything is about you," he snaps.

This pulls me up short. "Then what *is* the fucking issue? Because I'm not going anywhere. And our friends are still my friends."

"Friends?" Tate practically spits. "You were like my fucking brother."

We *were* like brothers. We were both a little rougher than Cortland and Clint. A little more reckless and daring. And I wonder where he's going with this thought.

"And you fucking left *me*." He smacks his chest.

What? "Tate." My throat clogs, the lump inside like a ball of acid. "I tried to talk to you, it's just . . ."

"Just what?"

"Trinity is your sister." I didn't feel comfortable telling him about our sex life. The disconnection. The separation between us. He didn't understand how deeply it hurt her to *not* have a baby. He didn't understand how it was killing me not to give my wife what she wanted.

I wanted to be a father. His dad had been a wonderful example of one.

"That's a poor excuse."

"It's not an excuse. And it wasn't all about your sister anyway. It was about me."

I sigh, turning my head and squinting in the morning light. "I was tired of feeling like a failure. I was just stuck." I glance back at him. "Not giving Trin a baby. Not fulfilling my promises to her."

His eyes widen.

"Even with Cort and Clint." I glance over my shoulder, as if they can hear me. "I'd been working construction for more than twenty years. I needed to do something different. Something I could control. Something I could win."

If anyone can understand the sensation of wanting to win, to be significant, it was Tate. He'd lived in the shadow of Cortland his entire life. Cort and his professional football success. Tate might have even been a better athlete than Cort, but he never got the break he needed to do more, be more. Part of that might have been because of his attitude. Tate acts like he's owed something. He's never seen how easy he has it, how much he already has.

"And you wouldn't talk to me either," I remind him.

Much like his sister, I called him. Tried to explain myself. Tate was all too happy to head to that old coal mine canyon and watch me race, but he wouldn't speak to me once I left.

I assumed his issue was about hurting his sister. Watching as he turns his head, his jaw tight, I realize something. "This is about you."

He whips his head back in my direction.

"You're upset because . . . I did something for myself. I was a success." It wasn't that Tate wanted me to fail. It's simply that I'd done something he hadn't exactly done himself.

His brother had gone off to be a football star.

Petty had been famous with his band.

Marshall was a success with his distillery.

And I'd been victorious, for a little while, as a race car driver.

"Tate." I sigh. "Don't you see, man? It doesn't matter?" He doesn't need to be a football star or in a band, own his own business, or race laps around a track. He is a success in his own right.

"Easy for you to say. You left."

It wasn't about leaving. Nothing ever held Tate back in this town, other than . . . him.

"And now I'm back. Because the most important things are here." I point at the ground. "Trin. And now Mirabelle."

Tate scoffs.

"Just because you don't want to be a dad doesn't mean I never did. You had the best father, Tate." My voice cracks at thoughts of Russell. His warm laughter. His kind heart. His belief in me.

"Don't," he demands, lasering his eyes on me.

"He was so proud of you, no matter what."

"Dart." He grits. "I'm fucking warning you."

"You have an entire family who loves you." I wave toward the house behind me. "When is enough *enough*?"

"You tell me," he spits. "You had a wife and a home, everything you ever wanted as well."

Tate knows my deepest desires, and he is right. I had what I'd always wanted, and I stepped away from it. I almost lost it, and now I'm scrambling to get it all back.

I lower my head, shaking it slightly. "I can't explain it all to you, Tate. Call it a midlife crisis. Call it a stumbling block. Call it a fucking mistake. I'm human, alright?"

Max Larsen saw it that way. A forty-something man feeling empty inside. He recruited me to race, to make a change in my life. But he also understood the value of a good woman. He wanted me to bring Trinity along for the ride. *I* wanted her there. But I'd still been lost.

I tucked into racing, and sped around a track, chasing . . . something.

Something I hadn't found until I came back to Trinity and Mirabelle.

Completion.

"I'm sorry I disappointed you." I blow out a breath and slip my hands into my pockets.

Tate snorts.

"And I'm sorry that I hurt you." I swallow thickly. "It hurt me that one of my best friends wouldn't listen to me. Wouldn't hear me out."

Tate stares back at me. His eyes so similar to his sister's, but more wild, almost cagey. He isn't any more perfect than I am. And one day, I hope he finds atonement for the things he's done.

"You left me, too, Tate." Sure, I still had Marshall and Hutch, and Petty on the fly, but Tate and I were the closest. He *was* the brother I never had. Family always forgives, Petty says. I want Tate to forgive me, but I can't make him do it.

When he doesn't say anything more, I turn away from him, take two steps, then stop to glance over my shoulder. "You should come back inside. Your mom made breakfast. Your sister is here with her new baby. Your family wants to spend time with you."

Family. That's what Tate was to me. A brother who disappointed me, like I disappointed his sister.

The difference between Tate and me is that I'm owning up to my mistakes. Trying to atone for them. He can accept me or not, but I won't let him walk out on the good thing he has inside that house.

His mom. His brothers. His sister. Their growing families.

Tate is blessed in more ways than he recognizes, and it is too bad he doesn't see it.

I've waved a green flag, signaling I'm ready to begin again. Be friends. Put the wreckage behind us.

Only Tate can decide to speed up or be left behind.

25

[Trinity]

To everyone's surprise, Tate comes back into the house shortly after Dart, who'd entered saying, "Anyone else want to air their grievances?"

Cort gives a crooked smile. Clint lowers his head. He had things to say to Dart as well, but he read the room. Perhaps, one Haven brother altercation at a time.

I look at Mom, who smiles softly and shakes her head. She knows how much of a hothead Tate can be.

I glance at Vale next, who smiles as well. She knows all too well how complicated brothers are.

When Dart finally comes to my side, he runs his hand up my back and squeezes the nape of my neck. A shiver runs down my spine.

The day is going to be a constant battle.

Memories of last night on the stairs. Memories of his care in the shower. Memories of waking up next to him this morning.

Lying next to Dart, I was reminded of when we first started hooking up. How we'd linger in bed when we could. How he'd tease me before we parted. Sometimes a simple kiss led to a morning quicky. A race against the alarm clock. Dart always made sure I was satisfied before I started my day and had something to remind me of him throughout it.

I never forgot.

We were so carefree back then. But then again, that's how one feels in their twenties, I guess.

Still, was it wrong that I wanted a little quicky this morning? A refresher on what we'd done last night.

Despite my emotions pinging all over the place, I felt calmer this morning. Dart's attempts to talk last night and his care in the shower made me feel seen by him. Made me feel special. Waking up next to him renewed that feeling.

He didn't slip out of bed like we'd done something we should not have done. He stayed.

"You okay?" he asks me, interrupting my thoughts.

"Are you?" I ask, arching a brow. An altercation with Tate could be fruitless. Tate was always determined to win, even if he was wrong.

"Never better," Dart lies, the heaviness of whatever happened between him and his old friend still weighs on him.

I slip my arm around his back and settle into his side. Then I glance across the room at Vale.

She grins like the Cheshire cat. Like she knows what I've done with the man beside me. She winks in solidarity.

I glance at Tate next, who purposely does not look in our direction, but takes a seat next to Cortland

"Who is ready to eat? I'm starving," Mom says, momentarily breaking the tension so everyone's focus shifts to breakfast.

The next hour includes the sound of plates being scraped clean and loud chatter about the baseball team Cort and Clint coach. The Haven Hitters, a twelve-and-under group of kids, are ripe with stories.

Mom speaks mainly to Vale and me about new romance novels at The Babbling Bean.

Dart appears like he's soaking it all in, holding Mirabelle in the crook of his arm while I eat. He casually leans back in his seat, with his arm draped over the back of my chair. A satisfied expression fills his face.

Dart Rivers is home. With his extended family.

Tate is unusually quiet before he stands abruptly and clears his plate.

"I need to head out," he states, looking only at Mom. "Summer camps start this week."

"It's Saturday," Mom reminds him, but Tate's excuse goes without further question.

As athletic director at the high school, he developed a summer sport camp program for younger kids. The six-week program builds community with the older kids and brings additional funds to the high school's athletic program.

Tate kisses Mom on the cheek and slaps Cort on the shoulder before heading out.

"Well, that was fun," I mutter as Tate's exit takes a bit of the stale air with it.

"Trinity, be nice," Mom warns, but she loosely smiles in agreement.

"Nice? I'm always nice," I tease, shifting sideways in my seat.

Dart chuckles while Clint snorts.

"Oh, I see how this is," I continue. "Two against one." I arch a brow.

"Sounds like a ping-pong matchup," Clint challenges.

I laugh until I realize he's serious.

When we were kids, our mother would send us out to the garage to clean up the countless pieces of sports equipment or wash our bikes. Any excuse to get us out from underfoot. We spent enough time in the garage that Clint eventually brought home a ping-pong table someone was giving away for free.

The garage became a zone we wanted to visit.

"I call Dart," Clint announces, pointing his fork with his final bite of waffles at my husband.

My husband.

I might need to get used to saying that again.

"I call Cort," I shout, raising my hand like a kid in a classroom, excited to have a little distraction and fun with my other brothers.

And that's how the four of us end up playing ping-pong, while Vale held Mirabelle and played commentator.

THE WEEKEND ENDED up being kind of perfect. After spending most of the day with my family, Dart and I spent the rest of the evening with Mirabelle. The three of us together.

After I gave Mirabelle a bottle near ten at night, prompting her back to sleep, I stealthily sneak out into the hallway outside my room, hoping not to wake her.

Dart stands in the hallway as well.

"Hi," he whispers.

"Hi." I lean against the wall.

"Just wanted to say good night." We finally finished watching *Bridgerton*, then Mirabelle woke up for this feeding.

"Good night," I whisper, but I don't move. Neither does Dart.

"I'll just . . ." He points down the hallway to the guest room.

"Oh. Okay." My chest aches. I don't know what I thought would happen tonight. We spent last night in bed together, but is it safe to do it again? Is it smart? Emotionally, I am still all over the place, so I don't want to confuse the issue any more than it already is for either of us.

"Unless you want . . . " He nods toward the bedroom door at my side.

"No, that's okay. You should probably go back to your room." Stating that the guest room was his room feels sour on my tongue. Disappointment settles in my chest.

He slips his hand against my cheek. "Why do I feel like I need to give you a good night kiss?"

"Why do I feel like I want you to?"

He smiles slowly, leaning forward. He runs his nose along mine before settling on my lips. Soft. Sweet. Tender.

He pulls away first, but I grab his shirt and pull him back to me. And he kisses me like a front-porch kiss. One that presses me against the wall and leaves me wanting more when we break apart.

"Good night, then," he says breathlessly.

"Good night," I whisper, just as swept away by him. Then I watch him saunter down the hall, glancing back at me with a satisfied smile before closing the door.

And I take comfort in his presence down the hall.

For a few minutes, it feels like all is right with the world.

In the quiet of the next early morning, I breathe in Mirabelle's lavender baby wash as she lies in the bassinet at the foot of my bed. To my surprise, she's still sleeping, and I take an extra minute to enjoy the silence before another day begins.

When I head to the kitchen, I notice Dart's truck is missing from the driveway. Surprisingly, I don't feel the panic I'd expect to feel. I feel lighter. Calmer. As if we've turned a bend in the road. It isn't always going to be perfect moving forward, but as long as we're together, we can handle the speed bumps and potholes.

Reaching the kitchen, I fall into the routine of no routine. This time won't last much longer. I have just over a week before I return to work, which means I need to go about the business of finding childcare. My six-week leave went so fast.

I still have a few months before the adoption will be final, and the one thing I am apprehensive about is leaving Mirabelle in day care or with a nanny. I'm not ready to leave her period, but I need to return to work.

The swirl of the front lock, followed by the quiet click of the front door opening, alerts me to Dart's return. I smile before taking a sip of my coffee to cover the grin.

When Dart enters the kitchen, surprise shows on his face. "You're up? I wanted to give you a little more time to sleep."

I took a later feeding last night. Dart took three a.m. We both wear the signs of tired parents.

Is that what he is? A parent to Mirabelle? Could he, would he, be her dad? It's a topic we haven't touched yet. Our relationship needs straightening out first.

Dart smiles slowly. I smile back.

Then my eyes drift to what's in his hands.

Flowers. A bouquet of daisies with a yellow ribbon around them.

"Happy anniversary, Forever." He holds up the familiar bundle.

Instead of taking it from him, I stare at the white petals and golden center of my favorite flower. The same ones that were my wedding bouquet. The ones that are significant to us.

After that tease of a proposal in my bed, Dart took me to an actual meadow and got down on one knee with a ring in his hand.

"Want to do this right," he'd said.

And every year since, including the years we were separated, a bouquet of daisies would arrive for me.

"Why'd you do it?" I ask, still staring at the offering. "Why'd you send them each year without a card or any other form of communication?"

The first anniversary he missed, he'd only been gone a few months.

The second one, I hadn't planned to honor, hoping the date

would quietly slip by on the calendar. I'd believed Dart and I were newly divorced. Papers signed and filed.

Last year, I stared at the bouquet, much like I am now, wondering how they looked so fresh, and so perfectly matched the flowers I once held walking down an aisle to meet him at the altar.

"I didn't want you to forget me, Trin. It was our anniversary. One of the best days of my life. And even if other days were difficult, that one day still meant everything to me. I'd hoped by sending you these flowers, you'd think of me. At least once a year, for one day, with a smile, not regret."

My mouth falls open, then I clamp my lips, taking a second to process what he said and how I reacted each year.

"It hurt to receive them," I admit. "They were a reminder that you left me."

His eyes widen, realizing his intention did not match the reception of his gift.

"But I never regretted you, Dart. Not once." I might have resented his decision to race and his absence from our marriage. I might have wished for more between us, like a full house and a continued life, but I did not regret *him*. He'd been the love of my life. A love I believed would last forever, and even if it hadn't, I'd known love like I didn't believe I'd ever know it again.

Because of him.

"I'm sorry they hurt you," he says, lowering his eyes, the flowers still dangling in his hand at his side.

"How'd you get them to me?" My heart begins to hammer, wondering what else I'm missing in that special bundle. "That exact bouquet, every year."

Slowly, he lifts his head. His eyes full of guilt and a secret.

You haven't placed your flower order yet.

The awkward conversation with Savannah Grant during RiverFest comes back to me.

"Savannah," I whisper. Her lavender farm outside of town has turned into a proper garden center with more than just lavender for sale.

Dart licks his lips and glances to the side before facing me again.

"No more secrets," he whispers, like this one is extra hard for him. "NASCAR always gets a break in June. That first year, months after I left, I came home. And I saw you."

"What?" The question wheezes out, like I've had the air knocked out of me. I clutch at my stomach.

"You looked better. Happier." He weakly smiles at me.

"Better?" I choke. I was dying inside. My husband was gone. The idea of future pregnancies gone. I had stopped considering adoption. I didn't want to go it alone.

I wanted my husband home.

"That first time, I picked them myself. Thought I'd make a grand gesture in coming back." He pauses, looking down at his boots. "But I don't know . . . I just couldn't do it. Start that cycle of pain all over again. I didn't think you'd be happy to see me, so I just left them. Like a coward."

I continue to stare at him, holding the island for support as my knees suddenly wobble.

Dart was here. He'd come back for me.

"Why?" I whisper.

"Just wanted to brighten your day," he admits again, but his expression is full of sorrow, his brows lowered, knowing that it'd hurt instead.

"Why didn't you come see me again?" I stress, clutching a fist to my chest while rounding the island, standing toe-to-toe with him.

Three fucking years. Three lonely years without him.

"Dart." My voice cracks, my heart breaking in a new way. "I fucking missed you. I was so lonely without you. I wanted you to come back to me."

Tears cloud my eyes.

Dart drops the flowers and tugs me to him, cupping the back of my head. “I’m sorry,” he says, “I’m sorry. I’m sorry. I’m sorry.”

I know he means it. The anguish in his voice. The way he’s holding onto me. He’s sorry he left, but is he back? Is he really home for good?

“Dart, we need to—”

Mirabelle cries out through the monitor app on my phone.

I don’t want to end like this. We have more to discuss. I need to know his plan.

“Dammit,” I whisper.

“I’ll get her,” Dart says, flowers still on the floor at his feet.

He runs his fingers along the side of my face, staring at me with so much sorrow in his eyes. Like he can’t get anything right. And I don’t want him to feel that way.

He stoops to pick up the flowers and silently hands them to me, then turns for the hallway, taking the stairs two at a time.

The pattern is heavy and familiar. A reminder that he’s in the house. The noise is a comfort more than an annoyance.

I bring the flowers to my nose and close my eyes.

He’d been so wrong. I wasn’t happier without him.

I was happier with him here.

26

[Dart]

After our *second* kiss, when I snuck to the hospital and kissed Trinity during her shift break, using some lame excuse when all I really wanted to do was see her again, we had a chance encounter on Marshall's property before it was his distillery and Savannah's lavender field.

Trinity was just standing there, like a ray of sunshine amid all these daisies in a field. Her hair was still strawberry-blond, and she somehow blended with the blooms around her.

I plucked a daisy from the field and held up the flower.

"Reminds me of you." Summertime and fresh meadows. Her smile bright as the white petals and golden center.

"Third time in four days, Dart River. What will the Star Gang think?" she teased.

I was there to help Marshall with something for the distillery he would eventually build. I couldn't remember why Trinity was present.

"They say the third time is the charm."

She laughed. "You already know you're damn charming."

I stepped closer to her and stroked the flower down her cheek. "Show me again how charming I am."

Then, I cupped the back of her neck, urging her toward me. She kissed me hard and fast, knowing we might be caught. Tate and Marshall were somewhere on the property. Still, I couldn't keep my hands or my mouth from her.

I thought sending her flowers once a year would put a smile on her face, let her know I was thinking of her. That I missed her.

She missed me? How would I know? She hadn't answered my texts. Hadn't returned a call.

My wife had me in a tailspin. I should have tried harder. I should have come home sooner, but I meant what I said.

She seemed happier without me.

The first time I got a glimpse of her, she hadn't filed for divorce yet. She looked better, healthier, less sad. And I'd been a coward.

My good intentions backfired, and I didn't know how to proceed. I didn't know how to undo what I'd done.

I'd hurt her again. A simple gesture like flowers, meant to brighten her day, only brought another layer of sorrow.

I'm such an ass.

My anger is further fueled when I whack my thumb for the second time while building the frame for the back deck. After tossing the hammer into the yard, I sit on the edge of the plank support and hang my head. Building a deck isn't a one-man job, but that isn't what's been on my mind the past few hours.

Trinity and I never fought. Not about the big things. We didn't have screaming matches or name-calling sessions, like I'd witnessed between my grandparents as the only married role models I had when I was a young boy. I was rather proud of the fact that we didn't argue, but it also meant we didn't communicate sometimes. We didn't open up enough.

I never heard Mary and Russell Haven argue either, but occasionally, I overheard some lively, contentious discussions.

Maybe a healthy level of argumentation might have been good for Trin and me.

We have a lot to work out, but being in the same vicinity is making a difference. I'm not running off to the racetrack. She isn't hiding out at work. We are here, almost forced to face each other. Even if we don't speak, we are still in close proximity. In my head, it sounded like the perfect plan to win her back.

But somehow, I still feel like I am losing her.

When the back door opens, I don't look up until Trinity stands beside me and hands me a glass of lemonade.

"Thanks." I take it from her but don't immediately drink. Instead, I stare up at her, take in her eyes, which had been too sad too often in our last year together. Her smile had been missing. Her spirit gone.

Standing in front of me now is a woman with a glow around her. Like that perfect moment in a daisy field. She has a new strength. An easiness I haven't seen before. A calm that's almost frightening.

She lowers to sit beside me on the narrow edge of the plank, and I take a sip of the lemonade.

"It's hard, right?" she begins. "Finding your way back."

I squint toward the yard. "I'm not making it easy."

She bumps into my shoulder. "*We* just need to put in the work."

I smile weakly at her.

"Speaking of work." She sits up straighter. "There are only so many home improvement projects around here." She pats the frame of the deck.

A deck had always been in the plans for this space, and now I want it more than ever. A space where we can sit and watch Mirabelle run around the yard, chasing fireflies. A place for Trin and me to share a quiet moment under the stars.

Still, I scoff. “Yeah. Well, besides us, I think I’m still in a bit of a midlife crisis. The only thing I know for certain is I want to be here. With you. With Mirabelle.”

Trinity watches me, the weight of her stare on the side of my face for a second, before I finally look at her.

“Will you take Clint up on his offer? Go back to work at Haven Exteriors?”

I sigh and glance back at my lemonade. “Trin, I don’t know if you can understand this, but I don’t want a job. I want something with meaning. For me.”

“And construction didn’t do that?” she questions.

“Don’t get me wrong. I loved working with my hands. The crew was amazing. Clint and Cort are great bosses.” I’m hoping she hears what I’m afraid to put into words. “But I was just part of the crew.”

She stares at me.

“Not all of us are fortunate enough to know what we want to do with our lives from such a young age.”

“Like me?” she clarifies.

“Like you.”

Trin had an experience in high school. A friend who had a miscarriage at the young age of seventeen. It happened in the girls’ bathroom, and Trin panicked. She never wanted to feel so helpless for either mom or baby again. She always knew her path in life. Her career path. She became a nurse.

“I was always a little jealous of you.”

“Me?” she says, aghast.

“You always knew what you wanted to be. And you were so smart, so driven, dedicated to that purpose. You had a true calling.” I pause and glance at the yard again.

Even with Mirabelle, Trinity has a role, but I don’t. Not officially.

“I wasn’t so fortunate,” I say. “I’d been floating through life until you entered it.”

I glance at her, and she blinks, startled by the truth. *She* became my purpose. Making her happy. Being with her. But happiness can't only be wrapped up in another person.

"Did racing do that for you? Give you purpose?"

The corner of my lip ticks. "In a sense." But not completely. "I think I was chasing something, Trin. Looking for control over the uncontrollable."

Us.

"I don't think I ever thought it would be more than a way to let off steam, but then I met Max." I wave a hand near my ear. "And he got in my head."

Could I really do this at forty-one? Start a new career? One that took physical strength and mental awareness?

"There had been guys who raced their entire lives, but Max saw something in me." Not much different than Trinity's dad.

"I felt alive when I raced." I didn't feel like such a loser. I squint toward the yard again. "But I never wanted to do it alone, Trin. I wanted you there beside me, which made me selfish. In hindsight, I see that more clearly. I asked you to move to give us a fresh start, but that start would have only been about me."

A new career. A new direction.

"I'm sorry I wasn't there for you," she says.

"And I'm sorry I wasn't here for you."

We sit in the quiet that follows, the summer breeze blowing around us. So many apologies lately.

"Speaking of work," she says again, and sighs, slapping her hands on her thighs. She's wearing jean shorts and a T-shirt. "I go back next week."

"Already?" I perk up. I knew she'd be going back, it just hasn't seemed like six weeks have passed.

"Monday." She looks back at me. "I need to organize child-care." Her head dips. "I'm not ready to leave her, though."

"You aren't leaving her, baby." I set my hand on her lower back. "You're providing for her."

I want to provide for them. And sitting around here finding home improvement projects isn't the way to go about it. Trin is right, there are only so many things I can fix or build. I need to start thinking about an income.

I'm being frugal with my race savings, but it won't last forever.

"Still, I feel funny about leaving her with a stranger."

"Let me do it." The thought pops out of nowhere, and yet, somehow, I think it was more present than I realized.

I reach for her hand, covering it with mine, shifting to face her better.

I want to be here for Trin and Mirabelle. And if that means an easier transition for Trin by staying with Mirabelle while she goes back to work, I want to do that for her. For them.

Trinity's head whips upward, her expression shocked.

"I'm already here." I squeeze her hand to reassure her. "And I love spending time with Mirabelle."

"Dart," she groans, chuckling like I'm joking, but she flips her hand, and now I'm holding it. Our fingers entwine.

"I can do this." The more I think about it, the more I mean it. More I want it. I might not be Mirabelle's dad, but I love her. I want to be with her. "I'm already changing diapers and feeding her. Mirabelle is easy, and on the days she's not, we'll take field trips."

"Like where?" Trinity stares at me, still disbelieving my offer.

"I don't know." My voice rises along with my other hand waving through the air. The rise could also be excitement. I clutch her hand harder. "I'll figure it out. You yourself are constantly saying parenting doesn't come with a manual."

Her coffee-colored eyes are bright and wide.

I clear my throat. "Not that I'm saying I'm Mirabelle's dad or anything."

I swallow thickly because I can't say that. I can't put a label on me that Trin hasn't given me. But I want that label. I want it more than I'll admit, because I don't want to pressure Trin. We're still trying to work out who we are as a couple.

"But I can do this for you." *Do this for our family.* "Let me be here for both of you."

Trinity continues to watch me, gauging my sincerity. Her eyes soften from my enthusiasm. Her shoulders relax.

"I do only work three days a week." She pauses, considering.

I recall her schedule. Three twelve-hour shifts within seven days.

"I don't know," she repeats more quietly.

I lift her hand, still entwined with mine, and kiss her knuckles in a silent plea. "Consider it, Trin. Really think about it." Please trust me. I'm here for you. Both my girls.

A squawk comes from Trinity's phone, and she checks the monitor.

"Duty calls." She waves it in the air and gives me a smile. A bright, genuine one that says Mirabelle is pure joy.

Like a field of daisies in sunshine.

She tugs her hand free from mine, but then she cups my jaw. The touch tender. Her eyes sweet.

And it's only after Trinity gets up and heads back into the house that I recall what she said.

We need to put in the work.

She said *we*, and I'm more determined than ever to make it happen for *us*.

27

[Dart]

"Okay, let's do it." The quiet comment jolts me from sleep.

Two nights ago, I was in Trin's bed in her room, but I've returned to the guest room, keeping my distance until I have her permission for more.

So, as I sit upright, I'm confused. I'd been deep in sleep, dreaming about her, so my first thought is she's waving the green flag to do something more.

I wrap my arm around her and slide her over me, landing her back on the bed.

"Really?" I ask, propping myself half over her. Leg between her thighs. Arm under her head.

"Yes. I think you should watch Mirabelle."

Oh. "Oh." I chuckle, pulling back from the way I'm over her. I fall to my back, my heart flooded, like an engine revved too much. I sling my arm over my face and lay my other hand over the thumping in my chest.

"What did you think I meant?" Trinity shifts beside me.

I can't look at her. I'm embarrassed by my quick reaction and instant hard-on.

"I thought you meant . . . It doesn't matter what I thought." I lower my arm and turn my head. "This is great news, Trin. Thank you."

While a smile comes to my face, I also want her to hear my sincerity. I'm genuinely thrilled for this chance.

I shift to my side. "Thank you for giving this to me." Time with Mirabelle. Trusting me with her. "I promise to take the best care of her."

"I know you will." Her faith in me is restored, at least when it comes to the baby.

"But let's get back to what you really thought I meant," she adds, still watching me. The room is dark, but the curtain is drawn back. The glow of the moon illuminates the space.

"I thought maybe . . ." I swallow. *Be honest.* "I thought maybe you wanted something more. With me."

"Oh." Her eyes drift away from my face to my bare chest.

The room is the perfect temp of mountain air coming through the sliver of open window, and I'm only wearing boxer briefs as I always do while sleeping.

"Yeah." *Oh.*

"Well, I did have another reason for sneaking in here."

I arch a brow. "Yeah," I say again, not capable of many words at this late hour.

She glances away from my eyes again and chews her lip. "I was wondering if I could sleep here with you."

She doesn't even have to ask, and I answer by slipping my arm around her and tugging her down to my chest. Her hair tickles. Her hand comes to my waist. Her palm is warm.

"Have a feeling your mind has been racing tonight, Forever," I tease.

She shifts, settling her cheek against my pec. "Yeah, just a little bit."

"Want to talk about it?"

She shakes her head. "I'm tired of thinking about the past."

I smile, only because I am too. "It's important to remember it, learn from it, but I don't want to keep dwelling on it, either. I only want to move forward."

I gently squeeze her arm. "So let's think about something else?"

"Like what?" she says, shifting her head to look up at me.

I run my hand over her shoulder. "Well, I got this new gig." I can't fight the smile, and it fills my voice. "And I'm wondering if you could offer some advice. What's a good field trip for a two-month-old?"

Trinity playfully slaps my belly. I clap my hand over hers.

"Let's see," I say. "I could take her on a walk." I tip-toe my fingers down her arm.

"We could visit the lavender farm." I twist, rolling Trinity on her back. Then I nuzzle my nose into her neck. "Smell all the pretty flowers."

"Dart," she giggles. "You're so ridiculous."

"We could watch the butterflies dance." I run my finger up her middle, between her breasts to her neck, where I skim my fingers over her skin.

Trinity ducks her chin while shivering.

"And what about you, Trin? What kind of field trips do you want to take?"

She stills beneath me, and I stare down at her, wanting to know what kind of plans she has for the future. We haven't taken many trips. Maybe it's time we do.

"I don't know. I don't mind a good hike." She walks her fingers up my chest and around my shoulders.

"What else?" I ask, noticing how my breath is raspy.

"We haven't been to the beach in a long time." She stares back at me, looking me right in the eyes, as her fingers dance over my belly.

The river doesn't have a beach, but there's a lake nearby.

"Swimming sounds good." My breath hitches as her fingers skate closer to my waistband.

"Ticklish?" she questions, arching a brow. "I don't remember that about you."

"I remember that you are." I dig my fingers into her side, forcing her hands from my belly, where she'll get a big surprise if she isn't careful.

She squirms and squeals, letting out a squawk, and then covers her mouth with her hand. Her eyes widen, begging me to stop, and as soon as she slings her leg over mine, I do.

Because I'm hard and she's soft, and she's lined up against me.

We both freeze.

"Is that for me?" she whispers.

"Always." This is what she does to me. My body reacts to her nearness. My heart races with her laughter. My soul calls to her.

She slips her leg off mine. "I only meant to sleep with you." *Rest*. She means rest.

"Then let's do that, baby." I straighten her nightdress over her hips and then pull her to me, tucking her head below my chin. With my arm around her back and her hand on my chest, my mind drifts.

I see us taking a hike in the woods, Mirabelle in a baby sling or infant backpack. I see us sitting by the beach, dipping Mirabelle's toes in the water. I see us pointing out butterflies and birds and teaching her about both.

And it's all such a nice dream, I'm afraid to close my eyes.

But when Trinity relaxes against me, I can't help but drift off to dreamland.

My dreams all sweeter because of her.

28

[Trinity]

Apparently, I'm being kidnapped. Or rather, girlfriend-napped.

Dart doesn't seem half as surprised as I am when he opens the door to Vale and Genie, both dressed for line dancing.

Wednesdays are Women's Night at Shenanigans. The local place is an old barn converted into a country bar, complete with pine-paneled walls, hardwood floors for stomping, and lots of space for dancing.

"Girl, get your boots on," Vale hollers, then quiets her voice, seeing Mirabelle in Dart's arms. "Time for Mom's Night Out."

I laugh at the thought when it hits. I *am* a mom. I'm Mirabelle's mom, and I smile at her tucked in the crook of Dart's elbow.

"Did you know about this?" I ask him, curious why he isn't reacting.

"Don't know what you're talking about." His smile gives him away.

"You start work next week, so we wanted to sneak in a night out before your schedule gets all wonky," Genie says.

My schedule will be hit or miss as I start back to work, and I glance at Mirabelle again, thinking I should stay home and suck up time with her. My time will be even more limited once I return to the hospital, and I know I'll miss Mirabelle. And Dart. I want to spend time with them. As a family.

But I don't have time to dwell on that final thought when Dart whispers, "Go." He nods toward the staircase. "Change."

I glance down at my loose sweatpants and cropped top.

"Are you sure?" I ask him. He hasn't been alone with Mirabelle yet.

"Consider this a practice run," he says, offering me a reassuring smile.

I rush up the staircase and fling open the closet, rustling through my clothes for a fun little dress and my cowboy boots. I'm giddy as I comb my fingers through my hair and put on makeup for the first time in weeks. A girl's night out might be just what I need.

As I saunter down the stairs, the heels of my cowboy hit the treads. Dart is still standing at the base, holding Mirabelle, and he does a double-take while watching me descend.

His amber eyes are like a sunset. Burnt orange, dull yellow, almost eclipsing the soft brown. His gaze stays pinned on me, like I'm the most stunning thing he's ever seen, even in an old dress and worn boots.

I hop off the second step, landing with a *thud*, which startles Mirabelle.

"All set." I glance around Dart at the girls who are still standing in the entryway.

"Let's go," Genie hollers, swinging her hand like a lasso in the air.

"Time to get our country groove groovin'," Vale teases,

opening the front door after saying goodnight to Dart. She steps out onto the front porch.

"We'll have her home before midnight, Dad," Genie jokes with Dart, before swinging out the door herself.

My gaze pings to Dart.

"She didn't mean . . ." I point toward Genie's exit.

Half his mouth smiles. "She was kidding," he confirms, but it makes me wonder once again if Dart still wants to be a dad. If he wants to be Mirabelle's dad. We still need to talk about that, but right now isn't the time.

For some reason, my gaze catches on the antique coat rack in my hallway. The one where two baseball caps now hang. One is for the days Dart plays ball with the guys. The other says Velocity on the front. Dart likes the bill of his caps rounded, not flat, and that Velocity one looks well-worn. And I marvel at how Dart has slowly started infiltrating the house again.

His boots by the door. His hat on that rack. His clothes mixed in with the laundry.

"I'm not certain I should let you out of the house like that." His voice is all appreciation, and my head turns quickly, catching him running his gaze down my form. Taking in the short, flirty dress that hits above my knees. The height of my cowboy boots, which show off plenty of leg.

"Excuse me," I counter. He can't tell me what to wear, but he's also looking at me like he'd like to take my clothes off.

"You look sexy, baby." His eyes snap back to mine.

I tip up my shoulder and twist my hips, twirling the dress a little bit. "Thank you, darlin'."

I step over to the coat rack, tug his hat off a hook, and settle it on my head.

I might have resented Velocity once upon a time. Been angry that the racing team took him away from me. But seeing him standing here, holding Mirabelle, waiting on me to go out with the girls, I can't find that anger anymore.

He steps closer to me. "Then again." He glances up at his cap on my head. "Go out looking sexy as that. Let everyone know you're my girl."

He tugs the bill of the cap downward, and I laugh.

"Dart Rivers, you are so ridiculous."

"And you are so beautiful." He leans even closer, then he glances at Mirabelle in his arms. "Don't look, Mirabelle. I'm gonna kiss your momma."

"Momma," I whisper, still disbelieving it sometimes.

"Momma," he quietly echoes, humming the word. "But how about that kiss, Forever?"

I cup his face and lean forward for a quick kiss, but Dart catches me around the waist, tugging me back to him.

His eyes light up. "Give me something to think about while you're gone."

I kiss him again. Taking his mouth and melting into it, while I hold his bristly jaw. The kiss lasts a little longer than it should and involves a little more tongue than I intended.

"Don't let me interrupt," Genie giggles. "But I'm on a time limit."

Turning my head, I catch her pointing at her breasts.

"On it," I laugh, before Dart softly pats my backside.

"Have fun," he says.

I glance back at him, staring at his lips, still wet from our kiss. "Did I give you enough to think about?"

"Plenty," he teases.

"Same," I whisper, before turning for the door and heading out with the girls.

The second I enter Vale's SUV, I'm bombarded with questions.

"So, I take it you and Dart are back together," Genie says, twisting in the front seat to look at me in the back.

"How is that going?" Vale asks me through the rearview mirror before reversing out of the driveway.

I glance at the house. "It's going."

"Is that wistfulness or frustration?" Genie asks next.

"Maybe a little of both," I admit, looking at them as the house disappears from view.

"What's going on?" Vale asks.

"We've been talking a lot. And flirting a little." I sigh.

"Have you had sex yet?" Genie asks, concern in her voice.

"Maybe." I shrug, but stare toward the front seat like that's the wrong answer.

Vale quickly glances at me over her shoulder. "How do you feel about that?"

"I think we needed to get it out of our system. We've been circling each other for weeks. Close proximity and all that." I huff, knowing my romance-reading girlfriends understand.

"Don't I know it," Genie admits, as she spent time living with Judd before their friendship-turned-fake-engagement turned into more.

"I'm the one who initiated it," I admit.

"Good for you," Vale says, tipping up her head to look at me again in the rearview mirror.

"So how was it?" Genie wiggles her brows.

"It was . . . hot." A little giggle escapes before I run my fingers over my lips, thinking about the kiss we just shared.

We haven't been kissing. We haven't been intimate again, but we have been sharing my bed. And all the little touches feel so intense.

His hand on my hip. My palm against his chest. Sometimes, I wonder what he's waiting for. Why haven't we done more again?

"Based on the kiss I just saw, I bet." Genie fans her face.

Vale smiles, but then her lips slowly drop. "How you doing with all this and Mirabelle?"

"Mirabelle is amazing," I say with pride. "And Dart is amazing with her."

"He's going to *manny,* or do we call it *danny* . . . Daddy nanny?" Genie laughs at her own joke.

"Yes, he's agreed to watch Mirabelle while I transition back to work. Until he finds a job." I turn my head toward the window, because there's still a twinge of fear that Dart will leave. The track will call him. Or Velocity will.

I tug at the hat on my head, torn between tearing it off my head and keeping it on.

Let everyone know you're my girl. While it might have sounded possessive, it was also said with pride. He'd be happy to call me his again.

I glance down at my naked fingers, wondering if I should have slipped my wedding bands on again. Wondering what he'd think if I did.

"You okay with letting Dart get close to Mirabelle?" Vale's question is asked cautiously. She had to think about her son when she got closer to my brother. But Hudson was also eleven when that happened.

"She's just a baby," I state as if that changes things. As if Mirabelle doesn't already love Dart in her infant way.

I'm certain Dart loves her. Could he leave her? Would he?

"Think Dart will stick this time?" Vale asks.

I shrug, squinting out the window once more. Because this *is* my only fear. I don't doubt Dart loves me. Or that he loves Mirabelle. I worry that he isn't fulfilled, doesn't have his purpose without racing. And what if racing wants him back?

"Do you want him to?" Genie adds.

I turn toward my friends. One straining against the seatbelt to glance at me over her shoulder. The other flipping her gaze from the road to the rearview mirror, assessing me.

"Is it wrong if I say yes?"

Vale chuckles. "I don't think there's ever a right or wrong when it comes to love, honey."

"You love who you love." Genie backs up Vale's statement.

"Yes, but is it wrong to want to love him when he hurt me so much?"

"If you can forgive him, and work it out together, then there's no wrong answer there either," Vale offers. She smiles softly, knowing she had to forgive Cort before she could give in to him again.

A story I know more details about than I care to admit.

I slowly smile at her. Do I forgive Dart? Have I forgiven him? Do I forgive myself for my part in our separation? Because I can't point the finger at him alone.

"I'd say we are a work in progress, but one that's progressing, and working for us."

Genie smiles. "I like that."

"Me too," I say, before adding. "And I'd definitely like to have sex with him again. Does that count for something?"

Vale glances at Genie, who only laughs. "Well, that's one way of working things out. Together."

I laugh, settling in my seat, telling myself to stop thinking so much.

"Okay, enough about me. This is Mom's Night Out."

"That's right, girl," Genie leans toward the backseat to give me a high-five. "Welcome to the club."

A new club with old friends.

I'm going to like it here.

29

[Dart]

Mirabelle is easy, like I knew she would be. That doesn't mean she's perfect. She cried for an entire hour after Trinity left. We went from pacing the house, to pacing the yard, to turning on black and white, hard rock videos from the 90s, which mesmerized her. When she finally took a bottle and went to sleep, I held her longer than necessary, enjoying the peace and comfort of her against my chest. Eventually, I set her down in the bassinet in Trinity's room, where she starts each night. I have the baby monitor app on my phone now as well, and I constantly check my phone's screen for the air temperature in the bedroom, Mirabelle's breathing rhythm, and her position in the bassinet.

Eventually, I turn on the television, randomly scrolling until I come across a list of recorded events.

Dart_Feb

Dart_May

Dart_July

The list spans three years. *Three years* of my races.

"Holy fuck," I whisper, staring at the screen, disbelief swirling inside me before my chest swells.

She was following me. She followed my career. The ups and downs. That's how she knew I'd had accidents prior to the last one. She'd been keeping tabs, or keeping up, or just . . . still interested in what I was doing. In me.

Maybe she hadn't been there. Maybe she didn't agree with my racing decision, but she'd been curious enough to watch me. To keep a record of it. Maybe, just maybe, she silently supported me.

Because she still cared about me.

I scrub a hand down my face, recalling our kiss from before she left. It was bold of me to ask and even bolder to want something deeper than a soft brush of our lips. I wanted to imprint myself on her, hoping she'd remember me while she was out with her girls.

And yet, this moment confirms that she never forgot me.

Maybe she didn't think of me as often as I thought of her, but she still thought about me once in a while. Not just once a year when I sent her flowers on our anniversary. But other days, other months, during the racing season.

She'd been in the corner, quiet and distant, but still somehow present.

My hand trembles as I lift the remote and click on the first race.

I watch with rapture at how I take each turn, listening to the announcer's comment.

A late entry.

A rising star.

One to watch.

Pride clutches in my chest, knowing what position I came in that first race. Not first place, but high enough to garner notice. To keep Velocity interested and move me up in their roster.

I get lost in the memories, watching another race, and another, until I no longer know what time it is.

When the whirl of the front door unlocking happens, I pause the race and shift on the couch. The house is mainly dark, other than the illumination from the television.

Trinity seems to fumble, tripping over something. “Oopsie.”

I smile, rub my hands down my sweatpants, and stand.

She enters my view through the archway to the entry, and then stumbles to a stop, facing me. Holding up a hand, pointing a finger in the air, she says, “I need water.” She turns toward the kitchen, and I hear the faucet turn on and water gush from it. A cabinet door gently slams shut.

Trinity reappears through the kitchen entrance to the dining room, rounds the table, and stands at the end of it, facing me. The couch is between us.

“You doin’ okay?” I ask, chuckling softly. Trin can hold her own with a drink.

“Yeah.” She pauses, chugs some water, and lets out a sigh as she pulls her lips from the glass. “Just thirsty.”

“Have a good time?”

“My friends are the best.” She leans back against the table and takes another long pull of her water.

“How was Mirabelle?” she asks after quenching her thirst.

“Perfect.” Just like her momma.

Trin nods and turns her head in the direction of the television. I’d paused the screen, so my car is front and center, frozen on the track.

“Oopsie,” she whispers again, before looking back at me.

“You watched me.” For some reason, I’m aware of the slow rhythm of my heartbeat. The stance of my feet on the rug. And the distance between Trin and me. “Why?”

She chews her lower lip, staring at that screen. “I just wanted to understand.”

Next thing I know, my foot is on the seat of the couch, and

I'm catapulting over it. My heart racing faster than my cars ever did. I move so quickly that she flinches backward, bumping into the dining room table and giggling.

"Ask me anything, Trinity." I pause in front of her. "I'll tell you everything. Anything you want to know."

"Always wondered what was more appealing about it. More appealing than me." She lowers her head, staring into her glass like water is the most interesting thing in the world.

"Trin," I sigh, stepping closer to her, tipping up her head by her chin. "Nothing is more appealing than you. *Nothing.*"

"But you needed it more than me," she says, holding my gaze a second before looking over my shoulder at the screen again.

"I didn't . . . I just . . . I wanted control in my life. Maybe barreling down a strip of asphalt at a hundred-ninety miles an hour wasn't the best example of control, but I needed something." I wave down my body. "Something to get out the energy, and the nerves. And the failure," I finish quietly.

"A hundred and ninety." Her eyes widen, almost comically. The brown is deep and dark in the low light of the room.

I smile because she's so cute. She's still wearing my hat, the ends of her hair damp from dancing, and I catch a few strands between my fingers.

"You know I've always loved racing, baby. Letting off steam that way." I sigh. "Maybe it seemed silly thinking a man at forty could start a new career. Join such an elite league."

Might have been silly to entertain the idea of something more professional than an old canyon and a dirt track. There were guys who'd been racing their entire lives. Guys with legacy in the sport. And then, there I was, forty-one-years old. Racing made me feel alive.

"I just didn't want to be a failure anymore."

"You"—Trinity jabs her finger toward me—"are Dart Rivers, and you are not a failure."

I chuckle at the ferocity in her tone. "How much have you had to drink tonight, baby?"

"Not that much." She lowers her eyelids and finishes her glass, then sets it on the table behind her. "But seriously, Dart. You're kind and strong. You're so good with Mirabelle."

I smile, appreciating the praise. "But am I good enough for you?"

She shakes her head. "You have *never* not been good enough, Dart." She waves toward the screen. "*I* didn't need that. Accolades or money to prove to me that you were exactly what I needed. Who I wanted."

I pause, staring at her. She's so fierce. So adamant. I was enough for her as I was.

"Those victories felt meaningless without you there, Trin."

"But you were happier without me." She leans forward, and I catch her shoulders.

"No. No," I say louder a second time. "I was not happier without you."

"It took three years and another accident to bring you back to me," she says quietly.

I shake my head again. "That accident scared me. Might have broken me a little bit, but it was not the reason I returned. I never stopped thinking about you, wanting you with me."

My head hadn't been in that last race, and Max knew it. He'd noticed even before it happened.

You're distracted, he'd said.

I was lonely. But I hadn't been able to admit it to him.

"Your accidents scared me too," she says quietly, leaning toward me and setting her head against my sternum.

"Oh, baby," I whisper, running my hand up her back and cupping her nape. "I'm here now."

She lifts her head, eyes big and bright, with a question in them. Her mouth opens, but she shuts it like she can't say what's on her mind or ask any more questions.

However, I have one for her. "Why did you record them? The races?"

She shrugs, glancing at the television. "I missed you." Slowly, she glances back at me. "I just wanted to be a small part of your world."

"Baby," I sigh again. "I missed you, too. So, so much. You're the best part of my life. The only part that truly matters. You *and* Mirabelle. And I'm so grateful you've let me be a part of your lives."

More grateful than she'll ever know. She's given me a second chance. One I don't want to fuck up.

"I want to be a part of your world, Trin. Yours and Mirabelle's. And I want you to be a part of mine."

Her gaze latches onto mine.

"Forever," I whisper.

She fists my shirt and pulls me closer, bringing her mouth to mine in a sweeping kiss. One that's instantly open-mouthed and all tongue and taking the breath from me before she pulls back.

"You know what else, Dart Rivers?"

I arch a brow, knowing she's about to enlighten me.

"You're too sexy for my own good."

"I'm too sexy for you?" I tease, leaning back and letting my gaze roam down that flirty little country dress with a string just above her breasts and her knees below the hem.

Have kneecaps ever been sexier?

Plus, my ball cap on her head. I tug the hat off her head and flip it backward on mine. "I think you got that wrong, Forever." I run my hands up her sides, setting my thumbs beneath her breasts. "You're the sexy one."

"Then why haven't you had sex with me again?"

I'm so stunned, I stand taller, hands frozen on her ribs, tucked under her breasts. "What?"

"We had sex weeks ago, but we haven't done anything else since then."

"I was giving you space. And time. And—"

"No more space," Trinity jabs my chest. "No more time."

"Trin?" I swallow thickly, but that finger at my chest becomes a sharp weapon, pressing me back with strength I wouldn't expect from her.

Or maybe I'm just under her spell as she walks me backward until my ass hits the top of the couch.

She slides her finger down my ribs, over my abs, and hooks it in my waistband.

"Damn sweatpants," she mutters, then glances up at me. "Is that for me?"

We both glance down at what's obviously long and hard beneath the dark cotton of my pants.

"Always for you, Forever. Only for you."

With her eyes back on me, she asks, "May I?"

"Please," I choke out. Please, please, *please*.

Her hand rests over my hardness, my cock stiffer than it's ever been. With a firm squeeze from her, I close my eyes. She moans. I don't make a sound.

I'm revved up but silent. Afraid to break this spell she has me under.

With one long drag up my length and a pinch at the tip, I choke. "Forever."

She tucks her fingers around the waistband, and I grip the edge of the couch as she slips her hand inside my sweats.

"No underwear?" Her voice is all syrup sweet, but I can't answer thanks to her confidently wrapping her hand around me, squeezing just the way I like it from her.

"Trin." I swallow hard before she's tugging my pants down. Just enough to set me free. The waistband of my sweatpants stretches across my thighs, just below my balls.

She cups me there next, kneading me, tightening her hold.

"Trinity." My voice rises. Blood rushes through my veins. One of my legs starts to quiver.

When she lowers to her knees in front of me, I see stars before she's even done anything. Just her hand around my shaft, her mouth nearing the tip.

She gives me a soft kiss, and I nearly come out of my skin.

"Baby," I whisper-choke, petting over her head once, then setting my hand back on the couch, letting her take control. Letting her lead this dance.

She runs her tongue up the hard length, and my hips buck forward. I might explode before she ever takes me in her mouth.

"So good," I whisper. No one has ever compared to her.

With one hand on my upper thigh, her other at my base, she opens wide and takes me into her warm, wet mouth.

My eyes close, the sensation too great, but I don't want to miss a second, so I look down at her.

"So pretty," I quietly say again. Her lips spread around me, taking me into her.

She smiles at the praise.

"You like that. Being told you're so good."

Her grin grows, and she glances up at me.

Damn. My wife is stunning.

She pulls her gaze from me and focuses, clamping her lips around me again and dragging me to the back of her throat.

"Trinity," I groan, eyes closing once more. The right suction. The right pressure. Her hand. Her mouth. She's fucking perfect.

She draws back, twirling her tongue around the tip before locking those lips around me again and dragging me deeper. She works me like only she can. Only she knows my body this well.

"Trin." I set a hand on the back of her head, then dig my

fingers into her short hair. Her name is a warning. I'm not going to last long.

How did I ever go so long without her? And not only because of this moment, but because of everything she is.

She is the compassionate, giving one. Tough as nails. And an amazing mother with a huge heart. All of which makes her sexy as fuck.

"Trinity." My voice rises, the warning louder.

She doubles down, sucking harder, taking me deeper. Saliva drips from the corner of her mouth. My hips buck forward again. I hold onto her head, trying to steady myself.

Suddenly, she slaps my ass, claps her hand on one tight cheek, and tugs me forward.

Stars float before my eyes like a freakin' firework display. Bright explosions and whistling sounds follow. I might even blackout for thirty seconds, and eventually I sag back against the couch, feeling that initial tremor in my leg turn to shaky knees.

"Baby." I cup her chin, and she gently pulls off of me, looking up as she wipes a corner of her lips.

"Fuck, Trin." All the reverence I can muster pours out of me. She might be on her knees in front of me, but I'm the one with weak ones. I'm the one in awe.

I release her chin and hold out my hand, helping her stand.

Then, I gently cup her throat and kiss her, humming against her lips.

"You're so good to me," I murmur. Because she always has been.

Slowly, seductively, she smiles. "Now let's see how good you are to me."

30

[Trinity]

L*et's see how good you are to me.*

Who says that? Apparently, I do, after feeling brazen and bold for bringing my husband to a rocking orgasm.

I step back but gently grip his shirt in my fist. I'm going to stretch this thing out with all the clinging I've done to it. Somehow, I don't think Dart minds.

With his eyes blown wide and a cheeky smirk on his lips, he tugs up his pants and follows me as I step backward toward the dining room table. Just before I hit the edge, Dart catches my hips and lifts me onto one corner.

"Want me to be a good boy?" he asks, his voice as seductive as the gleam in his eyes.

"The best boy," I tease until his mouth captures mine. Kissing me like only he does. His tongue sweeps over mine. His lips take command.

He moves to my jaw and my chin. "Did you behave yourself tonight?" he teases.

"I'm always a good girl," I sigh, jerking my head to the side as he moves to my neck. I've never considered myself reckless or particularly wild. And while I might have embraced my individual sexuality, I considered that self-preservation more than being a rebel of any sort.

"So good," Dart hums before he nips the juncture of my neck and shoulder. A sweet spot Dart knows well. His teeth scrape over my flesh. The pressure just right, sending a crackle between my breasts to my lower belly, like an invisible lightning bolt right to my core.

I spread my knees, allowing him more space between them. He tugs me by my backside to meet where he's becoming hard again.

Always for me, he said. Only for me.

That's how I feel about him. Only he can create this rush inside me. This desperate need to be close to him.

He moves his lips down my chest, dragging his tongue along the edge of my dress. The top scrunches, pulled together by a string. He tugs at it, allowing the bodice to open. And while he squeezes me over my dress, causing me to cry out on the pinch of my already hard nipple, he's a man on a mission, lowering for the hem.

"You like that," he teases, knowing I did. He's always been this cross between rough yet tender.

He shoves my dress to my lap.

"You have sexy kneecaps," he says, stroking his hands over my thighs and staring at the bend in my legs. "Might want to fuck you with those boots on one day."

"Promises, promises," I tease until he lifts his head and kisses me again, hard and fast, like he's imprinting that promise on my lips.

Like we have one day, someday, on the calendar ahead of us.

He lowers to one knee, spreading my thighs wider, and bringing me to the edge of the table. He just stares at my center.

"Never thought . . ."

I cover his lips with my fingers. "I don't want nevers. I want now."

"Yes, ma'am," he teases, eyes simmering with lust, as he glances back between my legs. He drags the back of his hand up my thigh and then swipes a finger down the damp strip between them.

"Looks like you made a little mess in this pretty underwear."

I'm wet, soaking the material, and giving him a show.

Reaching for my hips, he tugs at my panties, and I lift, allowing him to drag them off of me.

With my hands on the table, I spread my thighs just a little bit wider, giving him an even better view.

"Stunning," he whispers, like those folds are the most beautiful work of art he's ever seen.

He kisses one knee and squeezes the other, working his way up my leg. Then he inhales.

"Heaven." He blows over where I'm soaked and ready.

"Dart," I whisper, needing him. Needing this. It's been so long since his lips have touched me there.

"I know, baby," he says, like he's just as hungry to taste me as I am to be tasted.

Then his mouth is there. His tongue, thick and flat, licks up my seam. I cry out at the suddenness, even though I've been anticipating it, wanting it.

"It's been so long," I whimper, flashing back to when things were only functional between us. Quickly, I pull my thoughts from that time.

"Too long," he hums against me, wiggling that tongue against my clit before sucking me, kissing me.

I reach for his head, slipping my fingers into his hair, tugging a little at the wavy strands.

The movement only spurs him on, licking and lapping, treating me like I'm precious.

I lift my booted heel to the edge of the table. The position opens me even wider for him, allowing his tongue to go even deeper.

"Yes," he whispers against me, like he's the one on the edge of something monumental. He's on the brink of coming undone.

With my dress open at my breasts and the rest of it in my lap, plus my foot on the table, I'm a mess. And I'm a fucking goddess, crying out in my head, *Feast*.

As if Dart hears me, he doubles down, digging deeper with that tongue, adding his fingers into the fray. Two slip easily into me, stuffing me, filling me.

I drop to my elbows, my body quivering. The leg dangling off the table bouncing. He hooks that leg over his shoulder, allowing my booted foot to rest on his back. He cups my ass, lifting me like a treasured dish.

And then he does this thing with his fingers and his tongue simultaneously, and I crack.

I shatter into pieces all over this table, spilling against his lips.

"Dart," I cry out, then clamp a hand over my mouth, remembering that Mirabelle is sleeping upstairs.

He doesn't let up even though I'm spent. His tongue continues, making my body convulse with aftershocks until a new wave starts building again.

"Dart?" A question rings in his name. What's happening to me? It's been a long, long time since I've had a double orgasm. Even with him. Even with all he knows about my body and what he does to it.

He smiles against me, knowing what's happening before I do.

"One more," he mutters against those sensitive folds, before getting back on task and tipping me over the edge again.

I feel like a teacup about to be poured out, and I'll never think of that nursery rhyme the same way again. I'm tipping. I'm leaning. I'm spilling again, fighting a scream and allowing it to be a guttural moan to match the relief.

I fall to my back, completely spent. Chest rising. Heart nearly beating out of my chest. I fling my arms over my head, letting the table take my weight.

Dart kisses me one final time, then slowly stands, pressing more kisses into my thighs and just above my pelvic bone before tugging down my dress and holding out a hand to help me sit up.

"Was that good enough?" he teases.

"More than good enough."

He's enough. And he's so good.

31

[Trinity]

Dart has been in my bed since before Mom's Night Out. Since the night I told him I wanted him to watch Mirabelle while I return to work.

Tomorrow is my first day back after six weeks.

"Ah." I wake with a jolt, sitting bolt upright in the middle of the night. My heart races. My hands are clammy. I'm too warm. I feel like I'm on fire, but I'm not.

Dart was.

In the dream I'd been having, he crashed into a wall, the car instantly engulfed in flames. He couldn't get out. He wasn't getting out.

My breath comes in stuttering waves. Like I'm hyperventilating. Like I've inhaled too much smoke and can't breathe.

"Baby." Dart's hand runs up my back, but I flinch. He pulls back, holding his hand up in the air as he sits beside me.

"You're okay," he says. Not asking me if I am, but reassuring me.

I glance around the room. I'm in the house. I'm in my bed.

A crack of thunder rumbles. The sound feels like it hit the roof. Mirabelle lets out a cry, but I'm frozen. Paralyzed.

Dart scrambles to the end of the bed, soothing her with his hand on her belly. The bassinet gently rocks.

"I'm . . . I'm sorry," I say, my voice as shaky as my limbs. My hands tremble as I swipe them through my hair. "I didn't mean to wake you."

"What happened?" he asks quietly, Mirabelle settling for the moment.

Dart scoots back toward me. Our legs are trapped in a tangle of sheets.

"You were racing again." I pause, trying to catch my breath. Visions of the crash still linger in my head. The flames. Dart. "You were in an accident."

Just saying it sets my heart raging. "And you crashed. The car caught fire. And the flames . . ." I gasp for air, breathing heavily again.

"The flames," I choke, falling toward Dart, who catches me, tugging me to his side.

"I'm right here, baby. I'm safe." I wrap my arms around his middle, clinging to him.

"It was so scary," I admit. "I'm scared."

He pets my hair and strokes my back. "I got you. You have me."

But did I have him? For how much longer?

Dart falls to his back, taking me with him, and continues to hold me as I hold him.

Another groan of thunder. A crack of lightning. Mirabelle cries out again.

"Is it silly that I want her closer?" I whisper, wanting to gather everything I love near me.

Dart shakes his head. "I'll get her." He crawls toward the end of the bed again and lifts Mirabelle, settling her to his chest.

"Shh, baby girl. I got you. Dart is here."

Dart. Will she call him Dart? Or should she call him something else?

The thought is not for now. He brings Mirabelle to me, and I tuck her against my heart, lounging back on pillows he props against the headboard. I know all the reasons why you shouldn't place an infant in a bed, but I want to hold her, keep her close for a little while.

I want Dart close as well, and as if he read my thoughts, he scoots lower on the bed, but wraps his arms around my stomach, laying his head on my chest as well.

"We're all safe," he says, whispering to Mirabelle. "We're all here."

Everything I love is in this bed, I tell myself. Every*one* I love.

Because I love Dart. And I love Mirabelle.

And I don't ever want to lose either of them.

IN THE MORNING, I'm headed back to work after a handful of tears and extra kisses for Mirabelle.

The morning is a rush of reacclimating myself with the nurse's station, being assigned a pod—a section of three private incubators with newborn infants—and getting stopped by coworkers endlessly asking about Mirabelle.

Most people only know I'm adopting an infant. I don't share how she was born right in this unit to a young mother, or how Mirabelle came to me. The story needs to settle. It doesn't matter how Mirabelle came to me, only that she will be mine one day soon. Only a few more months.

When Mirabelle is older, perhaps I'll tell her about how she ended up on my back porch, maybe make a little fairy tale out of it.

The beautiful stork who delivered her.

The innocent maiden, willing to give her to me.

The protective mama bear I became.

It's a work in progress.

And not even an hour into my shift, I get a text message from Dart.

When is your break?

I instantly burst into laughter, easing all the tension of the morning. The text reminds me of the first one he sent me, which I surmise is his intention. With a quick response, I tell him the time and get back to work, almost forgetting about the message when a new baby boy is brought to my pod.

As I stare down at him with tubes and tape stuck to him, my heart breaks even more than it used to for the innocent babies I've cared for in the past. I picture Mirabelle. Wires and medical tape all over her little body. Under LED blue lights, to break down bilirubin. A 'bili' blanket beneath her. Halogen spotlights. Her little eyes taped shut for protection.

My stomach pitches a little bit imagining her so tiny. So fragile. And yet a fighter. A survivor.

When I get buzzed that someone is waiting for me outside the NICU doors, I don't even second-guess who it could be. I exit the unit to find Dart standing there with Mirabelle sleeping in her car seat.

"What are you doing here?" I laugh, relief in the sound at the sight of them. "Is everything okay?" I glance at Mirabelle again, my thoughts from only moments ago still lingering in my head.

Then I glance at Dart. He looks good in his jeans and a tee with a car logo on the front.

I try not to think about the dream I had last night.

"We're all good. I just thought I'd bring you lunch." He holds up a brown paper sack.

I typically just grab something from the cafeteria, and I

hadn't even thought about a noontime meal this morning when I left, too emotional about leaving them.

"I forgot all about lunch." I twist my arm, glancing at my watch, noticing he's right on time for my break.

"Well, let's share this one." He nods toward the sack.

"You okay?" I ask, squatting down to adjust Mirabelle's head, hoping not to wake her, but still wanting to touch her soft skin. A subtle reminder that she's my little fighter.

"I think Mirabelle misses you." He scratches the back of his neck.

I stand and smile. "Rough morning?"

He shakes his head. "Not at all. She's an angel."

I continue to stare at him, wondering what he's doing here. I mean, I'm excited to see him, but he looks a little . . . vulnerable.

"Okay, I might have missed you, too." He sheepishly glances at me and slips his hands into his jeans pockets.

I tuck my arm into his, leaning against him. "I miss you guys, too."

"You kind of scared me last night."

I raise my brows, as if I don't know what he means.

"That dream," he says, untwining my arm from his so he can wrap his arm around me and pull me into his side, pressing a kiss to my temple. "You were really scared."

I was scared. Afraid of what it might mean. Was it a premonition? Or was it just stress about returning to work? Did it reveal deep fears that I try not to consider but still linger inside me?

I didn't know.

"I'm sorry about that." Like I can control what my mind does during the night. I pull back so I can look him in the eyes.

"Just want to reassure you that I'm still here." His whiskey eyes are dark when he's serious, concerned about something.

"I know, baby," I say, cupping his cheek.

"Guess we should go eat. I know you only have thirty minutes."

The not-so-glamorous life of a nurse. Lunch on the fly.

He glances down at Mirabelle. "I can't take you out to my truck and make out with you, can I?"

I laugh, reminded again of our second kiss. The one where he made an excuse to see me.

"Probably not a good idea." I pat his chest. "But you can still kiss me."

I lean forward, and he cups the side of my jaw. The kiss is short but sweet.

As sweet as the daisy I find in the sack when we get to the cafeteria to share my lunch.

32

[Trinity]

That night, I'm exhausted from my first day back, but unable to unwind. I take my time giving Mirabelle a bath and tackling the nightly feeding, absorbing more of her love. The day was long but passed quickly enough. I held Mirabelle a little tighter that night, full of gratitude for her arrival and good health. She is such a blessing.

As much as I want to keep Mirabelle in the bassinet near my bed, I set her down in the crib. She'll be three months old this week, and it's time to move her on to the bigger space. Not to mention, her little coos and coughs and squirms easily wake me. Or maybe I wake her, like I did last night. She's ready for her own space.

As I enter my bedroom—our bedroom again—Dart is coming out of the ensuite bathroom. His hair is damp, his chest bare. He wears only black boxer briefs. As he's aged, Dart only grows more handsome. The scruff on his jaw. The powdery effect of gray here and there in his hair.

He gives me a smirk, catching me in the act of ogling him.

"I know you like to read before bed," he begins. "Maybe we should read that book." He eyes the top one on my nightstand.

The one my mom recommended.

Dart stretches across the bed, giving me another sexy view of his toned side and the length of his biceps.

When have I ever been attracted to a man's obliques? And yet, here I stand, transfixed by Dart's muscular physique.

When he pushes into a seated position, propped on pillows against the headboard, he holds up the book and pats the bed beside him. "Bedtime story."

I snort and shake my head. He's so ridiculous sometimes.

Earlier, almost immediately after returning home, I took a shower to wash off the hospital stench and germs, and I'm wearing soft shorts and a tank top without a bra. I've caught Dart checking me out throughout the night, chewing his lower lip a time or two.

He's just as attracted to me.

We haven't done anything sexy since the other night.

We don't need to have sex once a day, the way we did in our twenties, but I also don't want sex to fall into a routine like it had become before he left.

Brush teeth. Have sex. Read a book.

I want spontaneity, and Dart wanting to read a romance my mom recommended feels a bit spontaneous.

Crawling up the bed, I drop to my side, propping up my head on my hand.

To my surprise, Dart flips immediately to a passage, like he's already been reading this book. However, it didn't appear to be bookmarked. It's like he knew exactly where to turn.

He begins to read.

"Dennis," she cried out as her husband teased her entrance, dragging his seeping tip through her wet folds. Her nails dug into his firm ass, suggesting she wanted more from him.

Dart does a very bad impression of the woman.

"Not until you admit it," he demanded, continuing to tease her with the bulge of his head, toying with her clit. "Give me the words, and I'll give you my cock."

Dart glances at me like the word is so scandalous.

"Dennis," she ground out, teeth clacking while desire rushed up her midsection.

He moves his hand down his bare belly as if acting out that rush.

"Say it, and I'm all yours again."

He arches a brow, glancing at me like he's on the edge of suspense about what the woman must say in order to earn Dennis's dick.

"I love you," she blurts." Dart gasps in false shock. "*Despite how much she hated him, she still loved him.*"

"*Finally*," he continues, now in the role of Dennis. *Then Dennis surged forward, filling her channel with his firm length.*

Dart glances back at me, snapping the book shut around his finger.

"Wow, that Dennis is a ballbuster. Holding out until she says I love you before he fucks her." He blows out a breath, like he's just read the most profound literature. He tosses the book to the side and shifts to mirror my position. Elbow on top of the pillow. Head propped against his hand.

"Is that the kind of romantic hero you want?" he asks. "Where the husband is one big tease." He runs his fingertip down my nose and around my mouth, then under my chin. He continues his trail along the side of my neck, and I tip my head, lowering my arm to rest my head on the edge of the pillows.

"Was he teasing? He sounded kind of serious," I mock of his reading.

Dart lowers to the pillows as well, running his fingertip along my shoulder, brushing aside the thin strap of my tank top.

"All the guys in those books have big cocks and hard lines in the sand, don't they?"

I shrug. "You watched *Bridgerton*."

He hums, remembering, and I close my eyes as his finger continues to trail down my arm. When he gets to my hand, he takes my fingers, tugging gently at each one of them, massaging them in a sense. He flips my hand, digging his thumb into my palm before bringing my hand to his mouth.

"Let me be your romantic hero again."

A soft laugh rumbles from me. "How?"

He turns my arm and peppers my inner wrist with kisses, moving up to the crease of my elbow. Then he moves to the outside of my arm, working up to my shoulder before nipping me softly in that sweet spot he knows sends wicked tingles through my body.

"For one, I won't hold out on you," he says.

I laugh a little harder, my eyes closing again. He pinches my chin, and my eyes flare wide.

"I'll give you anything you want."

We've already made those kinds of promises to one another, knowing they can't always be upheld.

"The only thing I want is you," I whisper. I want him to stay, but it's still something I can't ask and don't want to assume will happen.

He hums again and moves to my chest, stamping kisses on my skin as he moves toward my breasts.

I fall to my back, scooting lower on the pillows.

Dart pauses over my heart, holding his lips there, as if speaking directly to the engine in my body.

"I'll love you like no other," he whispers. "I've never not loved you, Trinity."

I gasp at his words and cup the back of his head, tugging at his hair, but Dart charges up my body and captures my lips, preventing me from responding. As if he's afraid I can't say the words back to him.

But the truth is, I've always loved him. Never stopped.

I hated him while I still loved him, like that poor wife in the romance novel.

And I want him.

Thankfully, the kiss distracts us both, and his hand moves up my middle, lifting the hem of my tank. He glides higher, toward my breast, slipping his hand beneath the material to massage the heavy swell. Then plucks at my nipple.

He shifts and removes my shirt, then falls back into position beside me, running his fingers around one breast and over my nipple before skating around the other breast to the tip of my sharp nub. Quietly, he strokes around and over and back, until I realize he's making an infinity symbol on my chest. The entire time he watches his fingers move, and I melt beneath the gesture.

He's marking me as his. Forever.

He leans forward, cupping one breast and bringing his mouth to it. His tongue twirls around my hard peak before he opens wide, taking more of me. My belly flutters. My eyelids shut again.

The homage is slow, calculated, like he's taking his time to sculpt me, memorize me.

I haven't really changed in three years, and yet I feel completely different.

More confident. Much bolder. Demanding even. Deserving of this attention.

He takes his time, like we have all night, and I allow him to play my body like only he can.

Running my hands through his hair, I massage his scalp, reminded again of that fictional couple.

I'd been hurt. The break painful. But I meant what I said to him a few weeks ago. I have no regrets about our relationship.

Our marriage. My only regret is that we let ourselves drift apart. We got lost in what we lost.

And I'm grateful we've found our way back to one another.

As Dart moves lower and lower, he hooks his fingers into my shorts and tugs them down, taking his time to undress me until I'm bare on the bed. We haven't been in this position yet.

Where we face one another.

Where we're missionary again.

Where I feel so raw and exposed to him.

I whimper, uncertain where the noise comes from as he tickles his fingers up my ankle to my knee.

"I know, baby," he says, as if he understands somehow. The need for him. The vulnerability I feel in this position.

"Let me love you," he says.

Once upon a time, I crassly joked that we were only hooking up. Only fucking.

Dart argued then that he was never fucking me, he was loving me.

He spreads my legs and takes me with his mouth like he did the other night, only slower. Torturous teasing. Frisky flirting. He's meticulous, purposeful, like he's painting me. Stroke by stroke, he's memorizing the spaces, the folds, the flavor. Like that poster that hangs in the entryway. Petal folds of black, blue, and yellow outlined in gray. Where the lavender shades are distinct, and the pink fold stands out the most.

Dart slices his tongue into me, and I whimper at the softness of his licks. The depth of his strokes. I spread my legs wider, allowing him to go deeper. He hooks his hands around my thighs and holds me open to him.

When I finally break, shattering like splatters of paint in vibrant colors, he pulls back and removes his boxer briefs, revealing how hard he is. How eagerly he wants me. How desperate he is to bring us together.

"All I need you to say right now is yes." His voice is rough, raspy and low, as he holds his base and drags his tip through already wet folds. He catches on my clit, toying with me there.

"Yes," I whisper.

Yes to this.

Yes to him.

Yes to us. Again.

Dart easily slides into me, releasing a deep moan of relief as we come together.

Slowly. Sweetly. Us.

When I'm full to the hilt, he pauses over me, staring down at me.

"I'm always going to love you," he says, before lowering and taking my mouth, cutting off my response once again. Or saving himself from a lack of one on my part.

We don't need to talk. Our bodies read the message.

He loves me. And I love him.

He lowers to his forearms, kissing me tenderly while he pulls back, dragging his heavy length to my entrance. Teasing me with release, before rushing inward again.

Like he shifts forward to pass in a race, then slips back, letting me lead.

Accelerate, then brake.

The tension is unnerving.

Eventually, we set a new rhythm. One familiar yet different than anything we've experienced before. Both of us are falling in line with a well-practiced dance that we haven't done in years. A dance with new steps.

The rush of his hips. The response of my own.

His hands are in my hair, and I cling to his shoulder blades.

He slips lower to cup my shoulders, and I slide my hands to his firm backside.

His forehead rests against mine, and I close my eyes, breathing in this moment. *Feeling* how much he loves me.

Sensing him holding back from saying the words. And yet, I don't feel lacking.

He's loving me as best he can.

I cannot ask for more.

"Trin," he grunts, straining at the pace.

I languish in the moment, feeling incredible and relaxed, lulled by our movements. I've already orgasmed, and I want this moment for him. I want to feel what I do to him, deep inside me.

"Yes." *Take what you need*. What you want.

I cling tighter as he moves faster.

He grabs one hip, glancing briefly between us.

"A perfect fit," he mutters, hammering quicker. "Always so perfect."

He's a liar. We weren't perfect. We were human. But he's correct on one matter.

We have always fit together.

"So perfect," I whisper

His head whips upright, his eyes the brightest I've ever seen them. Sunshine in the night. Full of hope and love . . . for me.

He moves even faster, digging his fingertips into my hip as he leads me to match his pace. I hook my leg over his hip, heel against his lower back, opening myself up for him.

"Trin." He grunts when I grab his backside again, tugging him deeper.

He skyrockets from sweet to desperate, and then he grunts, "Forever." He stills all but one part of him, which thunders inside me, filling me up like he used to do.

Dart falls over me, smothering me a second before spinning to his side, taking me with him.

"Holy shit, Trin." He breathes heavily. "I'm seeing stars."

I giggle at the break in tension. The tenderness that grew too intimate. I kiss his shoulder, and he grabs my hand, bringing it to his chest, where his heart races.

Then he moves my hand to his mouth, stamping a kiss into my palm, lingering there.

He has something to say, but he holds back, tucking the words away.

I love you, I whisper in my head, knowing I'm not ready to share them yet either. I've always loved him and always will.

He's been my romantic hero in so many ways.

Maybe he truly can be one again.

33

[Dart]

The first week Trin is back at work goes relatively smoothly. She's on three days and then off until a new week begins. Her shifts are long but manageable for both of us. It gives me time with Mirabelle and provides Trin the break she needs to follow the career she loves.

I'm still floundering with what I want to do next for me, and I'm reconsidering the job offer from Clint. As a single dad, he's understanding about childcare, and he suggested I could work part-time to start.

Since Trinity isn't pressuring me and we're only in *her* first week back to work, I'm in no rush to make decisions. I've got about six months before I really need to worry about finances. For now, time is about finding my purpose, and my purpose is Mirabelle.

Every day is something new. A new skill. A new expression. A new experience. And I'm just soaking it all up. When you've wanted something for as long as Trin and I have, you catalog every moment, making a mental note of even the smallest stuff.

I'm grateful again for the time Trin has given me. Grateful for Mirabelle, too.

As much as I don't like spending time away from my girls, Trinity reminds me I deserve time to myself. A break with adults and my friends. So, her first week ends with me heading out to the ball field.

We have a decent team for the thirty-five-plus crowd. The games are supposed to be more about fun than competition, but Marshall and Tate can't seem to hold back their competitive nature.

Tate just caught a pop-fly, making it the third out for the other team, and we slowly make our way back to our bench, when I spy Trinity approaching with Mirabelle in the stroller.

"Hey!" I blurt, rushing over to them. I clock Mirabelle first, her little brown eyes wide from the bouncy ride over the grass terrain in her stroller. "This is a pleasant surprise. Everything okay?"

Trinity chuckles. "Nothing's wrong. We just thought we'd come watch your game. Cheer you on."

"We did, did we?" I eye Mirabelle, as if a three-month-old has any say in the matter. Reaching for the light blanket over her legs, I jiggle her covered toes before I swipe my hand over her head. She's so stinkin' cute, wearing a pink jersey-like onesie.

Speaking of cute, Trinity is wearing my Velocity ball cap again with shorts and a fitted tee.

I lean toward her. "You know what it does to me to see you in my ball cap, right?"

A sweet shade of pink climbs up her neck before she sighs. "I don't want to intrude on your guys' time. I just wanted to get outdoors tonight."

She is never an intrusion.

"I'm glad you're here. Both of you." I glance at Mirabelle again.

"Let me hear your cheer, baby girl," I tease. Mirabelle smiles at me, and that's all the inspiration I need.

"Go One-Eyed Snakes." Trinity raises her fist, weakly chanting, before making a cringe face. "Really? That was the best name they could think of?"

"Want to guess who picked it?" I arch a brow.

"Tate." She grumbles, shimmying with disgust. "He's so immature."

I chuckle and wrap my arm around her, kissing her temple. "Thanks for coming to the game."

My girls are here to support me.

Trin and I are making a real effort at home, being present with each other. She has her book club, and I have baseball, but we enjoy being together. I never want us to be strangers in the same house again.

Sharing a bed every night, becoming reacquainted with one another, is a big help. Some nights we just talk; other nights are a sex fest before exhaustion takes over.

I'm loving it, and loving her, although I haven't told her how I feel. The timing still feels too soon. Trinity still has a fence around her. Not a brick wall but an iron gate where I can glimpse a future, but sense her still keeping me at arm's length. Like she doesn't mind reaching through the bars, but isn't ready to open the gate to let me in.

Doesn't matter tonight, though, as my girls are here for me.

I lead Trinity toward the edge of the ball field. The public park doesn't have a formal bleacher stand, just a collection of fans in camp chairs and blankets along the baselines. Trinity parks the stroller and stands while I need to return to the bench. I'm up soon.

"Hey, Forever. Check me out in these baseball pants." I wiggle my hips, emphasizing my ass in the new baseball pants I bought myself.

We've been reading more snippets from her romance

novels, and she especially liked an excerpt involving a silver fox coach in snug baseball pants.

Her laughter follows me as I grab my bat, feeling a few more eyes on me than just my wife's. My friends are staring, and not just because I'm up at bat. At the games, we don't chat much about our personal lives. That shit happens once we reach a bar afterward, but I keep most things to myself.

Tate still isn't talking to me. Hutch listens, though.

While I wait until I'm up, I take a couple practice swings. My concentration is a little whacked, knowing Trinity is watching me, but when I'm at bat, I connect with the ball, sending a line drive down the third base line, and I hustle to first.

Tate follows me in the batting order, and something in the set of his jaw shows he's determined to smack the shit out of the ball. He doesn't disappoint, sending it sailing right into the glove of an outfielder.

With Marshall up next, I lead off first base until his hit allows me to steal second. I might be showing off a bit when I run like I'm being chased and slide into the base.

"Out," the umpire calls, swinging her arm in a sharp, chopping motion.

"What?" I snap at the same time Tate booms, "Bullshit."

Tate's been wound tight tonight, and something says he's suddenly spun even tighter. He's storming the field, approaching the volunteer umpire with fists at his side. "That is BS."

I intercept him, setting my hand on his chest to hold him back. "It's fine." I can be as competitive as the next guy, but I remind myself that this is a public league, not professional-level baseball.

He swings his head in my direction. "It's not fine. You were safe as the nose on my face." He turns toward the umpire and waves in front of his face. "Safe."

"Out." The ump glares back at him.

"Do you even know the rules of baseball?" he mocks the slim blonde staring back at him. With her hair in a ponytail and the baseball cap shielding her eyes, I hadn't recognized her as the same woman who occasionally waitresses at The Ferryman's Rest.

"I know enough that if I feel harassed, I can kick your ass out of this game."

A couple *oohs* and laughter come from both benches. Tate turns the deepest shade of red I've ever seen.

"You watch yourself, Gallagher."

"You watch yourself, Haven," she snaps back, fisting her hands at her sides.

Wait. *What?* Is this girl related to Pete Gallagher? Tate's college friend?

I don't have time to connect all the dots as I shove Tate. "Step back."

Tate continues to glare at her, nostrils flaring. Like he can't decide if he should charge her or kiss her.

Somehow, I think kissing tops the list. Although, he also looks like that might be the last thing he wants to happen.

With my hand on his shoulder again, he finally turns toward our bench, shrugging me off.

"Sorry about that, blue," I address her as the umpire.

Her shoulders sag. "I'm good. And you're still out."

I salute her and jog after Tate, his shoulders high and tight, steam practically coming off him.

"What was that?" Trinity teases when I near her.

"Who is that?" I ask. "He called her Gallagher."

Trinity narrows her eyes. "Is that Prudence Gallagher? Pete's sister?" She laughs. "Oh boy. They kind of hate each other."

She nods toward Tate, who has thrown himself onto the bench, leaning forward with his hands clasped together and his attention arrowed at the umpire near second base.

"Uhm, I'm not convinced hate is the right term. I can feel the sexual tension from here," I admit, chuckling at Tate's expense.

Trinity laughs as well, and it reminds me of how we used to be. Observing people, making up stories about them.

However, Trin and I are being watched in return. An approving grin from Hutch. A smirk from Marshall. Dancing brows from Petty.

They can write whatever story they want in their heads. I know the truth.

I'm in love with my wife.

The game goes on, and the evening sunlight fades.

"Need to get Mirabelle home soon?" I ask, as we near the ninth inning, behind by two runs.

"Probably." Trinity sighs. She's been holding Mirabelle in a way she faces outward, as if she's watching the game. "But we'll stay until the end."

On my last at bat, I knock the snot out of the ball, sending a guy on second and third home, plus myself. Not a grand slam because bases weren't loaded, but I still ride the high of winning the game for our team.

Our meager crowd goes crazy while the One-Eyed Snakes bench explodes with excitement. Just your average middle-aged guys pumped over a park district ballgame.

With high fives along the third base line before I tag home plate, it signals the end of the game, and I head toward Trinity.

Grabbing Mirabelle's foot, I wiggle it. "What do you think, Mirabelle? Did I do good?" I laugh. "Did you see Darty hit the ball?"

Trinity had been doing the mom-bounce, jiggling up and down to keep Mirabelle content, but she stops cold at my question.

"Daddy," she whispers.

I stand tall. "Darty," I correct. I wouldn't dare to dream of being Mirabelle's dad, although that's what I hope to be when Trinity and I stay together. *When*, not if. Because as Trinity's husband, I want the role as dad to Mirabelle.

I want the three of us as a family.

"Daddy?" Hutch claps me on the back, and I angle toward him.

"I said *Darty*."

"Like Farty." Petty chuckles behind Hutch.

Marshall wrinkles his nose. "He kind of smells like one."

"Okay, guys. What are we? Five?" I sass.

"Six, at least," Petty counters.

"And way to embarrass me in front of my girls."

The entire circle goes quiet.

Trinity clears her throat. "On that note, I should get this little one home."

She lifts Mirabelle and kisses her cheek. "Great game, Snakes."

"That's One-Eyed Snakes, darlin'," Petty says.

I smack him in the stomach with the back of my hand. He chuckles harder.

"You should come out with us, Trin," Hutch offers.

I stall, glancing from him to her. I should have asked her first.

With her eyes on me, she slowly shakes her head. "Nah. We've intruded enough on your night."

I step closer to her. "It was no intrusion." I liked them being here. Knowing they were watching me, rooting for me, even if it was only an old guys' baseball team.

I cup the side of her neck and run my thumb up the front of her throat. Fuck, she's so pretty.

She shrugs. "It's time for bed for Mirabelle, anyway."

Going to sound selfish, but when Mirabelle sleeps, it might be a favorite part of my day because I have Trinity all to myself. And I should be heading home to take advantage of that time.

"I'll come home, too."

"What?" Tate snaps somewhere behind us. "No. Stay out with the guys."

All heads turn in his direction, surprise smacking me the hardest. This is new, and I'm almost suspicious of his intentions.

Trinity arches a brow in shock as well.

"Hey, sis." He acknowledged his sister earlier, wiggling his fingers at his new niece. Tate isn't a fan of little kids. He's used to dealing with teenagers at the high school level.

"Hey," she addresses him in return, narrowing her eyes at his sudden pleasantness toward me before she turns to face me. "Go. Have fun with your boys."

She pats my chest, but before she pulls away her hand, I capture it and tug her toward me. Letting her feel how my pulse beats for her. Even with Mirabelle between us, I lay a kiss on Trin. One with tongue and heart and heat. Promises of what will come later.

Throats clear near us. Someone chuckles.

"That's still my sister," Tate grumbles.

I don't fucking care. Let them watch me love my wife.

When Trinity pulls back, her eyes are stunned, twinkling in the low light. I should go home with her, but I also don't want to turn down this olive branch from Tate.

Trinity slowly shakes her head, like she's erasing some thought, and settles Mirabelle in the stroller.

"Let me help you." I set my hand on the handle, but Trinity gently brushes it aside, wedging herself between me and the stroller. Her back hits my front, and I groan.

"I got it. You enjoy your night." She glances at me over her shoulder and winks. The teasing look sets its hooks. "Behave."

With my hand over my heart, I pledge I wouldn't dare dream of stepping out of line.

"As long as I can misbehave with you later," I tease, leaning in so only she can hear me.

She chuckles and shakes her head again, before walking away, giving that ass an extra wiggle as I watch her retreat.

When I turn back toward the guys, I feel ten feet tall, and they stare at me like my head is actually in the clouds. I'm grinning like a loon.

"Man, you've always had it so bad for her," Hutch says, smiling almost as big as me.

"What love songs are written about," Petty adds, grasping my shoulder and jostling me.

"Did you really call yourself Daddy?" Marshall questions, tilting his head in disbelief. Or maybe it's disgust. He's a sworn bachelor after having raised his sister.

"Daddy?" Tate chokes. "Fuck no." Still, he stares at me, reality slowly registering. If I'm married to his sister, and she adopts Mirabelle, then I could be Mirabelle's dad.

"Aw, fuck." Tate whistles.

I'll gladly take on any role Trinity allows me, but I correct all of them. "Darty. I said Darty."

"Still sounds like Farty." Petty laughs.

"It almost sounds like Daddy, though," Marshall adds, watching me.

It sure does.

"First round is on Daddy," Petty says, still holding onto my shoulder.

Yeah, *Daddy's* got the first round.

He won the game, and his girls saw it.

As we collect our gear, I end up near Tate. "Hey, man, thanks for the invitation to join you guys for beers."

Tate lifts his head, his tone tight. "You always join us for beers."

"Yeah, but the invitation came from you."

He hitches his bat bag over his shoulder. "Look, don't make

it weird. You're part of the team. The team goes out for beers afterward."

I have more to say, but I bite back the words. Instead, I change topics as we start walking away from the bench. "You went a little hard on the ump tonight."

Tate got into it with Prudence a second time. Marshall intercepted Tate that round. I was kind of in awe at how she stood her ground with him. The way he came in a little too hot the second time. He'd never harm a woman, but he can be a hothead. I've seen him break hearts.

"She doesn't know baseball. She's into band," he scoffs.

"Got something against band kids," Petty adds from in front of us.

"Of course not, it's just—"

"It's just what?" Petty stops short, lowering the bat he had lazily lifted against his shoulder, like he's ready to defend the honor of musicians at any level.

"Nothing," Tate counters, continuing to walk toward the parking lot.

"Didn't look like nothing to me," Petty comments, situating the bat at his shoulder again.

"Just drop it," Tate grumbles over his shoulder, walking a little faster.

Petty glances at me, but I shrug, not having a clue what's going on. He wiggles his brows, mischievousness lighting his eyes.

"Into band, huh? Think I'll ask her out then."

Tate drops his bag and rounds on Petty. "The fuck you will."

"The *fuck* does it matter to you?" Petty stands toe to toe with Tate.

"She's just . . . Pete's little sister." Tate's nostrils flare.

"So?" Petty doesn't back down, smiling wider, teasing Tate, pushing him to the brink.

"Oh, right. I forgot." Tate scoffs. "You're into younger

sisters." He sneers in my direction next. "It must be a trait of those who leave."

What the fuck?

Petty and I stare at Tate as he quickly turns, aggressively hoists his bat bag from the ground, and stalks toward his truck.

I glance back at Petty, wondering what the hell Tate meant about sisters and leaving, but also realizing that the olive branch I thought Tate offered me was still fragile.

And suddenly snapped in half.

34

[Trinity]

Summer moves on, and every day brings us one day closer to Mirabelle's adoption.

Dart and I fall into a routine. I work. He watches Mirabelle.

One day in August, ten days out from Mirabelle's adoption date, I'm at work and get a call from the waiting room desk clerk that I have a visitor. Typically, I have a hint from Dart when he's about to visit. A silly text with sexual innuendos about meeting in his truck for meal breaks, me being his meal, which *doesn't* happen with Mirabelle present.

I'm surprised to find a young woman seated in the waiting room outside the unit instead.

Strawberry blonde hair. Blue eyes. College age.

"Hello," I hesitate as she doesn't look familiar to me.

"Trinity." My name seems like a relief to her. Slowly, she stands holding out a hand like she's about to interview for a job. I am no longer in the director of nursing role, nor do I have hiring power. Still, I shake her hand.

She smiles cautiously. "You don't remember me, do you?"

"I'm sorry. Should I?" I question, the fine hairs on my arms rising.

"I'm Marissa Olsen. Mirabelle's mom." She swallows thickly. "Well, the woman who had Mirabelle." The clarification sounds almost as painfully said as her first statement. *Mirabelle's mom.* A label on her that feels like someone punched me in the gut.

Sweat trickles down my back, but I'm suddenly cold to the bone.

"Would you like to take a seat?" I point toward the row of green waiting room chairs. I'm not certain we're allowed to speak to one another, but she looks so young, so fragile.

Marissa shakes her head. "I won't take much of your time. I just . . . I wanted to know how she is."

Her concern drops like an anvil on the eggshell of my heart.

A million questions fester fast and furious.

Is she going to contest the adoption? Does she want Mirabelle back?

My knees begin to tremble, and I desperately want to sit down, but if she isn't willing to take a seat, neither will I.

"She's . . . she's wonderful, and beautiful, and perfect in every way," I admit because I cannot hide the truth. She's an angel. One I suddenly, overwhelmingly fear might be taken from me. A fear that's been an undiagnosed nausea in my stomach for weeks.

With shaking fingers, I reach for my phone in my back pocket. "Would you like to see a picture of her?"

Slowly, Marissa shakes her head. "I don't think so."

My brows squeeze. She wants to check on Mirabelle, but doesn't want to see her?

Pain slashes the young woman's face. "I just want to know I made the right decision. Giving her to you."

I blink. Tears burn at the back of my eyes. "Yes. Yes, absolutely. I love her with everything I have." I clasp my hands and press them to my chest where my heart hammers and my breath saws at my lungs. That nauseous sensation grows more prevalent, and bile tickles the back of my throat.

She nods, as if agreeing love is a good thing.

"I didn't know you were married." She glances at my hand, where the rings are still absent from my finger.

How would she have known? Did it even matter? She left Mirabelle with me because of our distant relationship.

However, the courts prefer a couple adopt Mirabelle.

It's one reason why Dart and I are still married. Why I haven't demanded we refile for divorce. Which isn't exactly true, either. But that information isn't relevant to her.

The most important thing this young woman needs to know is that I am still legally married to Dart.

We hadn't discussed Dart's role after the adoption yet. But we're in bed like a couple every night and working as devoted partners raising Mirabelle every day.

Unless this girl changes her mind. It could happen. The courts will always rule in favor of biology.

"His name is Dart," I tell her. "He loves Mirabelle as much as I do." I have no doubt about Dart's feelings for Mirabelle. What I haven't considered yet is how he'll feel once Mirabelle is adopted. Once she's fully mine.

A tomorrow problem. Or rather, an issue in ten days.

Marissa licks her lips. "Good. That's good. I want her to have what I had."

I tilt my head.

"Loving parents." She blinks hard at the reminder that hers are gone. "A family."

"I'm sorry you're alone." The motherly nature in me has me itching to reach for her.

She shakes her head. "But I'm not, though." She smiles weakly. "I head back to school soon." She doesn't tell me where she attends, and I don't ask. While I'm well aware of open adoptions, our situation will not be like that. She's relinquishing all rights.

Which leads me to wonder, again, if she's changed her mind.

"What are you studying?" I ask, deciding the question is neutral.

"I want to be a lawyer. Like my mom." Her smile remains soggy. "I think I'll be good at it."

"Good." I struggle to find my own voice. "I'd bet she'd be really proud of you." Her daughter following in her footsteps.

Marissa glances toward the ground, blinking hard. "One day . . . if she ever asks about me . . . will you tell her I did it for her. I wasn't being selfish." She snaps her head up. "I wanted her to have the best."

Loving parents. A family.

"Of course," I whisper, my thoughts still a riot of emotion. Unable to stop myself, I rub my hand up and down her arm.

I don't consider Marissa's decision selfish. If anything, she's acting *selfless*. Giving up a baby must be incredibly difficult, for hard reasons and complicated circumstances, but it's also a blessing to another couple, another family.

"Anything else?" I hold my breath, still concerned she might change her mind, even though she stands here with her future planned.

She shakes her head, her lip curling timidly. "Just take care of her."

I nod, offering a shaky smile in return. "And you take care of you, okay?"

She nods once, holds her head higher, and offers a final, sad smile.

As she walks around me, I can't help but watch her retreat until she enters the elevator. Then, I reach for my phone again and call Dart.

I'm visibly shaking when he cheerfully answers. "Hey, baby."

"Dart." I choke on his name.

"What's wrong?" The joy in his tone instantly drops. "Are you okay?"

"Can you meet me in the parking lot?"

"Trin," he groans. "You're scaring me."

"I just . . . I need to see you." I need him to hold me and tell me it can't happen. I can't lose Mirabelle. *We* can't lose her.

"Fuck. What happened?" he repeats.

"I'm okay. I just . . ." I choke around a sob, uncertain if it's relief or fear or a combination. The nauseous sensation shifts to real concern that I might vomit. "I can explain everything when you get here. I just need you."

"I'm on my way." He grunts. "I'll text you when I get there."

THE NURSE MANAGER is understanding when I tell her I'm suddenly not feeling well. It's evident I'm shaken by something, and she lets me clock out early. I wait for Dart near the staff parking, pacing the sidewalk, until I eventually see his truck whip into the lot. Relief washes over me, although I still clutch at my belly. Hands trembling. Heart sprinting.

When Dart stops alongside me, he bursts out of his door before I can reach for the passenger door. Instantly, I'm in his embrace, my arms around his neck, holding him like I'll never let go.

"I'm here," he coos near my ear. "I've got you."

He doesn't even know what's happened, and yet, he's here.

"Get me out of here," I whimper.

Dart pulls back, scanning my face for a second, before tugging open the passenger door and helping me inside. I immediately swivel toward the backseat, panic momentarily seizing me.

"Where's Mirabelle?" I spin toward Dart.

"I took her to your mom's. You sounded . . . I don't know what you sounded like, but it scared the fuck out of me."

I take a deep inhale, absorbing the faint scent of comforting pine and asphalt.

Dart runs his hand down the side of my face. His eyes ping over me, concern filling them to the brim.

Once he shuts my door, he rounds the truck and re-enters it. He shifts to Drive and sets his hand on my thigh. Through the thinness of my scrubs, his warmth seeps into my skin. The bone-cold chill is a direct result of the rattle in my nerves.

I grip his wrist, holding onto him like I need the reassurance he's actually present. He's here beside me. He's here because I called him.

"Start talking, Forever." His tone is terse, full of worry.

"Marissa came to see me."

His head swivels in my direction, eyes questioning before he glances back at the road.

"Mirabelle's mom."

"*You're* Mirabelle's mom." Razor-sharp and clear, he squeezes my thigh to emphasize his words.

"Her biological one."

His mouth pops to argue, then snaps shut. "What did she want?"

"She wanted to check on Mirabelle." Or maybe she just wanted confirmation for herself. For her decision.

Was I overreacting? She didn't want to see a picture. Didn't want to know more about Mirabelle. Her height. Her weight. Her development. Her easy personality, already present at nearly five months.

I swipe my other hand over my forehead, noticing the continued tremor in my fingers. "I think . . . I think I just panicked. Like, what if she wants her back?" I turn my head toward Dart. My eyes cloud with the tears I've been holding back. Dart blurs in my vision. "What if she takes her from us?"

Suddenly, Dart is pulling off the road. The truck jostles and jolts over a rugged path before he pulls between a set of trees, shielding us from the road.

He cuts the engine, pushes his seat back, and reaches for me all in one smooth move. I'm in his lap before I can process how quickly he moved, clinging to him as hard as he is clutching at me.

"No one is taking her from us. No one." He sounds so certain and emphasizes every word with an extra squeeze. He pushes me back and cups my face, so I focus on him. Look him in those whiskey-colored eyes.

"Nothing is going to happen to her." The determination in his tone does little to ease me yet. "To you. To me. To us. I won't let anything happen to anyone."

He pulls me back to him, fusing me tightly to his chest, peppering the side of my head with soft kisses.

"Gonna always be here for you, Trin. We'll get through anything together."

As he kisses me, I kiss him in return. His ear. His neck. His jaw.

I need him closer. I need to feel the certainty radiating off him.

Together, we'll get through this.

How often had he said it before? How many times did we make it through difficult situations? Together.

While I'm still in my scrubs, Dart is wearing jeans and a white tee, plus one of his favorite ballcaps. Reaching for the hem of his shirt, I tug it free from his jeans.

"Whoa." He chuckles, rough and confused. "Trin?"

"I need you," I whisper, hasty and low. "I need to be closer."

With a hand on his belly, I absorb more of his heat before I cup the back of his head with my other hand and bring his mouth to mine, linking us in some way. Lips and tongue. Awkwardly, I shift until I'm straddling his lap. The thinness of my scrubs and the stiffness of his jeans are still too much of a barrier between us.

With every stroke of his hand over my head and down my back, touching me all over in an attempt to soothe me, the frenzy to be closer rises.

"Closer," I demand against his mouth, grinding against him, like I can break through the cotton and denim and bring him into me.

Dart's hands move to my hips, tugging on the waistband of my scrubs. I shift off him, banging my knee as I twist to sit beside him and remove my pants.

When I scramble back on top of him, he has shoved his jeans below his knees.

I don't need foreplay. I just need him inside me, and I balance on the tip before bringing him into me. Taking him deep until there's nothing more to give. He and I are one, and I cling to his neck, coiled around him, like it still isn't close enough.

"I've got you," he says again, running his hands up my back and down my arms. Over my hair and down my back again.

We don't move. We settle. Absorbing the warmth of each other, soaking in the nearness.

"Forever," he whispers, every ounce of his love for me in the word.

Something inside me ignites. Placing my hands on his shoulders, I peel myself from his chest and move, disappearing in the moment. Him inside my body. Inside a part of me that's deep and hollow without him.

He fills my soul. He is my heart.

"Can't lose her," I whimper, closing my eyes and setting my forehead on his. "Can't lose you."

Dart claps his hands on my backside and thrusts upward, bucking like a wild bull.

My eyes open at the rush of movement, and we lock gazes.

"Not going to lose anyone," he groans, lifting and lowering me, dragging me to the tip, and then dropping me to engulf him.

I'm so alive like this. With him. Only him.

And I can't go back to where I've been. Trudging through life, feeling empty without him. Empty without her.

"Dart," I grunt, riding him hard and fast in return, needing him to let go inside me.

He slips his hand between us, stroking his thumb in that place that triggers everything.

"I don't need it." I don't need to come. I just need to feel him.

"Not without you."

My head is a mess. I can't think. I can't process. I can't relax like I need to.

Suddenly, Dart presses the door beside him open. He swings us in the direction of the open space, but we break apart in the awkward attempt to move.

"No," I cry, slick between my thighs, sweat trickling down my back.

"Need to get at you better."

Within seconds, my spine is plastered against the sunshine-warm metal. My toes in the dirt beneath us.

Dart bends a little, grips himself, and lines up at my entrance, rushing into me again. He curls his hand around the edge of his truck bed and the other around my thigh, lifting my leg to his hip, opening me up to him.

While I didn't think I could come, I flash from zero chance to sixty in a matter of moments. Clutching at his shoulders, surprise laces my voice when I cry out, "It's gonna happen."

"Damn right it will, baby. Nothing will stop us." He moves

faster, pistoning into me like a man on a mission. The sound of us coming together mingles with the late afternoon breeze and the call of a bird somewhere above us. The river rolls in the distance, just on the other side of the trees. But all that matters is us.

I arch my back, my clit hitting his pelvic bone. The pressure is just right. The release is a rush, cresting over me and drowning me. I scream in surprise, in relief, in ecstasy.

Dart slams into me, stilling, while I'm breaking into a million pieces around him. His orgasm follows, feeling like it's pulling those pieces of me back together. We are magnetic, drawn together, bound to one another.

"Holy fuck," he eventually exhales, dipping his forehead to mine as he breathes heavily.

"I needed that," I whisper, a weak chuckle following.

He huffs a laugh, the sound rough and uncertain. He lifts his head, eyes matching the sunshine's brightness, searching my face.

"You needed me."

"I needed you," I quietly admit, because my addle-brained, shaky-knee state can't garner more than repeating him.

Running my hand along his bristly jaw, I pull him back to me, kissing him slower this time. Sweeter. Calmer.

Eventually, he slips from me, but we aren't distracted by the loss. We continue to kiss, lazy and slow. Like we can freeze this moment. Press pause on time.

Where we are together.

Where Mirabelle is ours.

Forever.

35

[Dart]

Trinity really scared the fuck out of me. The fear in her voice. The need in it.

I couldn't get to her fast enough, but I also knew I needed to get to her alone. Dropping Mirabelle off with Mary took a few extra minutes. When I got to the hospital, seeing Trin standing there, head down, shoulders slumped, my genuine concern turned to real fear.

I hopped out of my truck before I hardly had it in Park.

When her crazed eyes caught mine, I worried even more. Something had spooked her. Frightened her. And I'd seen that look before.

I didn't want a rearview mirror to exist for us. We only needed to look toward the future, even if we didn't know what the next turn would bring.

We had each other, and we had Mirabelle.

When she told me about this Marissa woman coming to see her, I could hardly compute the words. The truth is that

Marissa still had time to change her mind and take Mirabelle from us.

Yes, us.

Trinity was the strongest woman I knew, and yet, I know she wouldn't survive the loss.

To love someone so completely, so wholeheartedly, so unconditionally, like Mirabelle, and then to have her taken away, would be unimaginable.

I didn't want to imagine it.

I wouldn't survive the loss either.

To tear that little baby from a couple who love her like we do, it wouldn't be fair. It wouldn't be right.

And for half a minute, I wanted to pack Trin and Mirabelle into my truck and run away. Run where no one could find us.

Instead, we stay put, and in each other's arms, holding tighter every day for the rest of the week.

The countdown until adoption day is in the single digits, and the date can't get here fast enough. I want Trinity's name on the dotted line. In the designated box for *Mother*.

Technically, she didn't have to fill in a father, but I was hoping she would. I was hoping she'd set my name right along with hers.

And I plan to discuss my thoughts when she gets home from work tonight.

We needed a little time to get through that bump of Marissa visiting Trin, but I didn't want anything to get in the way of Mirabelle's future.

Two parents were better than one. Heaven forbid something ever happened to Trin, I wanted her to be assured Mirabelle would be taken care of. *I* am here for her. And being listed on her birth certificate is a start.

I've just settled Mirabelle for a morning nap when I get a call. The caller ID identifies a name I easily recognize.

Max.

While I always thought my first instinct would be to jump at the idea of Max calling after all these months, I hesitate a second before I click to answer.

"Hey, Max," I say, noticing a slight tremor in my voice.

"Dart Rivers," he says, in a slight Floridian drawl. There's a smile in his voice, which is a positive sign.

In some ways, Max reminded me of Russell Haven, Trin's dad. He saw potential in me, a man just dipping his toe into his forties. He knew I was sad. Not unhappy, just aching for something. A purpose. A direction. A focus.

Max had seen me race in the canyon, a slightly uncommon spot to recruit drivers, but not completely unheard of.

He'd been a good mentor, a decent manager, and a bit of a manipulator.

"What's up?" I ask, my voice still clipped.

"Gonna be in your area. Thought we could catch a race together."

"I haven't been driving," I admit, more important things to chase than the taillights of another car. Like my wife's heart.

"What have you been doing?"

I pause, not certain I want to tell Max that I've been making home improvements, babysitting a child, and falling back in love with my life.

I'd never stopped loving my wife.

"What can I do for you, Max?" I ask instead, still hurt about how things went down between us back in May.

He hums. "Was wondering if you could still meet me at the race. Let's talk. In person."

"You makin' me an offer to come back." I felt a little kicked to the curb after that last accident. Granted, I'd been bruised and battered. That close call was closer than I thought. I was rattled by it like I'd never been rattled before.

Max and the team doctor suggested rest and maybe a therapist.

I came home to Rogue River instead, knowing deep down what I really needed.

My wife back.

Max chuckles. “Let’s talk.”

My curiosity is piqued. I want to hear what he has to say, so I agree to meet him. But I have no intention of going alone, and I worry about how Trinity might feel attending a race with me.

On one hand, I want to show her what I love.

On the other, I respect her fears. That dream she had before she went back to work still haunts her. She doesn’t really like to watch the races on TV, but she does. She sits beside me and supports me, often sharing popcorn, snuggling against each other.

Still, I’m nervous when Trin gets home from a long shift. I pour her a glass of wine as she cuddles Mirabelle, smothering her cheeks with kisses.

After handing her the glass, I take Mirabelle from her and set her in a baby swing I pulled into the kitchen while I made dinner.

“I got a call from Max today.” I blurt out the news like I can’t hold it back any longer.

Trinity stills, wine glass mid-lift to her mouth. She lowers it back down.

“Max?” Her voice tight.

“There’s a race tomorrow, and he asked me to attend. He says he wants to talk to me.” I lean on the island between us.

Trinity sets her glass down and stares at the red liquid. “Okay.”

She doesn’t sound okay, and I step closer to her.

“Tell me what you’re thinking.” I rub her arms, feeling her bristle beneath my touch.

If she tells me not to go, I won’t. I don’t want to do anything to jeopardize where we are, but I’m also curious what Max has to say to me.

She shakes her head like she doesn't want to say her thoughts, or maybe she thinks nothing of this situation.

Maybe my own nerves are in the way.

"I'd like you to go with me."

"Really?" she says quietly, keeping her eyes on me.

"Really." I smile wider, relief washing over me. "We can make a date of it."

We've been on a few dates in the past months, but not many. Family is always open to babysitting, especially Mary, but Trin and I like to spend time with Mirabelle. We also realize it's important for us to have alone time together. Just adults.

"It will be fun," I add, still sensing her apprehension.

"Okay," she says, her voice low. "I'll call my mom."

She pulls her phone from her pocket. She isn't even out of her scrubs yet.

Watching her, I'm a little caught up in my own thoughts. I'm excited to see the track again. Even a little excited to see Max. But most of all, I'm excited to spend time with Trinity, sharing the track *with* her.

THE CLOSER WE got to the canyon, the more anxious I become. I've had my hand on Trinity's thigh the entire ride here.

She's wearing another floral dress, which is flirty and country, like the dress she wore out with her friends. She's also wearing those cowboy boots that drive me wild. She has my Velocity hat on her head, giving a valiant effort to support this night. Support me.

She might be just as nervous as I am.

Once we park, my anxiety shifts to excitement. There's a buzz in the air, mingling with the riotous roar of race cars in the distance.

The grandstand here isn't nearly as grand as the one in

Daytona. Still, the metal structure rises in front of us like a wall. A fortress holding back the dragon within.

The scent of burgers on a grill mingles with gasoline and burning rubber.

This is a dirt track compared to the asphalt of more polished racing.

Once we claim the tickets Max left for us at Will Call, we step through the tunnel between the stands, and I inhale, taking in the beauty in front of me.

The track is a breathtaking sprawl of combed dirt and color. Pit road gleams with polished cars wrapped in bright sponsor graphics. Crew members move with focused urgency, tightening lug nuts, checking tire pressure, wiping windshields. The smell of racing fuel is sharp, almost sweet.

Surprisingly, we find Max almost instantly along the barricade fencing that separates the crowd from the beast of the track. He shouts a greeting and shakes my hand. I lean in to introduce him to Trinity.

"Max," I yell. "This is my wife, Trinity."

I pull her into my side, as excited to show her off as I am to be here again.

Max gives me a knowing smile. He bore witness to me setting those divorce papers up in flames after losing my wedding band somewhere on the track in Daytona.

"Nice to meet you," he hollers back at her, shaking her offered hand. She smiles hesitantly.

"I see why you stole his heart," Max adds, winking at me with his appraisal of my wife. I'd be upset if I didn't know Max was a dedicated family man himself.

"I have something for you," he addresses me over the roar and rumble of engines. Reaching into his pocket, he pulls out a set of keys, and I instinctively open my hand to take them.

Shit. My keys. I curl my fingers around them, feeling the familiar bite of metal teeth into my palm.

"Watch number eleven." He slaps my shoulder. "And then we'll talk."

I nod, knowing he doesn't mean the car in the eleventh position, but the car marked with a giant 11 on the hood.

When the drivers fire their engines, conversation becomes impossible. The noise isn't just loud—it's physical. Pressing against your chest, rattling your teeth, making your heartbeat sync with the growl of eight hundred horsepower idling just yards away.

Trinity and I make our way to our seats.

I give Trin another glance. My wife is hot in her flirty dress, with her knees exposed, and I'm like a kid on my first date. I have the girl of my dreams beside me.

But it isn't just her looks. Trinity exudes patience, and she's giving it to me tonight. She might be just as curious as I am about what Max wants from me and what number eleven has to do with anything.

When she glances back at me, I cup her chin and draw her mouth to mine, probably smudging the bright pink lipstick she's wearing. Don't care. Let everyone see me kissing my wife.

Sure enough, a Jumbotron catches us, and I sling my arm around Trin's shoulders as a notice appears over the screen.

NASCAR welcomes DART RIVERS.

People near us turn and clap. Someone wants a selfie. Another wants an autograph.

I'm humbled that a guy from the middle of the pack, who won a few races, is recognizable in this crowd. I'm also honored.

And a little embarrassed. I glance at Trin again, but she smiles softly, pride in her eyes. Like she knows I worked hard. How much I wanted to be something. Be better for her.

When the people around us settle back into their seats, I reach for Trinity again and kiss her cheek.

She chuckles. "What was that for?"

"Just . . . thanks for being here with me." For being here *for* me, because I still don't know what Max wants, but those car keys in my pocket are digging into my thigh.

Trinity continues to watch me as I glance back at the track.

"You really love it here, don't you?"

Being here isn't just about a race. It's atmosphere. Tradition. It's the shared gasp when someone bumps the wall and the collective roar when your favorite driver takes the lead.

Strangers will high-five like lifelong friends.

Being here isn't quiet, polite, or subtle.

It's thunder, heat, horsepower—and the unmistakable thrill of speed.

I can feel it rattle in my bones.

I shrug. "I do," I sigh. "I mean, I did." Even standing here in all this bounding excitement, I know my race days are over. I can't get in a car to drive at high speeds and risk something happening to me. Risk leaving Trinity and Mirabelle without me.

Or me losing them.

"You miss it," she says, not really a question but an observation.

"Yeah," I say, the sound more a sigh.

I glance toward the fence caging in the racers. The main event will start soon, although people are still moving along the barricade and up the stairs. The energy among the crowd is like a living, breathing thing. The movement is mesmerizing. The sensation intoxicating.

What's not to love about this collective excitement?

But then again, I've taken so much pleasure in the quieter times spent with Trinity and Mirabelle these past months.

We've been enjoying the new deck. Trin comes to my games. We've gone dancing together, something we never did before.

I'm reminded of that giddy first date feeling from when we

first took our seats. Trin and I are new again. We're whole again.

Engines rev louder. The sound is almost deafening. The purr is like an aphrodisiac. The pull of wild beasts ready to be unleashed.

My heart rate accelerates, as if I'm a driver about to hit that dirt course.

"I never wanted you to feel like you were floating."

With my arm around Trinity, I lean closer, trying to hear her better.

"I only want you to fly."

My head turns in her direction, our faces close. We recently watched *F1*, a fictional movie about a former NASCAR driver who moves to a new division of racing. The main character describes getting in the zone while driving is like flying. That moment of pure bliss. Adrenaline high. Heart full of awe.

"I'm not floating," I argue. My purpose is clearer now. Perhaps clearer than it's ever been.

Some of us don't have definitive answers to what our calling is in this life. We don't have a constant high from doing what we love, where we love it. We aren't born with a gift or talent or have an experience that shapes our life, drives it in one direction, like Trin did. Some of us fight and fumble and make big mistakes. Some of us wait and wait and wait before we reach for the brass ring and take destiny into our own hands. Some of us have multiple starts and stops and breakdowns before we hit the road again on a new path.

There isn't any right or wrong course.

But I know I'm meant to be with Trin and Mirabelle. Wherever they are, I have purpose.

"We should all feel special about what we do," she continues. "Who we are," she shouts, her brows creasing, concern circling her eyes.

Racing made me feel special.

Sure, it was entertainment, but on a personal level, I had focus when I raced. I constantly pushed myself to do better, be better. An insistent push and pull between potential and success.

And I was successful in some ways.

But I feel more successful being with Trin. She makes me feel important. Her and Mirabelle. Maybe being a dad isn't for every man, but it's something I've wanted for a long time, and it was rewarding for me. Rewarding in ways that don't lead to dollars, trophies, or accolades.

I'm looking forward to that day I might get a homemade bracelet and a handmade award.

World's Best Dad.

I wish.

With my arm around Trin, I squeeze her against me. "I do feel special, baby." I kiss her temple again. "Because you love me."

She hasn't said it. She doesn't have to. I know she loves again. Or never stopped loving me, just as I never stopped loving her.

And that is more special than anything in this world.

"I do love you, Dart."

Stunned by the admission, I pull back, staring at her face. "I love you, too, baby," I say, caught up in the moment.

My girl. Our love. The race.

The green flag drops, and I tighten my hold on Trinity.

Go time.

"But sometimes love alone isn't enough," she says.

I turn toward her again, my heart sinking to my booted feet. "What?"

My brain pings from the excitement of the race, and the revelation of our feelings put into words, to sudden dread in my gut.

"What are you saying?" I yell back at her, knowing this isn't the time or place to have a deep conversation. It's suddenly too loud, too hard to think. I don't know if the fog in my ears is the cars whizzing past us or the whooshing of my pulse.

Trinity cups my jaw and leans toward me, kissing the corner of my mouth.

"I'm gonna go home, but I want you to stay."

I'm pinned in place, too stunned to move. Like watching a bad crash in slow motion and not knowing how to respond as an observer.

Or worse, being the driver. Knowing you need to get out of the flames, but you're suddenly so cold inside, you don't feel the heat. You're stuck in this time warp of rippling speed flipping to lazy, curling rolls, like moving through mud.

Trinity slips past me before her words and actions register. She hastily weaves between latecomers who are clambering up to their seats, or stalled on the stairs, taking in the first minutes of the race.

Fuck. "Trin," I holler as she bops through the mayhem.

I start after her, fruitlessly calling her name, knowing she can't possibly hear me over the thunderous roar.

She gets farther and farther away from me, the crowd almost moving her forward while holding me back. Eventually, she reaches the tunnel entrance and disappears, like she's been swallowed.

I continue rushing after her, apologizing as I press forward, pushing people aside, until I reach the tunnel as well.

I swear I'd recognize Trinity anywhere. Find her in a crowd of faceless people. Sense her in the myriad mayhem. But I can't see around or over or through the jam of race fans in the concourse.

I've lost my wife.

And this time, I worry it's forever.

36

[Trinity]

Attending the race was the last thing I wanted to do, but Dart had invited me. He asked me to be there for him, and I wanted to. I really wanted to. I wanted to understand what Dart loved. Wanted to witness what brought him such joy.

But triggers were going off inside me like the warning lights on a dashboard. Ones that I can't interpret but somehow know mean danger.

That probably, as in Dart's career was *probably over* flipped through my head on repeat. Because on the other side of probably over, was probably not.

And just hearing Max's name accelerated my heart rate.

Met a guy named Max Larsen tonight. He works for a race team named Velocity.

That Max Larsen guy I told you about . . . he thinks I have potential as a driver.

Trin, what would you think about moving to Florida? Getting a fresh start?

I want to be a racecar driver. Come with me.

This time, I didn't want to tell him no. He wasn't asking me to move or give up my life, he simply wanted a date night . . . at the track.

I was even a little excited to see what he loved so much. See the enthusiasm on *his* face.

But so much happened at once.

Meeting Max and the drop of those damn keys into Dart's hands. That Jumbotron welcoming him. The fans seeking photographs and autographs.

I was so damn proud of him, so thankful for getting a glimpse of his world, but I was still conflicted inside.

Dart's overall excitement was so much more than I expected.

And I could never ask him to give that up. To give up something he loved so much. That made him feel so special.

He missed it. His quiet *yeah* haunted me.

As we drove to the event, Dart was silent at first, but then he grew more vocal, sharing race stories and shenanigans from the circuit. Not like I hadn't heard tales before, but this was different. His animation grew with every mile, and I wanted to be just as enthusiastic for him, but I couldn't seem to settle the unease in my gut.

Was he happy at home? Was he happy with us? Was he happy with Mirabelle?

Dart revved my engine, but was revving enough?

When we pulled into that lot, cold shivers of dread chilled me.

An intuition that something lingered around the bend of the dark road ahead.

Dart's love for the sport.

Dart missing it.

I had to set him free. I couldn't take any of that away from him, that sense of purpose he felt, he deserved.

I wanted him to fly through life, like I said. Not just float.

I shouldn't have left like I did, but I also couldn't sit there and watch the race. Watch the expression on Dart's face shift between love for a sport and the pain of losing it.

I had no doubt Dart loved me. Loved Mirabelle.

But I knew who I was. I'm a nurse, a mother, a homemaker. Those things bring me joy.

I couldn't take from Dart something that brought him so much pleasure.

After a quick text to Dart, once the ride share picked me up, I return home. The ride was long, time added because I initially had to wait. The canyon wasn't exactly on the edge of a town.

Mirabelle was with Mom, and I should have gone to collect her, but I needed more time alone.

I'd walked away from Dart.

I'd severed my own heart to let his be free.

Dart would always hold a special space inside me. He'd broken me and put me back together, patching up the cracks he initially made, then made me even stronger.

I could do this for him. I could let him go.

Once upon a time, I had given up on a dream—motherhood—until a miracle placed a baby at my door.

But Dart has struggled to find something that drives him, stumbling upon it because of our repeated tragedies.

I couldn't take that away from him.

When I finally reach my house, I stumble inside, finding my legs almost too weak to carry me. My pulse is slow, sluggish even. I move like I'm forcing myself through deep snow. I shiver in the imaginary cold, despite the mid-August temperature.

Inside the house, I pause, staring at the poster in my front hallway. The giant pussy. The gorgeous flower.

This is my happy place. My home, once remodeled by Dart, additionally decorated with love because of Mirabelle.

Most recently, Dart replaced the roof, fixed the shower, and added a back deck. He'd been telling me about his plans to build Mirabelle a playhouse and rehab the detached garage. He'd been excited to continue his found projects . . . or so I thought.

The joy of a new garage or a fun playhouse had to pale against the allure of racing.

I cared for Dart. And I refused to hold him back.

I hang his hat on my coatrack, wondering if he'll leave it behind for me. A painful yet bright reminder of the reconciliation we had. The new love we shared recently.

As I slog up the staircase, I hold the railing to balance my efforts. Once inside my room, I try to ignore the large bed. The space where Dart and I have reconnected. His scent lingers in the bathroom. Pine and asphalt forever burned into my senses.

I tug off my boots and peel myself out of my dress.

I stare at myself in the mirror. In only my underwear and bra, I study my subtle curves. The swell of my breasts. The flatness of my belly.

Once upon a time, I cried that I'd never earn stretch marks. My stomach wouldn't swell. I wouldn't bear a child from my body.

But now I have Mirabelle.

She is my purpose.

Tears fall, fast and furious, and I slip out of my bra, pulling on a comfy pair of loose sweats and a T-shirt that was draped at the end of the bed, realizing too late that it belongs to Dart. I'm engulfed in fresh pine and another hint of asphalt when I bring the collar to my nose and then wipe my tears with the edge of the shirt.

My feet clomp, feeling too heavy to lift, as I traipse back down the stairs in need of an oversize glass of wine. I pass the living room without a glance and head directly for the kitchen.

But my feet suddenly stall, trapped by the wood underneath them. My heart bangs against my ribcage. I blink like that will help me process what I think I saw.

I spin, racing the short distance back to the archway between the living room and the hallway.

Dart stands beside the pink couch. The same one he laid on after breaking into the house months ago. The same one where I kissed him with hurt in my heart while confusingly still attracted to him. The same one where he's cuddled Mirabelle and held me countless times.

"How?" My breath escapes me like a cloud. "What?" I thunder, low and restless. "Why?"

Dart rushes toward me, stopping short of reaching me, and tugging a ballcap off his head.

"Because I fucking love you."

"But racing . . ."

"Fuck racing," he practically shouts, setting his hands on my upper arms. "I love you more, Trin. So much more."

"But the keys?" I whisper, my throat burning. "You took those keys from Max."

Dart chuckles, and I'm startled by the sound, struggling to pull out of his grasp.

He holds me tighter. "Those keys are for the Camaro."

The Chevy Camaro he'd gotten for a steal and fixed up on his own. I hadn't exactly forgotten the car, I'd simply put it out of my head.

"Max brought it back to me." Dart pauses. "Well, he brought it somewhere to the race."

Dart stares at me, his eyes wild, pinging from one of mine to the other.

"I'd given Max the car as collateral when I first started racing. Until I had my first big win. But as I traveled often and used Velocity's cars, he's been holding onto it for me."

"I thought . . . " I swallow thickly. "I thought he was giving you a car again. A team car."

Dart chuckles, sliding his hands to the side of my neck and pausing there. "No. No, I am not going back to racing."

I'm stunned, and I blink like that will make me hear him better. Like that will make the words clearer.

"But you want to go back," I state. A fact I saw written on his face while I stood beside him.

"Says who?" His brows lift, his tone teasing. "I'm not going back to racing, Trin. My life is here. With you. With Mirabelle."

"But you love racing," I argue. "The speed. The rush."

"I do. And I'll love to watch it, but I'm not going to participate in it anymore. I don't want to. I'm happy to slow down. Time with Mirabelle is going to go faster than we think."

I'm still flabbergasted. "You need purpose."

My hands have been hanging by my side, but I wave one, which knocks into his chest. He releases my neck and catches my hand, pinning it against him, dragging it up over his heart.

"*You're* my purpose, Trin. You and Mirabelle." He lowers his head so he meets my eyes, holding them, like he wants me to really hear him, feel him.

"I'd been chasing a high that never felt fulfilled. Never fully complete. My situation had become a racetrack metaphor, Trin. I'd been chasing taillights, going round in circles, but feeling like I'd never catch up to whatever I was following. Even crossing a finish line hadn't made me feel like a winner. Not in a long time. You're my win, Forever. You and Mirabelle."

"Then what did Max want?" I ask, my voice cracking as I'm still trying to process how I'm enough for him. How Mirabelle is enough.

Dart shrugs. "I have no idea. As soon as *my wife* ran off, I chased her."

"You didn't have to do that." I lower my voice and drop my gaze.

"Yeah, I did. Because I'm always going to chase you, Trin. I'm sorry I took a detour. A bump in the road, but I love you.

You are my dream, Forever. You and Mirabelle. I love you more than any track or car or whatever else you want to compare." He tips his forehead to mine. "There is no comparison."

"I don't want to hold you back," I admit on a sob, fighting to swallow it back.

Dart lifts his head. "Trin, you have never held me back. Not once. You let me go, and then you took me back. I'll always be so . . . grateful. Did I want you there? Of course. But did I maybe need to do it alone? I think I did. And look where it brought me, right back to where I should have been all along. Beside you."

"But what if you grow bored? What if you tire of diapers and bottles and taking care of Mirabelle? What if you feel restless again? What if I'm not enough again?" I make a fist, clutching it to my chest, because he's always worried that he wasn't enough, but what *if* I'm not?

"You are enough." He chuckles, like it's the most absurd thought he's ever heard. "You were always enough, baby. Racing was about me, but now . . . I'm done. It was thrilling but risky, and I don't want to risk missing out on us. On our family. Watching Mirabelle grow up. Loving you."

"Our family," I whisper-choke. Because he is part of our family. We are three. Mirabelle, me, and Dart.

"Am I somehow failing her?" he chokes. "Failing you? Right now. Right here. No what ifs."

I shake my head. He's been so present. More than I ever imagined because I never imagined Mirabelle. I never imagined this second chance with him.

"Sure, some days are tiring, maybe even stagnating, but it doesn't mean I don't feel like I have a new purpose." Dart stands taller. "I love Mirabelle. She's my purpose. We are my priority." He waves between us. "And I want to be here for all of it. The good, the bad, and the boring." He chuckles, the sound soggy, as he removes his hands from my neck.

"I am here for us," he chokes, swallowing hard.

Dart Rivers, who I have never seen cry in my life, has tears in his eyes.

"This is home, Trin." He points at the floor. "You and Mirabelle are home. You're all I need. All I've ever wanted."

He swallows thickly, licking his lips. "I know we haven't talked about it. Not directly, but I want to be Mirabelle's dad. I didn't bring it up before because the adoption felt fragile. Unreal until it was real. But with Marissa coming to visit you and Max's return, I just want it settled. I want you to know where I stand. What I really want. I want her as mine too."

"Dart." His name is tremulous and wet, matching the tears that don't seem to stop flowing.

He pinches the corners of his eyes. "I've been eternally grateful for the second chance you gave me, Trinity. *Forever* grateful. So, don't ever run off on me again. Okay? Don't shut me out. *Please.*"

His voice cracks, and I lunge for him, erasing the distance between us and clinging to him. His arms circle around me, binding me to him as well.

"I love you so much, Trinity," he chokes again.

"I love you, too, baby." I pull back and kiss him.

Through the salt on our lips and the blur in our eyes, we kiss like we can't get close enough.

Dart pulls back first, setting his forehead against mine again. "Thank you." He whispers. "Thank you so much, Trin."

I stroke my fingers through the hair on the back of his head.

"Are you wearing my shirt?" he suddenly asks, breaking the tearful tension. "You know how I feel about you wearing my stuff."

I do know how he feels, and I know how I feel putting on his things.

Like he's mine.

"Now." He pulls back, still looking at his shirt draping over my body. "Speaking of speed, let's see how fast I can get you out of those clothes."

I chuckle despite my wet cheeks. "Dart Rivers, you are so ridiculous."

"And that's why you love me?"

He kisses my cheek. Then the other cheek.

"One of many reasons," I admit as he moves to my neck.

"Hey, Trin," he whispers.

"Yeah?" I swallow as he moves toward the spot that will bring me to my knees.

"Honey." He whispers against the juncture of my neck and shoulder. "I'm home."

Then he nips me, and as my knees go weak, he scoops me up, taking me to our bedroom, where we can celebrate that he's home.

Forever.

37

[Trinity]

"Are you nervous?" Dart asks me the morning of adoption day. We have a set time at the court.

"Very." I sigh, giving my hair one last scrunch as I look at myself in the mirror.

Do I look like a mother? Is that something you can tell by looking at someone? Is there a scent that other mothers recognize? The tired gleam in my eyes? The weight of the world on my shoulders while my heart is so full of love? Is it a badge? A handshake?

Do I really have what it takes?

"What are you thinking?" he says, as he stands behind me in the bathroom.

Mirabelle is oblivious to all of this in her honor, peacefully sleeping through her morning nap, while I've been a wreck. I don't think I slept at all last night.

Dart chuckles, and I notice that I'm scowling at myself.

"Think they'll say no," I whisper, when it's not really a fear.

Cassidy Lane said it's very cut and dry. Some forms. A judge. A photograph.

Afterward, there will be a party in the yard.

Dart laughs harder. "Not a chance." He kisses the side of my neck.

"Do I look like a mother?" I ask him, smoothing my hand over my belly for some reason.

"Yes. You look like Mirabelle's mom." He smiles at my reflection over my shoulder. "And I have something to make it official."

He scoops his arm around me and dangles something from his fingers.

A long chain with a delicate pendant.

"It's called Mother and Child," he explains of the larger figure with circular arms, extended toward a smaller one. I've seen it countless times. Wanted one for so long.

"I've been holding onto this for years."

Our eyes meet in the mirror.

A dozen years. Three angel babies. Gone but never forgotten.

And yet we have a new angel to guard.

"Dart," I whisper, tears filling my eyes as I watch him open the clasp and fasten the chain around my neck. He straightens the latch, and I hold the pendant in my hand, staring at myself once more in the mirror.

"Now, you really look like a mother," he says, lowering his voice and his head toward my ear. "One hot momma."

I laugh through the tears, blinking them away.

This man. His ridiculousness.

"Thank you," I whisper. "For everything."

He sets his chin on the top of my shoulder. "Forever." He winks at me. "And we should get going."

I'm wearing a dress. Dart has on tan slacks and a button-down shirt, sleeves rolled to his elbows. It's the most dressed up he's been in years. And Mirabelle, she's in a sweet pink dress that matches mine.

We ride to the courthouse, just the three of us. We don't need the fanfare of family and friends. We're saving that for the backyard. For now, I want this moment to be private, monumental.

And it is, especially as the judge holds out a pen to Dart.

"What?" He stares at the form in front of him. A legal request to change Mirabelle's rather generic birth certificate.

My name is in the box designated for mother.

And Dart's name fills the one marked Father.

"Trin?" He looks up at me, surprised, shocked really, but so full of hope.

Before we talked about Dart being Mirabelle's dad, I knew I'd put him on the birth certificate.

He is Mirabelle's father.

But Dart wasn't present when the social worker walked me through the final paperwork, and I asked her if there was a way to surprise him.

He's certainly surprised, and eager.

"Do you really mean it?"

"We really mean it," I say, jostling Mirabelle in my arms.

Dart looks at the judge and practically rips the pen out of his hands, his fingers shaking as he firmly, confidently signs his name in the box.

Father: Dart Rivers.

He drops the pen and tugs me to him, wrapping his arms around both of us.

"Am I allowed to do this in a courtroom?" he says, not releasing Mirabelle and me, as he first peppers her cheek with kisses and then lays a rather inappropriate one on me.

I giggle when the judge clears her throat.

"Congratulations, Mr. and Mrs. Rivers. It's a girl," the judge says.

She's more than a girl. She's pure joy.

I don't think my heart could be any fuller.

Much like Cassidy said, we sign forms, the judge rules, and we take a picture. Cassidy Lane and Stone Sylver are our witnesses as they've been such a huge part of our journey.

It all passed in a blur.

When we get home, our yard is full.

Mom. Cort. Clint. Tate.

My girls: Vale, Genie, Halle, and Mavis, and their significant others.

Their kids.

Hutch and his boys are here with Petty.

A real gathering of all the people we love, celebrating the one person Dart and I love most.

As Mirabelle gets passed around, Mom swooping her up almost as soon as we arrive, Dart is handed a beer by Petty.

"How'd it go, Farty Darty?"

"Dear God," I chuckle.

"Hilarious," Dart retorts, offering me a sip of the beer Petty already cracked open.

I shake my head. A celebratory bottle of wine has my name on it somewhere around here.

"Actually," I interject, slipping my arm around Dart's middle. "Do you want to tell them or me?"

"What?" Hutch says, standing there as well, brows lifting as he glances from me to Dart.

Dart looks at me, all the love in his eyes. All the hope solidified.

"Actually," he repeats, staring at me a second before looking at his friends. "I'm Mirabelle's dad. So I think the name you're looking for is Sexy Daddy."

"Oh, brother," I pat his belly and pull away, but he tugs me back to him.

He leans toward my ear. "We can role-play that later."

"Hide Daddy's sausage in—"

"Watch it," Dart warns Petty, pointing a finger at him while holding a beer can.

"Are you ever serious?" I ask the goofy guy in a band.

"I try not to be." He winks.

Late arrivals enter the yard. "Is that Savannah with Marshall?" I ask.

"Where?" Petty says, his face sobering as he looks toward the corner of the yard. The midnight-haired beauty leaves her brother's side and heads toward a group of women.

Marshall stalks toward us.

"Excuse me," Petty grumbles, making tracks toward Savannah.

I glance up at Dart, who slowly smiles. *Uh-oh, there's a story there*. One I'm certain I'll hear more about later.

For now, as Marshall joins the guys, I break from Dart and make my way around the party, greeting guests, passing out hugs, and taking in all the congratulations, before Mirabelle is fussing and I excuse myself to take her upstairs for a nap.

The party can continue, but the honored party girl needs a little reprieve, and I take an extra minute to hold her in the chair Dart gave me to celebrate my first Mother's Day.

Eventually, I step into my room to use the bathroom but stop near the window overlooking the yard. I clutch the Mother and Child pendant between my fingers, running it back and forth along the chain, watching Dart move around our guests before disappearing.

When I hear soft steps coming up the staircase, I smile to myself, knowing true to his word, he'll always chase me.

"Hey, baby," he says as he enters our room, softly closing the door behind him. "Whatcha doing up here?"

"Just needed a little break." I love our family. I love our friends, but the day has already been a lot. Between the lack of sleep last night and all the jitters today, I'm suddenly exhausted.

"You okay?" he asks, stepping up behind me like he did earlier today and wrapping his arms around my middle.

"Just taking in all the love, I guess."

With his cheek pressed to mine, he smiles. "So much love," he marvels. "All for one precious little girl and her mom."

"And her dad," I say, smiling myself.

"Dad," he whispers. "I didn't think this day would ever happen."

"Me neither. For either of us."

We stand in silence for a minute, letting the sad memories quickly pass. We stand here stronger now, because of our love, but also because of Mirabelle.

Wonderous miracle.

I spin in Dart's arms, looping mine over his shoulders. "I love you."

He smiles, slow and wide. "I love you, too, baby."

I tip up on my toes, setting a tender kiss to his mouth, but the longer we kiss, the deeper it gets.

"Trin," he groans against me.

I wouldn't be opposed to a quicky.

I'm reminded of another memory. The first time Dart came to dinner at our house *after* we started hooking up.

He'd followed me up to my bedroom, much like he did today. What always started as a heated kiss led to more, and soon Dart was inside me. My dress at my waist, his pants at his hips. I don't think we even locked the door.

It was thrilling and reckless, and I loved him so much I blurted it out.

He stilled inside me. He'd wanted to make our relationship more public for a while, but I'd held fast to keeping him to myself. Keeping us to us.

"I love you, too, Forever," he breathed against my mouth, showing me how he felt by finishing what we'd started.

When we went downstairs, my brother asked where we'd been.

"Kissing," I said to the room. "I'm in love with Dart."

Dad and Mom weren't as shocked as I expected.

They were just happy for me.

I am happy for me.

"We can't start this now," Dart continues, rocking his forehead against mine.

"Later, then," I whisper.

"Later," he says.

"Promise?" I tease, pulling back to look him in the eye.

"Promise."

38

[Trinity]

"Is she asleep already?" I ask Dart later that night.

"She is." After an incredibly long day, he apparently had the magic touch, soothing Mirabelle with a bottle and a song.

He steps up behind me.

I just finished a shower and have only a towel wrapped around me. Another towel in my hands for my hair. Dart takes the towel from my hand and gently rubs the soft terry material over my short strands. The length is slowly growing out again.

I close my eyes as he massages the towel over my head and then tosses it on the bed, using his hands to continue what he's started. A tender squeeze against the back of my neck. A firm scrub at my scalp with his fingertips, combing his fingers through the short, damp length.

"Feels nice," I whimper.

He moves his hands to my shoulders, digging his thumbs into the back of them, before moving down my arms. He kisses the side of my neck.

"You feel nice," he whispers just below my ear.

My skin pebbles.

He travels his hands back up my arms, returning to massage my shoulders and neck. Then he cups my chin and turns only my head, bringing our mouths together. We kiss softly. The touch tender.

When he pulls back, he says, "It was a good day."

"It was," I agree. "A special day."

"Every day is," he says, turning me so I face him. "Because you and me are together."

"Forever," I whisper.

"Exactly." He runs his nose along mine, his new way to tease me. He brings his lips whisper close to mine as well but doesn't kiss me.

"Tease."

He chuckles. "You're the tease, wearing this towel." He pulls back to look down at the short strip of terry cloth wrapped around my middle.

"Is it later yet?" he asks.

"It's later," I say, a smile forming on my lips.

"Want to celebrate today." He runs the back of his hand down my arm again, punctuating his desire.

"I know the perfect way." I step back and release my towel, letting it fall to my feet.

Dart stares blatantly at my breasts, raising a fist to his mouth and biting the edge of it. "My wife is a smoke show."

I chuckle and shake my head. "You're so—"

"Right?' he counters, bringing his eyes to mine and stepping forward to walk me backward.

I shake my head.

"Seductive?" he tweaks one brow.

I chuckle, although he isn't wrong.

"Good at loving you." He doesn't ask it like a question.

"Yeah," I say, low. "That one."

"Get on that bed, baby."

A shiver runs down my back as he spins me to face it, guiding me to climb up. He removes his sweatpants and cups my hip, holding me in place, silently telling me to stay on all fours.

Then he crawls up behind me.

"Gonna love you," he says, as his chest hits my back and his hard length meets the crease of my ass. He kisses along my shoulders and down my spine, worshipping me like only he knows how.

"Want to take my time with you," he says.

And he'll do it, if I tell him to go slow, but tonight, I just want to feel him. I want to let the time take us where it will.

I arch my back, seeking him behind me.

He nips one cheek, and I flinch, giggling after the sting.

"You want something from me, baby," he teases.

"You," I admit, strong and eager.

He skims his hand up my back while the other reaches between my legs, instantly finding where I want him most.

I whimper at his touch. A soft tickle. Not hard enough.

Then his finger enters me, and I hum, arching my back again.

"So ready for me. So good," he moans.

"Always for you," I say, lowering my head to the bed, while keeping my backside in the air.

"Don't know if I can go slow with you in this position."

We've been in numerous positions, and he almost always says the same thing. Since his return and our eventual reunion, we've been insatiable for one another, like we'd been when we first started.

When we kissed after a car ride.

Kissed again on my shift break.

And then started making out whenever we had the chance.

But the real change came when we started having sex. When

I said we were hooking up, and Dart said he was loving me, even back then. Even before we fully defined our relationship.

He always knew it was love, he said.

When Dart says he *never thought*, I almost always stop him, but the one area I don't is when he says he knew he'd never love anyone the way he loves me.

Fully. Completely. Forever.

He adds a second finger to the first, easily entering me, filling me, like only he can.

"So good," I whisper, clutching at the bed cover.

"Gonna be good for you," he says.

I smile as he continues to tease me, wrapping his other hand around me to get to that sweet spot.

I wiggle and whine, and just give in to his touch.

I come slow and steady, like the river that runs through this town. I languish in the release, letting it ease out of me, letting it carry me away.

"Wow," I whisper, as I come down from the high.

Dart leans forward, kissing my shoulder blade. "Scoot forward, Trin."

I do as he asks, getting as close to the headboard as I can. Then Dart is there, his tip at my entrance. His cock inching into me.

I press back to meet him, to draw him forward.

He wraps his arm around my middle, tugging me upward, and I use the spindles of the headboard to help me climb, until I'm seated in his lap.

"This is new," I smile, full in a new way. My legs spread wide. My back to his front.

"Gotta keep things fresh," he says into the side of my neck, smiling through his saucy comment.

Using the headboard as leverage, I lift myself, then lower back onto him.

"Trin," he hums, gripping my hips.

"Like that?" I ask, glancing over my shoulder.

"Love it." He kisses my shoulder. "Love you, Forever."

I turn my head, but our kiss is quick because our pace picks up. The headboard taps the wall. The mattress shifts. And I stay on Dart's lap, meeting his thrusts with my own, drawing him deeper, riding him faster.

"Yes," I cry out. Yes to him, to us, to this. To our life, and our love.

He slips one hand between my legs, finding that sweet spot again.

"I—"

He nips my neck near my shoulder, another sweet spot he knows well. "You will."

Confident, cocky, certain that he's enough for me. That he'll give me anything.

He teases my clit and fills my channel, and I'm clutching at the top of the headboard as I pitch forward and silently scream, afraid to wake Mirabelle down the hallway.

Dart moves even faster, surging harder, taking me to a higher level.

Leaning back, I wrap my arm around his neck. His forehead rests on the side of my head. He breathes heavily.

"Love you so much," he grunts, until he finally stills, letting go inside me.

"I love you, too."

We're both a little sweaty and sticky, but we stay together for another second. Dart slips one arm around my breasts. His hand between my thighs lifts to my lower belly.

Once upon a time, we'd make jokes about what might have happened after having sex like we just did. And touching my soft stomach would bring me to tears, knowing nothing had happened.

But tonight, I smile, especially when Dart says, "Congratulations, Momma."

"Congratulations to you, Daddy."

We just celebrated our baby girl down the hall.

Dart chuckles, "I know what you mean, but that sounded dirty as hell."

"You like it dirty," I tease, glancing over my shoulder at him.

"Only if I'm dirty with you."

"Always," I say to him as he cups my chin and brings my mouth close to his.

"Promise." It's not really a question.

"Promise."

EPILOGUE

[Dart]

One week later

I'm standing in the front yard, about to head out for my newest home renovation—a revamp of the free-standing garage. It's the last project on my list before I take Clint up on his offer for part-time work.

Trinity and I talked about me finding a purpose. Not just husband, father, friend, but something for me. For now, I just like staying busy.

I'm about to open the garage door when a car pulls into the driveway.

A Chevy Camaro that's as familiar as my right hand.

She's loud. A beauty and a beast.

A young guy unfolds himself from the driver's side door. He's tall and thin, wearing loose-fit jeans and a Chevy t-shirt.

"Hey." His voice cracks like he's still in puberty. "Are you Dart Rivers?"

"I am." I step toward him, offering my hand, although a

faint trigger about the last time a stranger approached me, asking me the same question in such a hesitant voice, comes to mind. A time when I was worried I'd lost my wife, and I had.

"Ryder Wesley." He shakes my hand with a firm grip. "Max Larsen said I should come see you."

Max shouldn't be passing along my private address, and I make a mental note to ream him out for it. After my early departure from the race track a few weeks back, I called Max. Told him I had a family emergency and never watched the race.

"Family always comes first," Max said. *"You make it your number one priority."*

"What can I do for you?" I ask the kid. "But a better question is, what are you doing with my car?"

I stare at the lean machine, almost afraid to approach her. Max gave me the keys the night of the race, but my only focus had been on chasing Trinity.

"Thought I'd personally deliver her to you. And then ask a favor." He slips his hands into the back pockets of his jeans, like he's anxious while excited at the same time.

"What do you need?" I'm not saying yes or no, just curious.

"I was wondering if you could train me."

I pause, pulling my gaze from the sleek lines on the wide hood of the Chevy. "Train you?"

"Yeah." He's still sheepish. "How'd you like my race the other night?"

The kid Max wanted me to watch. Number eleven.

I scratch at the back of my neck. "Sorry, kid, but I didn't end up staying for the race. I had a family emergency."

"Oh." His face falls. He only has a speckling of scruff on his jaw. He looks so young. A guy in his twenties with dreams.

"Everything okay? With your family?" He nods toward the porch, and I see Trinity standing on it, holding Mirabelle on her hip.

At six months, our baby girl is healthy and lively, showing us every day even more of her individual personality.

I give Trin a reassuring smile before turning back to him. "It's perfect."

My girls are the most important people in my life.

"So, Max sent you here to ask me to train you." I pause a beat. "Do you need training?"

He shrugs, squinting in the morning sunlight. "I guess so. He said you were local but a legend."

I choke out a chuckle. Good old Max, always embellishing the truth. "I don't know about legend."

"He said you hit the circuit at forty. A midlife crisis redemption story."

My face falls. "Well, that makes me sound like shit more than a hero."

He laughs. "Yeah, well, I don't want to wait until I'm forty." There's a quiet confidence to him. A little cocky as one is in their twenties.

I get it. I totally get it. And I appreciate his candor. He has a goal and wants to act on it. He's already smarter than me.

Then I check myself. We each take our own path, setting our own pace. Some race to the finish line, like Trin, knowing at a young age who she wanted to be. Some of us need more time. Either way, it's okay to change course. Adjust the speed with which we achieve our dreams and complete our goals.

"What would training you look like?" I hadn't ever considered being part of a crew. My position was always behind the wheel. But that didn't mean I couldn't teach this kid a thing or two.

"Watch me race. Maybe give me some pointers."

"Play Doc Hudson to your Lightning McQueen?"

He stares at me. He can't be so young that he hasn't ever heard of Disney's *Cars*, right?

"Sure," he eventually says, appeasing me.

I glance back at Trin. "I'd have to think about it."

When I look back at Ryder, he's looking at Trinity and the baby. "Sure. I get it."

Does he? Will he eventually learn there are greater things to achieve in your life? That people are more important than trophies or accolades. That love is the ultimate victory.

Still, there's something about the awkward way he stands and the hunger in his eyes that reminds me so much of myself.

Trin's dad comes to mind, telling me I reminded him of himself. Potential. His favorite word for me.

I want to know Ryder's story, but first, I want to talk with Trinity.

"Why don't you give me your number?" I pull out my phone, taking down the digits he gives me. "I'll get back to you in a day or two. And in the meantime, maybe watch *Cars*. Appreciate the small stuff before you hit it big."

He smiles like a kid.

He finger-guns me and winks, like that flashy cartoon race car in the movie. Apparently, he's already perfected a smirk for the media.

"Alright. I need to get to the hardware store."

He gazes toward the car and clears his throat. "Think you can give me a ride into town?"

Glancing at my Chevy, I realize he doesn't have a way to get anywhere. "Sure," I chuckle, mimicking him. "Can you back out the Chevy? Let's trade positions."

I swing into my pickup, reversing into the street to switch parking spots. When he approaches the truck, I set it in Park.

"Give me a sec, okay?" I hop back out of the truck and cross the yard for the porch.

"Everything okay?" Trinity asks me as soon as I reach the steps.

"Gonna give this guy a ride into town."

She eyes him suspiciously.

"Max sent him. He wants me to train him." We don't have time to have a full discussion right now. "Can we talk when I get back?"

"Of course." She smiles while pressing a kiss to the back of Mirabelle's head. Mirabelle's limbs go wild. Arms and legs and a smile of her own.

God, I love my girls.

I hop up the steps and kiss Trinity one more time before giving Ryder a lift.

Once I'm back at the house, I find Trinity in the living room. Mirabelle squeals in a new baby seat contraption.

"So, about Ryder . . ." Trinity pauses, looking up at me from her spot on the floor. "You should do it."

I chuckle, surprised and confused. "I don't even know what it involves."

"I want you to love it again, Dart. Even if it's from the sidelines."

I fold down to the floor, stretching out on my side, Mirabelle between us.

"You sure about this. It might mean days at the canyon. Or nights at the track. Could mean weekends away." I grimace. "I'm not willing to give you up again, Trin."

"You're not giving us up, Dart. We're here to support you."

"God, I love you." I press up and lean over Mirabelle, giving Trin a quick kiss. Then I lean down and kiss the top of Mirabelle's head. "What do you think, baby girl? Think Daddy will make a good coach? A good mentor for a driver?"

"I think he'll be perfect at it," Trinity speaks for Mirabelle, her eyes warm, her confidence in me unwavering.

I don't deserve her, but I also don't intend to ever let her go again.

EPILOGUE 2

[Trinity]

September

Hammering out details on how Dart could train Ryder did not take us long. With my three-day work schedule, Dart had other days to mentor Ryder.

We made an effort not to be like cars in passing lanes.

If Dart had a race to watch, we went together.

I promised not to rush off from the track ever again.

He promised he'd always come home to me.

Ryder Wesley turned out to have great potential. That's all we can ever strive for. Potential to do our best. Use our talents and skills. Find something we love to do. And love those around us.

Dart and I still have days where I get in my head, and he struggles with his purpose, but we work through those times together.

In the hard times and the easy, as our vows once said.

Fall is definitely in the air as I stand on the back deck. The

September sun is still warm, but the nights are cool. Autumn is almost here. I can smell a change in the air when a sharp yowl catches my attention.

I step off the deck, down into the yard, and glance toward the lattice that decorates the base of the deck.

Bright yellow eyes belonging to one orange tabby stare back at me.

"Oliver." I smile widely. "Where have you been?"

Assuming all Dart's construction projects scared the cat away, I haven't seen him for months. Not since the day before the night I assumed he was mewling at my back door, and it turned out to be a baby instead.

I make soft *tsking* noises, hoping to lure him forward, but he scurries deeper beneath the deck. Thinking I'll bring him some milk to tempt him from the darkness, I re-enter the house and hear the sweetest giggles.

Distracted by the sound, I weave through the kitchen and dining room, finding Dart on the floor in front of the couch. He leans into Mirabelle's belly, growling softly against her solid tummy, and she giggles. The sound is tinkly and bright like sunlight dancing through a window.

A prism of light even glows against the walls like a work of art.

"What's going on in here?" I grin, lowering down beside them.

"Mirabelle and I were just chatting."

"Oh, you were, were you?" Skepticism fills my voice about the ability of a six-month-old to speak. "And what were you discussing?"

"Well, first I was trying to get her to say Dada."

Ever since Dart learned that one of the first sounds a baby makes is often *da*, he's been encouraging Mirabelle to call him a name he longs to hear.

"Okay, Dada," I tease. "Give it a rest."

"She's gonna be so smart, like her Momma."

When he calls me that, I soften. Then I notice the prism of light again and catch on a yellow ribbon Dart dangles over Mirabelle. Her little hands reach up for the object, but she doesn't have the skill yet to catch what he's holding. Not to mention, he keeps tugging it out of her grasp.

"What's that?" My throat thickens as I narrow in on the object looped through the ribbon.

Dart slowly sits upright, bending one knee upward and holding up the ribbon. I watch the object dangling from it, mesmerized like Mirabelle had been.

"That's the other thing we were discussing."

I swallow hard as my eyes cloud.

"I was asking Mirabelle if I could ask her Momma to marry me."

Dart reaches for my hand and sets a kiss over my vacant ring finger. "I thought we could renew our vows or something."

I chuckle through the thickness in my throat and blink away the foggy tears. "Dart Rivers, is there a question in there?"

He scoots closer to me and winds the ribbon tighter around his fingers to give me a better view of a gorgeous diamond ring.

One that's different from the first one he gave me. A little bigger and square cut on a silver band.

"Trinity *Rivers*. Will you marry me? Again." He lifts my hand and stamps the inside of my wrist with a kiss. "Make new promises with me, to love each other. Forever."

"Forever," I whisper.

He arches one brow. "Is that a yes?"

"That's a hell yes, I'll be your wife again."

And I know the perfect place to renew our vows.

A riverside ceremony symbolizing how life moves on. You never stand in the same water twice, just like Dart and I are not the same people we were three years ago. Or in our twenties.

But one thing remains constant.

We're stronger together.
And with Mirabelle in the mix, we are whole.
A family.
Full of promise.

+ + +

Thank you for taking the time to read PROMISE.
If you enjoyed this book, please leave review were ebooks and paperbacks are sold and discussed.

Want a little more of Trinity and Dart?
Read about their vow renewal here.

PROMISE: BONUS CONTENT

Up next in Rogue River - PATIENCE
When a single father meets a single mother stranded during a snow storm, he quickly learns she's his new neighbor, and Clint Haven will need a little patience, if he wants to win her heart.

MORE BY L.B. DUNBAR

Rogue River

A spin-off from Sterling Falls, following the Haven siblings

Promise

Patience

Prudence

Sterling Falls

Seven small-town siblings muddle their way through love over 40.

Sterling Heat

Sterling Brick

Sterling Streak

Sterling Clay

Sterling Fight

Sterling Touch

Sterling Stone

Lovewell Landing

The Holiday Post

Fall Love

Midsummer Mishaps

Chicago Anchors

When your eyes are on the silver fox coach more than the ball.

Elevator Pitch

Catch the Kiss

Parentmoon

When the mother of the groom goes head-to-head with the single father of the bride.

Holiday Hotties (Christmas novellas)

Holiday novellas certain to heat the season.

Scrooge-ish

Naughty-ish

Grouch-ish

Elf-ish

Road Trips & Romance

Three sisters. Three destinations. Second chances at love over 40.

Hauling Ashe

Merging Wright

Rhode Trip

Lakeside Cottage

Four friends. Four summers. Shenanigans and love happen at the lake.

Living at 40

Loving at 40

Learning at 40

Letting Go at 40

The Silver Foxes of Blue Ridge

Small mountain town, silver fox brothers seeking love over 40.

Silver Brewer

Silver Player

Silver Mayor

Silver Biker

Sexy Silver Foxes

When sexy silver foxes meet the feisty vixens of their dreams.

After Care

Midlife Crisis

Restored Dreams

Second Chance

Wine&Dine

Collision novellas

A spin-off from *After Care* – the younger set/rock stars

Collide - Caught

The Sex Education of M.E.

The original sexy silver fox.

When a widowed professor decides she'd like to date again, and a local fireman volunteers to give her lessons.

The Heart Collection

Small town, big hearts - stories of family and love.

Speak from the Heart

Read with your Heart

Look with your Heart

Fight from the Heart

View with your Heart

A Heart Collection Spin-off

The Heart Remembers

BOOKS IN OTHER AUTHOR WORLDS

Smartypants Romance (an imprint of Penny Reid)

Tales of the Winters sisters set in Green Valley.

Love in Due Time - Love in Deed - Love in a Pickle

The World of True North (an imprint of Sarina Bowen)

Welcome to Vermont! And the Busy Bean Café.

Cowboy - Studfinder

THE EARLY YEARS

Legendary Rock Stars Series

A classic tale with a modern twist of rockstar romance and suspense.

Paradise Stories

MMA romance. Two brothers. One fight.

The Island Duet

Intrigue and suspense. The island knows what you've done.

Modern Descendants – writing as elda lore

Magical realism. Modern myths of Greek gods.

ABOUT THE AUTHOR

www.lbdunbar.com

L.B. Dunbar loves sexy silver foxes, second chances, and small towns. If you enjoy older characters in your romance reads, including a hero with a little silver in his scruff and a heroine rediscovering her worth, then welcome to romance for those over 40. L.B. Dunbar's signature works include women and men in their prime taking another turn at love and happily ever after. She's a *USA TODAY* Bestseller as well as #1 Bestseller on Amazon in Later in Life Romance with her Sterling Falls, Lakeside Cottage, and Road Trips & Romance series. L.B. lives in Chicago with her own sexy silver fox.

To get all the scoop about the self-proclaimed queen of silver fox romance, join her on Facebook at Loving L.B. (Dunbar) or receive her monthly newsletter, Love Notes.

+ + +

CONNECT WITH L.B. DUNBAR

www.ingramcontent.com/pod-product-compliance
Lightning Source LLC
Chambersburg PA
CBHW051457030726
47592CB00006B/1969

* 9 7 8 1 9 5 6 3 3 7 7 8 5 *